Praise

'F...................................mundane . . .

'Unsettling, horribly gripping and touched with genius'
Daily Mail

'An acutely unsettling folk horror with a superbly unreliable narrator'
Metro

'Fletcher has a most distinctive voice, and convinces me that there
may be some truth at last in those rumours about a renaissance in
British supernatural fiction'
Lisa Tuttle, *The Times*

'Terrifying, slow-burning, exquisitely wrought'
Lancashire Evening Post

'Daniel's traumatic back story makes it easy for the sceptic not
just to accept but to enjoy and admire the supernatural element as
projections from a deeply troubled mind. This gives the novel a
political as well as a psychological edge, which I particularly
appreciated. One of this year's favourite reads'
Anne Goodwin, author of *Sugar and Snails*

'A remarkable horror story with superb world-building. The
book weaves the horrors of war and climate change into the larger
narrative, merging fantasy and reality. It makes for a haunting
and poignant read. *Witch Bottle* is an intense and atmospheric folk
horror that leaves an arresting impression'
Read by Dusk

'If you enjoy Andrew Michael Hurley you will devour this dark and mysterious read . . . the perfect balance of a perfectly created fictional world and a realistic portrayal of an unsettling atmosphere and a wonderfully unreliable narrator'
On the Shelf

'An impressive book, a fusion of classic horror with a story of modern life and broken relationships which left me feeling deeply uneasy'
Blue Book Balloon

'Absolutely pitch-perfect literary horror, gorgeously written and paced, and blends its folk-horror and supernatural elements with an extremely fresh use of the cosmic'
Sublime Horror

'Impressive . . . *Witch Bottle* is both a great and beguiling read'
Gingernuts of Horror

'Fletcher's imagination is truly boundless'
Avid Fantasy Reviews

'This novel grips, tugs, claws at you from the very first page. Fletcher really displays intelligent, fresh writing from the get-go. The mundane is turned to the intriguing'
Fanfiaddict

'Literary horror at its finest'
Bookka

'It explores the human emotions of loss, of grief, of loneliness and of self-preservation, one of those really unsettling reads. A haunting, dark and twisty story'
Books and Me

'A dark and twisted gothic style novel, Tom Fletcher's *Witch Bottle* proves to be a perfect pick for this spooky October'
Ellie Jayne Taylor

'A distinctive and personal voice . . . Fletcher knows how to ratchet up the tension'
Ends of the Word

Tom Fletcher is a writer of literary horror and dark fantasy novels and short fiction. His first three horror novels, *The Leaping*, *The Thing on the Shore* and *The Ravenglass Eye*, were followed by the dark fantasy novels *Gleam* and *Idle Hands*. His latest novel, *Witch Bottle*, is a deeply atmospheric modern gothic tale of grief and guilt. He lives in a remote village in Cumbria with his wife and family.

TOM FLETCHER

Witch Bottle

Jo Fletcher
BOOKS

First published in Great Britain in 2020
This paperback edition published in 2021 by

Jo Fletcher Books
an imprint of
Quercus Editions Ltd
Carmelite House
50 Victoria Embankment
London EC4Y 0DZ

An Hachette UK company

A CIP catalogue record for this book is available
from the British Library

PB ISBN 978 1 84866 263 6

10 9 8 7 6 5 4 3 2 1

Typeset by CC Book Production
Printed and bound in Great Britain by Clays Ltd, Elcograf S.p.A.

Papers used by Jo Fletcher Books are from well-managed forests and other responsible sources.

For Beth, Jake, and Arlo.

The Giant

I'VE SEEN THE GIANT only once, but in seeing it I knew that it was entirely real. So once was enough. It was not directly in front of me, nor in my presence; I saw it through space. It was the day I left Ellie and Marianne. I headed from the front door of the flat that Ellie and I had – until that day – rented together, dragging a backpack along the ground, and I headed to the bus stop and rode the bus to a Travelodge on the edge of town. I opened the door to my room, and saw it. The door had become a window into another place, and in that other place was the giant. I stood in the doorway and looked down into the place where the giant was. A black coldness gripped me. The kind of cold that feels like metal being pushed into your body.

The giant was sitting at a square table in a dark, dank stone room. Its chair was draped in tattered, colourful fabrics. The giant was naked. Its skin was saggy, pocked and sweaty, and a terrible stink arose from it. Its long thin hair hung lankly down its back. The giant did not have eyes, or a nose, or ears. It just had a mouth, a mouth that arced downwards between one dented temple and the other. Behind its bloody lips were crowded yellow teeth.

On the square table was a mountain of some unidentifiable material. The giant was gathering handfuls of it and shovelling it into its mouth, forcing it in, smearing it across the skin around its lips. The material was mostly wet, but there were hard things in it, things that I could hear crunching between the giant's teeth. I watched as the giant just about cleared the table. Before it could, though, yet more of the slop suddenly dropped from above, piling up on the table and splattering the giant and the floor all around. The giant grunted in approval, and resumed eating with a renewed vigour.

The more it ate the worse it smelled. The sweat ran in constant streams. The giant did not stop eating. The substance (flesh, it was flesh, it was flesh and bone, I knew it, of course I knew it) kept coming, and the giant was insatiable.

I knew I was witnessing a real thing that was happening somewhere beneath the surface of the world. The icy coldness, the dank stone of the walls, the stench. These were real. Just in another place that I had somehow gained an unwanted access to. The insatiable giant was real.

I did not hear a word leave the giant's mouth, and nor did I see it interact with another living thing. But I knew, as well as I knew it was real, that it was a cruel creature. Cruel and intelligent. It ate like a wild animal – messily, greedily and shamelessly – but it was not a wild animal, gorging itself on its latest kill while it could. It was cruel and intelligent like a man. I could feel its cruelty like I could feel the cold. It was a sickening sensation that penetrated through my skin. Its insatiable appetite for the bloody substance constantly being served was not only mirrored by its insatiable appetite for cruelty: they were one and the same. The same appetite. I didn't know how this could be, but I knew it was the truth. I knew this instinctively. There was no doubt in my mind that if it had been presented with something alive, it would torment and torture the thing before killing it, and take delight in the pain it inflicted.

Something alive, like me. I thought I was alive. I felt that if I moved, the giant might notice me, and reach up with one of those wet, over-knuckled hands, and close it around my waist, and squeeze me and molest me and peel me, and then eventually kill me and eat me. So I stood still and watched. I dared not even blink.

Some time later a door that I hadn't noticed opened, and a small figure entered the giant's space. The figure was a human in a white coat, and if it had stood next to the seated giant it would have perhaps reached its ankle. It was only then that I realised the giant was a giant, and not the size of a human.

The giant stopped eating and stared at the newcomer. I stepped backwards and slammed the door shut. After a minute or two I opened it again, and found myself looking into the drab order of the hotel room.

Two hours earlier I had been in another bedroom, the bedroom Ellie and I shared, picking up a pint glass half full of water in order to hit her with it, and then, realising what I was doing, smashed it over my head instead. The glass had had to break, it seemed. And then I had screamed at her. And I should have known that's how it would end.

I went and lay down on the hotel bed. I curled up. Later, I dreamed that it was a hot day, and Ellie and I were swimming together in a blue lake.

The Job

I GET FOUR HOURS IN bed before the alarm goes off. I paw at my phone on the bedside table, trying to stop the alarm, but I can't see and I can't think. It's four a.m. I silence the sound – it's the same gentle, repeating melody as the one I was using when Ellie and I first met, the same tune that woke us on our first morning, but it's years later now, years later and phones later – and roll out of bed. I'll brush my teeth, but there's no point in having a shower. I put on my old jeans and a thick, soft shirt. I pull the waterproof overtrousers from the drawer.

Upstairs, I grab a couple of breakfast bars and fill the flask with coffee. Get my sandwiches out of the fridge. The flask was a birthday present a couple of years back; it's one of those Penguin Classics things, with a leather *On the Road* sleeve. Orange and cream. Covered in brown drippy stains now, though. I stick it all in my backpack. I put on my old, filthy, waterproof coat. Heavy boots. Ten past four. Backpack on. I leave the house. Step out into the early autumn pre-dawn. I close the door behind me as quietly as I can, and lock it. The air is fresh and cool. No clouds; the sky is thick with stars. Breath misting. I walk across the grass to the shed. An owl softly hoots from somewhere in the copse at the back of the garden, and is answered from the hills beyond the field. Something – a cow, presumably – shifts heavily on the other side of the hedge. There's no frost yet, but there will be soon. The shed is barely still standing; it only just keeps the weather off. The door's difficult to open quietly – it's wonky and warped. I yank it open, worried as ever that I'm going to accidentally pull the whole thing over. Inside, shelves bend beneath the weight of jars, bottles and pots. The pots were left behind by the man who used to live here – a potter – and the jars and bottles are mine. I retrieve my bike and helmet, lock up the shed and wheel the bike through the yard to the pool of yellow light beneath the street lamp that marks the yard entrance like a sign. At the roadside I turn the bike lights on, put on the helmet, mount the bike and point it down the hill towards the big road. The hamlet is like something out of a fantasy novel: a deep, slow river, a bridge, a farm shop, a pub, and a few houses clustered around. I wonder sometimes why I want to write a fantasy novel; why I'm not content just living in one. In my novel I envisage the aftermath of a centuries-long, planet-spanning conflict. The entities that were at war – states, nations, whatever – are now at peace, but are negotiating the return of the war dead to their homelands. The problem is, the war was so long, and so long ago, that the dead have all decomposed into the ground. So powerful magic users are engineering the extraction, lifting and transport of particular soils from one side of the world to the other. The book will focus on one particular magician, who's got to manage this huge landmass that has been a mass grave. And she's dealing with

6

the bureaucracy and the politics and trying to maintain her skill and her energy and it's incredibly difficult and she's worried she can't do it, and she can't sleep for fear of dropping this gigantic inverted mountain into one of the new cities.

THE BIKE COASTS SILENTLY down the hill, on to the big road, and I pedal across the bridge. For a while I'm under the overhang of trees. I keep an eye out for foxes and badgers, but don't see any this morning. After a right turn towards Saltcoats, I can see the depot glowing. Cold industrial lights casting a haze upwards amid the expanse of darkened fields. And I can hear the faint humming of the van refrigerators.

The Bean is changing a tyre as I arrive. 'You're going to have to peg it,' she growls. 'I haven't loaded the van yet. Found this fuckin' flat. Why didn't you change it yesterday?'

'Didn't know about it.'

'It's your van.'

'I'm sorry. I didn't know about it.'

The Bean can get grumpy but as long as you don't bite back she doesn't stay grumpy. The flat tyre is a pain though. Certain customers want their deliveries by certain times, so if you're late getting away you've got to rush, and any of the myriad little things that can go wrong become significant. And now I'm going to be very late getting away. I watch as Graham leaves, his van rocking gently as he fails to avoid the potholes in the lane. Usually, the Bean has the vans loaded and ready to go by the time we get here.

We call her the Bean because she looks like a big long runner bean. Tall and flat and tough.

I head through to the fridge and start pulling the trolleys out.

The trolleys are old and wonky-wheeled. The fridge floor is rough concrete with drainage channels, covered by metal grilles that have long-since bent and broken. Getting the full, heavy trolleys across the floor, out of the fridge, through the cluttered link corridor, out through the loading bay and up the ramp to the sliding van door takes a knack. I'm familiar with these trolleys now and I can do it, but in the early days there were some near-misses. Trips, slips, tips, drops. The trolleys are as tall as me and packed solid when they're full.

I heave this one up the ramp, battling gravity. At least it's dry; doing this in heavy rain and gales is that much more difficult. The ramp is metal, and it does have an anti-slip texture on it, but it's just a gesture really. Well-meant. I leave it at the top of the ramp, on the flat bit; the Bean is still working on the tyre.

By the time the Bean's finished, I've got three trolleys at the top of the ramp. She slides open the van door and I kick the metal plank over, to make a little bridge between the ramp and the van. Wheel the trolleys in one-two-three, as she brings more up behind me. I need six for this round. I have to line them up inside the van just so, for them to fit. Then we pile in the Orders.

On the round, there's the File, and then there are the Orders. The File is a list of the customers, with their daily deliveries detailed – usually these are the core products: the bottles and cartons. It's printed out monthly. The Orders are additional requests, phoned or emailed in, and the Bean boxes those up every night for the next morning. The trouble is, you end up memorising the File. You can't help it, you just do. And so the Orders are easy to forget. Sure, the Bean writes them down for you on a separate list, but remembering to check that extra list in the first place is the tricky bit. It sounds easy, I know; I mean, it *is*. But sometimes, at that time of day, if you're rushing – as I will be, today – or if your night's sleep was broken and haunted, or if the weather is rotten and the roads are a bit hairy, it's easy to forget.

'Wait a minute,' I say, as we check everything over. 'Where's my carrier?' My carrier is like a basket for milk bottles, that enables me to carry eight bottles in only one hand.

The Bean shrugs. 'Dunno.'

'Great,' I say. So I'm setting off late, and once I get out there, I'll be slower than usual too.

Today I'm heading north, up along the A595 to Calder Bridge, Beckermet, then Thornhill, and then on up to Westlakes Business Park, and finally to Craggesund Paperboard. There's a customer in Beckermet who wants their delivery by 7 a.m.; that's going to be tight, today. And you've got to hit Westlakes by 8 a.m., 8.15 a.m. at the latest – get there before the office workers. And then Craggesund by 9 a.m. Those are the beats, on this round. The first one is always the one that puts the pressure on. Because if you can get to that house by 7 a.m., then generally you know you'll get to the others on time too. If you're late for the first one, then the pressure builds until you hit your second, and so on. But the truth is, if you're late by 7 a.m., you'll be late all the way around, because that's when the traffic starts piling on to the A595. Netherhall workers, and farmers, and in the summer, tourists with their caravans. And today I'll be having to jog back and forth to the van more than usual, because I don't have my carrier, and I can only carry four full bottles in one hand.

Other customers probably want their deliveries by certain times too, but we only know for sure about the ones who complain if we're late. That's what drives the beats: the complainers.

The Orders all loaded up, I set off, sipping coffee from my flask cup. Normally I'd use the toilet before going, and immediately upon swinging out of the potholed lane I regret not doing so today. The Bean's outdoor toilet is truly horrible: a crusty old throne with taps that don't work and a towel that is more fungus than fabric. Not to mention the spiders. I have never seen so many fully grown spiders in one place. They lurk motionless in the upper corners, swaddled in thick white web. But, it's the last toilet you get the chance to use before heading out.

By the time I'm dropping off at Hold Engineering, I'm almost on track. I've finished my coffee and feel a bit more human. The sun is just coming up; normally I'd be leaving Hold in the last moments of darkness. The Hold yard is a good place to be for the sunrise. The first red light sharpening the purple mountains to the south, dark grey clouds stretched across like streaks of paint. I briefly gaze at the view – the dark fields, the small plumes of smoke rising from Gosforth houses, the sunrise – as I put my foot down.

I'm not checking the File as thoroughly as I should be, because I'm so desperate to hit the 7 a.m. house in time *and* I'm desperate for a piss. I can't stop anywhere before hitting that house. I've got to hold it until then. But, after I've hit that house, there won't be a handy pissing place for a good couple of hours. When caught short up on the housing estates to the north, you've got a problem: the few public toilets that are still around are all locked up in the early hours. And there's no privacy to be had anywhere. You've got to get inventive. Fucking customers. It would be a much easier job without them.

So I'm jogging down driveways with numerous full bottles in each hand, returning to the van with an empty on each finger, hoping I don't slip and fall and land on my hands. Leaving the sliding door open when I shouldn't – the sound of the refrigeration unit has been loud enough to prompt complaints to the Bean before – and driving just a little faster than I should.

I hit the 7 a.m. house at 7.10 a.m. I can see the occupants through the window, moving around their kitchen. They look out at me as I approach the doorstep. I drop the delivery and dash back to the van before they come out to bring the delivery inside and catch me. I hurry out of the cul-de-sac and pull into the next. The sun is up now and the sky has that blue-yellow watercolour wash look to it, with a bit of pink bleeding up from the horizon. Geese in vees overhead.

I'm just trying to give you a sense of the job here. How time passes. What's really important is that I spend most of the day on my own. That's what makes it a job I can keep. I do have to spend some time talking with other people, especially at the depot, but not for so long that I can't keep the mask on.

IT'S A WET MISTY morning and up on Corney Fell visibility is down to just a couple of meters. The Corney Fell road is twisty and narrow – mostly single-lane – and it winds up and over the fell, providing a slightly shorter route if you want to head south from the Western Lakes to the M6. The alternative is to stay low and drive all the way around the fell; this takes longer, is more miles and denies you the views. But ostensibly it is less hair-raising. I like the fell road though; even in one of the Bean's vans, even though the roadside is marked by jagged rocks, even though it's a rat run for half-mad

Netherhall shifties, even though it's often blanketed in thick cloud . . . I like it. I like the blasted heath that rolls out in all directions like a wild sea. I like the stone circles. I like the old Herdwicks that move out of the road for no man. And on those days that the clouds stay up in the sky, or do not manifest at all, then yeah, I like the views. I like how all the 'PASSING PLACE' signs have been vandalised so as to read 'PISSING PLACE'. I didn't do it; it had probably been Ryan. I like to imagine that I live in one of the old farmhouses that dot the lonely moors, even though the thought of living in one of them makes me feel cold and afraid.

I've been taking it easy because of the weather, but am once again desperate for a piss. On Corney, though, I know of a few good lay-bys and lonnings in which I'll be hidden between the van and the high hedgerows. Especially in this mist.

So I'm rushing in order to get to the next appropriate lay-by. The next pissing place. I have to drop off six pints and four loaves of bread at Mrs Atman's farm, which is at the end of a long, bumpy lane – not ideal – and then I can press on to the field gate I've earmarked for a toilet stop.

Radio 4 dissolves into static as I swing into the Atman lonning. I take my foot off the pedal a moment and fiddle briefly with the tuning dial; no luck. Weird. I don't usually lose reception here. I accelerate once more and swerve around the potholes at speed. Things are getting serious. Sometimes Mrs Atman likes to chat; I'll have to give her short shrift today. I swing the van around in the great muddy turning circle outside her yard, brake hard, jump out into a puddle and sling her bread over the drystone wall and into the big metal bin she uses to keep the dogs from eating her deliveries. In there is a bottle holder I quickly fill with full pint bottles. Somewhere the dogs start barking. I sprint back to the van and, as I slam the door, I see Mrs Atman gesticulating from inside her glass porch. I pretend I haven't seen her and pull away.

I don't bother trying to avoid the potholes on my way back to the road. I hear the trolleys clattering in the back of the van each time I bounce. I'm gritting my teeth. I'm beyond plain old discomfort and actually on the verge of pissing myself. The clenching hurts. Stop for a second at the lonning mouth, listen out for any other motor. There is none. Nothing. I put my foot down, turning left, and then about thirty yards later swing off the main road again to the right. My next customer's a good ten minutes down the road, but here – ah, right here—

I pull into the left, slam the brakes on and jump out. I briefly check that I'm not blocking the road and then run around the other side of the van and scrabble for my flies; then remember I'm wearing my thick, waterproof overtrousers. I yank those down, unbutton my jeans and let the piss burst out. I close my eyes and listen to the sound of it. Sheep are bleating out on the fell. I feel as if clouds of steam are billowing up into my face. Beyond the smell of urine is the sharp, clean tang of fully fledged autumn. The stream doesn't slow down. It just goes on and on.

And then there's another sound. An engine, getting closer and louder. It's probably going to head straight past this road and on up and over the fell. Or – no. No, it's coming this way. Still, I'm hidden behind the van, obscured by mist in a field gate hedge gap. They won't see me. They're going too fast for this road. Way too fast.

The vehicle suddenly tears the morning open with a blare of its horn, screeches across the tarmac and crashes.

I button myself up and go to investigate.

It isn't in too bad a state: it's simply run into the hedgerow on the other side of the road, tearing into the dyke. It's a distinctive truck – a normal cab, if small, but with a big dark boxy metal behind – and I recognise it immediately. It's the Fallen Stock wagon. Almost cuboid, the box is galvanised metal with some sort of structural reinforcement along its exterior sides. Along the top of the side of the box, the words FALLEN STOCK are stencilled in black. The Fallen Stock wagon goes around picking up dead livestock from farms. They must have changed their design – they used to bear blue decals with white writing. Dark streaks along the tarmac mark the path of its last swerve before impact. It had swerved to avoid my delivery van, which it could have passed safely if the driver had been going at a reasonable speed. My van's white too, which no doubt didn't help in this weather. At least I haven't been hit. I won't have to go crawling to the Bean to explain myself. Small mercies.

The box truck is still upright, but its front end has become elevated by the muddy dyke, so that the whole thing looks as if it's going up a steep ramp, or taking off into the misty air. I clear my throat.

'Hello?' I call. My voice comes out quite quietly. Nerves and mist conspire to deaden it. 'Hello?' I call again, raising the volume. At first, there's no response at all – no sound, no movement. I walk slowly closer. Then, all of a sudden, the passenger-side door opens and a man slides out through it. He slithers down the side of the cab and the dyke until he reaches the road, and then he turns and looks at me.

In the mist all of his clothes appear black at first, but upon closer inspection he's wearing baggy plus-fours tucked into his wellingtons and a long, dark green waxed coat. He's very large – both wide and tall. He wears a tweed cap, from beneath which long blond hair protrudes messily. His face is round and smooth. Blood streams from his nose, but he's smiling all the same.

'Hi,' I say. 'Hello. Listen, I'm sorry about your nose. And the van. I had to pull over to take a phone call. It wasn't important in the end, but it might have been. I mean, I was expecting a very important call, but the call I answered wasn't that call.' I pause. 'And it wasn't important.'

We're quite close together now. His eyes are watery, as well they might be after a knock to the nose. I watch blood drip from his chin. He makes no move to clean himself up. His pale eyes rove up and down as he takes me in. It's not a very nice smile, close up. Barely a smile at all. It's a smile-shaped hole, through which large brown teeth are visible. His lips are pink and wet. Somehow wriggly.

'Did your face hit the wheel, then?' I ask.

He doesn't say anything. I get the distinct impression he's sizing me up.

'You didn't hit your head, did you?'

His smile-hole widens and he very deliberately and slowly shakes his head. 'You don't need to worry about me, old chap,' he says. His voice is deep and plummy. He does not have a local accent.

'Do you need any help? Can I call the doctor?'

'The good old doctor, eh? Rushing out to aid the villagers with his bag and his stethoscope? I can barely imagine such a thing any more. That's not how it works these days, is it?'

'No, but – can I call anybody?'

'No, thank you.' Blood is running down his neck and soaking into the open-necked gingham shirt he wears beneath his khaki jumper. He chuckles and shakes his head. 'Call the doctor! Well, I never.'

'Listen – do you want to borrow my handkerchief?'

'Hardly the done thing.'

'I might have some tissues in the van.'

'No!' Blood flecks outwards as he snaps, 'No, thank you! I'll be quite all right!'

'Yes, well – okay. Do you want any details?'

He looks me up and down again. 'What I want . . .' he says, trailing off. Then he snatches at my hand, drawing white lines of pain across the back of it with his fingernails. 'I just want to walk this world like it is mine again.' He's yanked me close and is staring into my eyes. His voice is a low snarl. 'That's what I want.'

I look down. Blood is beading beneath his grip. His fingernails are long, yellow and ragged. 'Get off,' I hiss.

After a moment, he releases me.

'I do not require insurance details, if that's what you meant.' He nods towards my van. His voice and eyes have returned to normal. 'Not a scratch on yours, is there? Most fortunate.'

'Are we done?'

He gazes absently at me and nods. 'I'll be on my way then,' he says, and he turns and climbs laboriously back up into his truck. I retreat to stand against my van as he restarts his engine.

He slowly backs the truck down from the dyke and on to the road, demonstrating quite excellent control of his vehicle. So he can be careful when he wants to be. As I watch, I notice something horrible.

As is usual, the back of the truck provides access to the interior – in this case via a back door that would lower down and form a ramp. The door of course is closed. From beneath it, however, runs a steady stream of blood. I've already seen enough blood coming from the man's nose, thank you very much, and yet here is even more. More blood. It spatters all over the road. It's dark and thick. As the truck levels out, the stream stops. The step at the back of the truck is slick with the stuff, though. The man hits his horn as he drives away, but I don't look up from the splashes of blood on the road. I thought the whole point of Fallen Stock was to ensure containment, especially since foot-and-mouth. After the sound of the truck engine has faded away, I hurry over and crouch down for a closer look.

The blood is indeed dark and thick, and there are small white things in it. I jerk up and back when I recognise them as maggots. Tiny little maggots, wriggling about.

That's it. I've had enough. I squeeze my scratched hand, trying not to think about the man's disgusting fingernails. I climb back up into my nice warm van, check the time and swear.

The Hands in the Sea

AFTER WORK I KICK my muddy boots off by the door, remove the thick plastic waterproofs and peel off the sweat-drenched underlayers. In the shower I think about Kathryn, from the La'al Tattie Shop. I think about her all the time. I stare through the small square window at the unruly hedge at the back of the garden. Beyond that are uneven fields, sloping generally down to the river. A vee of geese moves slowly across the darkening blue of the sky as hot water courses down my back. I need a haircut, but I've needed one for about two years now. I haven't had a haircut since my marriage ended, and nor have I shaved. My hips ache from the getting in and getting out of the van, and my arms ache from carrying around two-litre sixpacks. The job keeps you fit. I run my fingers through my beard. I don't like to see my old friends any more because I can't relate to their lives at all – functioning relationships with their spouses and kids, careers, mortgages. The last time I saw Hoof he asked me if it was true that I was a milkman.

'Yes,' I said.

He nodded appraisingly, and then clapped me on the back. 'Don't worry about it, man,' he said. 'We've all had to take weird little jobs at some point.'

Some of my old friends now have multiple mortgages. I rent this house from my uncle. I pay less than market rate, because he's doing me a favour. Or, rather, he's doing my mother a favour and I benefit from it. He doesn't believe the moon landing really happened, and he refers to the old man who lived here before me as 'the pottery puff'.

My hourly wage is low but I work long days, and with no expensive hobbies, no social life and no real desire to own a home, I can get by all right.

I put the TV on. News 24. Refugees fleeing the war in Syria. Whether or not the war in Syria is its own discrete war – separate from the wars against ISIS, and before that the wars in Afghanistan and Iraq – I'm not sure. Everything is connected; banal but true. More refugees fleeing drought. Yet more fleeing floods and wildfires. Refugee kids being taken from their parents at the borders, and being put in cages. Scrapyard rafts bearing desperate families sinking in the Mediterranean. Navy ships setting sail to *stop* refugees from reaching the shore. Refugees being captured and sold by slavers. Put to work in British factories. Put to work in British pubs and on British farms. Children being sold for sex. Small brown bodies washing up on European beaches. British tourists crowding round the small dead bodies. We won't understand it even when the dead are washing up on our own shore. We'll just stand and stare and scratch our heads. Prod the dead body in the sand. Call somebody to come and pick it up. We don't see the wires that connect them to us. We don't see cause and effect. We'll feel sad that it happened, but no responsibility.

No guilt. What a terrible world. Look out at the sea. What deep, cruel waters. Imagine an overcrowded vessel, not seaworthy, taking on water. All the kids faced with the heartless ocean, crying out. Picture a shark. Picture a pair of giant hands reaching up from the depths, and somewhere even deeper, a ravenous mouth, waiting.

Marianne has to grow up in this world, and survive it. Marianne. I hope – I pray to whatever's out there, whatever primary creative force birthed and guides the universe – that your life is not made short and nasty by water wars, resource scarcity, failing states. I'm sorry. A small, scared part of me still thinks we shouldn't have made you; however, the whole of me wants to reach out across the shadowed face of the country to see you, speak with you, even just email you. But I don't trust myself not to hurt you now, any more than I did back when I left. There is still something in me that I don't trust.

I wake in the armchair. I've spilled whisky across my stomach and it's cold. I shudder. It's dark outside now. Behind me is the Juliet balcony. Double doors, glass, through which you can look out over the fields, over the river, across the fields beyond and at the mountains. I normally close the heavy curtains across them before it gets dark. Now I don't want to face them. I have this sudden and awful feeling, new to me, that something terrible approaches. There have been nights in the past, maybe after watching a scary film, that I have spooked myself, but this is different. There's a certainty to it. I get up and move behind the chair to close the curtains, trying not to look through the glass as I do so. Breathing is difficult. And there, on the grass: there's a person. I feel fear trickle through my body, from the top of my head all the way down into my bowels, like water. There's not much moonlight so I can't make out their features.

Their silhouette is familiar, though I don't know where from. Arms outstretched, pointed head, a ragged cloak or cape flapping around their knees. Bare feet. They look like a scarecrow, or Christ on the cross. They look like somebody in a black Ku Klux Klan costume.

They don't look like they're looking at me. Their head is angled downwards, as if looking at the ground. I feel like if I move, if I close the curtains, then I will draw their attention. I close my eyes instead. When I open them, the figure is gone. My bike is on the grass there, though. I squint, but I can't make the bike look like the figure I just saw.

I snap the curtains shut. Then I hurry downstairs to the dark hallway. There's a small glass panel in the door that looks out towards the same grass that the figure was standing in. I quickly steal a glance through the glass and then duck down. They're still not there. I look again, for longer this time. Definitely not out there. Not where they were, at least. I imagine them standing directly outside the door, just to the side of the glass. I duck down again.

Later, after another whisky, I go outside and put the bike in the shed. On the way back to the house I break into a run and once inside, slam the door carelessly. The sound is loud and sharp, like a firework, and I imagine it bouncing from the mountains.

The Magic

GRAHAM IS STORMING ABOUT, breaking up boxes and stuffing them into the recycling cages. Graham is the same shape and size as the Bean, but a little younger. His skin is weathered and thick – so much so that the lines of his face look like cracks. They look sore. He's been a milkman since before he worked for the Bean. He's been a milkman since leaving school – at sixteen, I guess, though really it might have been earlier round here, back then – and now he's in his sixties. He speaks quickly and has a stammer and one of the strongest Cumbrian accents I've ever heard, and he talks to himself. I just quietly get on with sorting out my empties because he's clearly angry about something. Graham and the Bean fall out sometimes: at the root of it, Graham wants more money and the Bean doesn't believe in paying her staff different wages. And the Bean can't put all the wages up, so she won't put Graham's up, even though Graham has worked here longer than the rest of us.

I am not sleeping well, for fear of seeing the man with the pointed hood again, and I don't feel capable of dealing with Graham. I stay clear of him and stack my crates of empty bottles at the side of the yard ready for Central to come and collect. I've emptied the van when the Bean bursts out of her house and strides across the yard towards me.

'The Woolpack,' she barks. 'Need to get down there now. I've boxed it up, it's in the fridge. Take them that. Then you can go.' She shakes her head. 'Bloody late getting their orders in, like. Always bloody late, them lot. And take a sack of carrots for Mrs Lindon. Y'know her, down the lane? For the horses. Drop 'em on the way back.' She nods. 'Aye, and *then* you can go.'

Pub orders tend to be a bit hefty. Bags of potatoes, bags of carrots, bags of onions, boxes of this, that and the other. Loads of meat. Graham is muttering something about 'them lot over the wall' as I carry the sacks through. I don't know what 'them lot over the wall' do. The wall is the back wall of the yard, but it divides the depot building too. You can hear a lot of machines from the other side, but never any talking.

It's a bit of a drive to the Woolpack, but it's a nice drive. It's a nice drive all year round, but I'm a fan of the autumn, so this time of year it's especially good. Now the dark grey clouds are out, accumulating above Wasdale and Eskdale. I'm on Irton levels when the wind picks up and blows a hail of bright yellow leaves across the brooding black sky, and at just the same moment a flock of crows rises from the fields and flies in the opposite direction. The leaves are like fire against all of the darkness. The crows make it look as if the wind is blowing in two directions at once. It feels almost hallucinatory. I slow the van, momentarily overwhelmed. The air turns to glass and everything freezes sharp-edged in time. I remember lying at the bottom of the river, looking up. I remember floating on the surface of a lake, listening to a tree talk.

The moment passes. This is the way we used to come as teenagers, just after we'd learned to drive. We'd go swimming in the rivers in summer. Hoof would steer and Ryman would change gears with his eyes closed, Hoof shouting out, 'Third! Fourth! Third! First!' as the car careened around the bends of those tiny Eskdale roads.

There was nothing better than the rivers in summer with the waterfalls and the rocks to jump off, lying on the grassy banks looking up at the deep blue sky, some bird of prey in the distance, sound carrying from one mountainside to the opposite mountainside. The water was always too cold at first but you got used to it; you had to jump in, there was no other way. Your body wouldn't let you do it gradually; if you tried to sit on the edge and dangle your legs you had no chance. You had to jump and then stay underwater while your body and skin adjusted. The water in those rivers was impossibly clean – it was so clear, you could open your eyes and look at all of the grey and green stone around you as if you were looking through glass, honest to God. The currents were playful but not dangerous, not dangerous at all unless you are so unintelligent that everything is dangerous. Or maybe it is dangerous if you have a weak heart. But none of us had a weak heart; we all had good strong hearts and brains to match. What did we do? I think we just jumped in and then floated and then clambered out again and then jumped back in, talking all the while. It was enough. I remember that sometimes the weather would change as we approached the river, switching from burning sun to warm, humid rain with a sudden rush of bulbous clouds, but our plans would not change. We would still go swimming, jumping, whatever you wanted to call it. I remember one time in particular, a summer storm: heavy rain breaking the surface of the river, thunder rolling down from the peaks like an invisible wave, lightning springing into existence between the mountains, touching down on all of them, joining them all together in the sky, and everything and everybody was so wet, water running across our skin, nobody really talking actually, all of us just basking in the constant turmoil, the stimulation of it, and it wasn't stopping, and we were grinning at each other, we all were, and we lay on the bottom of the river and looked up, watched the rain hitting the water from beneath, and I think we could all just hold our breath for pretty much for ever. We didn't bother getting dried or changed on the way back to the cars that day, because it hadn't stopped raining and we'd just get wet again; we just ran barefoot back down the riverbanks – not running to avoid the rain, just running because we were going downhill.

What I'm trying to get at is that there's a magic here, a magic in the place. It is easier here to plug into the world than it is in other places. It's easier to open yourself up to it. I've always found nature and the physical world itself a more comfortable companion than other human beings. Having said that, as a teenager, I found it easier being around other people than either before or afterwards. Partly I think because everybody else was in flux, too. There was chaos in everybody – not just me. Not that I understand why I feel the way I do. Generally, I just have this sense of guilt, and a feeling that I shouldn't spend too much time around other people.

The Fallen Stock Drivers

WHEN OUT DRIVING FOR the Bean, we see lots of other professional drivers out too. Often, on the later valley rounds, we leapfrog with the postal worker. We deliver dairy products and fruit and veg to the pubs, alongside specialist food wholesalers from whom the pub chefs buy more exotic ingredients – so we see their vans around. Many a time I park up at the end of a lonning waiting for the laundry van to make its slow way out. And there's the butcher, whose Cumberland sausage is famous. There are the independent couriers in their battered old Transits, subcontracted by Yodel or whoever. We often meet each other in muddy farmyards, or prim courtyards, or briefly block each other in on gravel driveways. Our relationships are more than cordial; we recognise each other as friends and colleagues, of a sort. There isn't really time for any camaraderie – if we were ever to stop for a chat, our vans would block the narrow country roads – but there is mutual respect. Even the drivers for Dawson's, our closest competitor, share a nod and a wave as we squeeze past each other between the drystone walls.

There has also always been the Fallen Stock driver. The Fallen Stock driver is the only driver I don't like running into – especially since the near-miss on Corney. I feel like up until that incident, I only saw the wagon very rarely. As the days and weeks of the new pattern pass, it's the Fallen Stock wagon – or perhaps it would be more fair to say the Fallen Stock driver – that starts to ruin things.

I start to see the wagon a little more frequently, just because I'm doing the Bootle and Waberthwaite rounds on top of what I had been doing, and there are a lot of farms down that way. Maybe the pattern change has simply revealed something to me; the situation hasn't changed, but my perception of it has.

It's the postwoman who first expresses her displeasure with them. I bump into her outside the little village shop in Eskdale, where I'm dropping off some punnets of tomatoes and picking up some newspapers for onwards delivery. The tomatoes aren't at their best this time of year, but they'll do for cooking. The village shop is an old slate building, vibrant with window boxes and hanging baskets. I get out of my van and retrieve the fruit from the back, and turn to find her pulling up. I like the Post Office van; it's so nice and red and bright. But as I'm about to smile and say hello, I notice the long deep scratches and dents down the driver side of the vehicle. I go and have a closer look. There's one particularly deep and sharp gouge that runs the length of the vehicle, just below the bottom of the windows. The wing mirror is badly cracked, though it's still functional. The postwoman remains in the driver's seat a moment, mobile phone to ear, then throws her phone down into the passenger seat and gets out.

'Bloody Fallen Stock driver, that's who it was,' she says. I think her name is Judith. 'Absolute bloody menace! Honestly, I'm so pissed off! And I can't get no signal to call the bloody office.'

'What happened?'

'They kept going when they should have stopped, that's what. You know – you know what it's like! We all do. Sometimes there just isn't room for two vans. But they had space to wait! If they'd stopped where they were when they saw me, we would've been fine. But no, they just had to keep on coming. Keep pressing. I pulled over even though there wasn't room. I tried to get right in. It was up by the old Jackson place, so you know – no point in me reversing, it doesn't get any wider back the way I'd come. They should've stopped.' She fiddles with her visor. 'Or they should've reversed. But they didn't. They just forced their way through. Big metal van as well. Not rounded and painted, like ours. All hard edges. Bloody men, that's what it is! No offence.'

'None taken. Did you see the driver inside the cab at all?'

'Briefly. A man in a hat. And those cabs are a bit too high, right? They're higher than ours. Couldn't see them very well. They pushed right past, my poor van squealing like a pig, and they just kept on going.' She shakes her head. 'Arrogant. That's what they are. Arrogant bloody men, just doing what they want.'

'They've changed their design,' I say.

'Aye. And they've taken the phone number off with it. I noticed that too. Anyway, I'd best get in there and use their phone.' She nods towards the shop. 'Ian!' she shouts, upon seeing the shopkeeper watching us from out of the window. 'I need to use your phone!' She makes the phone sign with her hand. Ian is in his early twenties but has gone almost completely bald. She grabs one of the boxes of tomatoes from me. 'Let me take one of them,' she says. We enter the shop together. I rotate the shop's tomato stock and collect all the empty boxes while the postwoman repeats her story for Ian.

I open the door to leave and the little bell rings. 'Look out for the fuckers!' she says to me, over her shoulder. Ian flinches at the language and drops his pen.

After that, I also start to notice that the Fallen Stock drivers are inconsiderate. They will not wait at the end of a lonning for you to emerge. They plough their way in and then just sit there, blocking the passage, waiting for you to reverse. They always expect you to be the one who pulls over if you encounter each other on the roads. They drive too fast. They don't bother finding out-of-the-way places to stop and eat, like the rest of us – they just stop on the sides of the road, narrowing them still further. And, unnervingly, they're around more and more. I see them heading towards the Allington farm. I see them coming out of the Race farm. I see them, from a distant hillside, parked up in old Mrs Goodwin's yard. I find them blocking the lonning to the Royle place. Correspondingly, I've been noticing more and more fallen stock for them to collect. Small heaps of corpses in the shadiest corners of the farmyards. I don't like that they're around so much, and I don't like their behaviour. And neither do the other drivers, from what I can tell. I notice their scowls. Sometimes I'll be behind the Fallen Stock wagon, and I'll see the butcher, for example, pull over to let them past. Then I'll let the butcher past in turn, and we shake our heads at each other in mutual disapproval of the wagon speeding away.

The Project Manager

ELLIE WAS A PROJECT manager for a construction firm primarily occupied with exclusive new-build housing estates around the outside of the city. She worked from a shared space in the city centre, the construction firm having made all office and managerial staff entirely mobile. She shared the space with a marketing person from the same company, an artist and a coder who'd never tell anybody what she was working on. Because Ellie worked from this shared space, she could wear whatever she wanted, but she'd always wear a suit. Her skills for juggling workforce, spotting efficiencies, optimising assets — it was like magic to me. It was a kind of four-dimensional modelling. Squeezing resource profiles through a sequence of business requirements that changed over time. She enjoyed her work, but of course she was underpaid for what she did. She probably saved the company tens of multiples of her own wage every year, just by finding ways for projects to complete early. We couldn't afford to buy one of the houses that her firm built, despite me earning the same as her. I was overpaid for the work I did: I was a Customer Insight Analyst for an unknown tech firm that thrived somewhere in the supply chain of a major, well-known tech firm.

She managed and drove every new development in our lives. Every move, every interview, every fitness regime – she planned it, drew it up as a Gantt chart, assigned milestones and deadlines and level of effort required on any given day. She couldn't bear dead time. She didn't read fiction, only business or management or self-improvement books with titles like *The Chimp Paradox* and *The 7 Habits of Highly Effective People* and *Sharpening the Sword*. She was creative – she was like a sculptor, working with time. And not only for the sake of efficiency – or at least, not efficiency for its own sake. Our being efficient meant that we then had time and space to enjoy ourselves and each other. She liked to go for walks together and take photographs.

'I've made you something,' she said, one night. She was sat on the sofa, legs drawn up, her face bathed in the light of the laptop screen. I was stood in the doorway between the living room and kitchen, running a teatowel around the inside of a pan and watching the TV news. A private security firm subcontracting for a private construction firm that was in turn subcontracting for our government had opened fire on a truck carrying medical supplies, killing several civilians. 'Here.'

She turned the laptop around to reveal a Gantt chart entitled 'First Novel'. She'd made a project plan for me, for the writing of my first book – a plan that accounted for research time, thinking time, note-making, world-building, first draft, resting period, reread, redraft, submission to beta readers, redraft, submission to agencies, waiting times, further rewrites, submission to publishers, the whole lot. The schedule ended with the delivery of traditionally printed copies into my hands. I looked over it, realising – not to my surprise – that she knew a whole lot more about the process of writing a book than I did. She'd obviously looked into it, whereas I'd never done more than just think about it. If you could even call it thinking; it was more like daydreaming.

'I only mentioned this to you last week.'

'You seemed serious about it.'

'I am.' I scrolled back to the start of the Gantt. 'Thank you.'

'It's nothing,' she said. 'Will you use it?'

'Of course,' I said.

'Good.' She turned the laptop back around and briefly typed. I felt my phone buzz in my pocket. 'I've emailed it to you. If you want to use it, work starts next Saturday.' She looked at me. 'I want you to feel like you can do the things that are important to you.'

'I do feel like that.'

'I mean, I want to show you that it's possible.'

'Thank you,' I said, again.

'I've made another Gantt,' she said, eyes returning to the screen. 'The start of this one is tied to the finish of the First Novel schedule. See what you think.'

This project was entitled 'First Child'. I felt a thoroughly unpleasant prickle of heat sweep my body as I forced my eyes to traverse the chart.

'Very good,' I said, but my mouth had dried up and the words came out a bit gummily. 'Very good.'

'What's wrong?'

'Nothing.'

'We've talked about this before. It's not a surprise to you.'

That was true. She'd always been very open about wanting children. I too wanted children, but when I imagined us as parents the children were walking and talking. For some reason, the prospect of us having a baby – being parents to a baby – utterly terrified me.

'No, I know,' I said.

'You want kids too, right?'

The pan was getting heavy in my hands. 'Yes,' I said. 'I want to be a parent. I want to be with you, for ever, and for us to be good parents together. I just can't get my head around the thought of us having a baby. It scares me.'

'It is scary. Doesn't mean we don't do it.'

'I can't imagine it. It's like there's a blank space where the baby should be.'

'That's because of Robert.'

'Yes,' I conceded. 'Yes, it probably is.'

'I understand,' she said. 'But you need to let me know whether this is a difficulty that we can work through, or a fundamental difference regarding what we want from the future. Obviously the latter cannot be overcome very easily.'

'It's the former,' I said. 'Absolutely.'

We were twenty-three.

The following Saturday I opened up my own laptop, opened up the Gantt and opened my notebook. I looked at the project schedule and put pen to paper, but then couldn't move it. I watched as the ink slowly blotted on the page.

The Stories

FOR THE SECOND TIME today I return to the depot, turn the van engine off and hear shouting. My heart sinks. Ryan. Now *he's* arguing with the Bean, probably. I've never argued with the Bean myself and I never want to. I've never seen her do anything scary but she's got this latent power that you can identify, if you're sensitive.

As I step down from the cab, Ryan storms out of the covered area, booting empty cardboard boxes before him. Ryan is tall and wide with a square head, red cheeks and deep eyes. His hair is thick and black and lies remarkably flat on his head, creeping closely down the sides, like moss on a stone. He wears pale grey jogging bottoms and a bright blue waterproof jacket. Never anything else. When he isn't carrying anything he keeps his hands down the front of his pants. His bottom lip is fat and shiny pink, and his lower jaw tends to jut. He's twenty-two. He's a father, with another child on the way.

He's scowling. He looks away from me as he passes, and I don't say anything. I'm about to open the van door when the Bean's voice erupts from behind me.

'That bloody Ryan! The great lump! I've had the bloody head-mistress on the phone!'

'Speeding again?'

'Aye. Bloody fool! I pay you by the hour so you *don't rush*. Speeding! What's in it for him? Speeding past the bloody school! Nobody wants to work, but he kills somebody, what happens? What happens? He's got a turnip in his head and nowt else.'

'You should maybe get somebody new.'

The Bean rubs her face. 'Aye, well.' She slaps the side of the van. 'I'll help you unload.'

IN THE BEAN'S KITCHEN between one round and another, Graham is gangling in the corner with a cup of tea. He's made me one and I sip at it, but it's a bad tea. As bad as the Bean usually makes.

The Bean comes in out of the yard with a loaf of sliced bread from out of the stores, and puts a couple of pieces in the toaster. Under her arm she's got a two-kilo bag of grated cheese. She pops the toast up before it's done, drops a handful of cheese on to a piece and folds it over. There's too much for the toast to hold, and bits spill on to the floor. I nurse my chipped mug.

'Old Mr Bibby's been banging around,' Graham says.

'Oh aye.'

'His footstep on the stair.'

'Who?' I ask.

'Old Mr Bibby,' Graham says. 'Haven't we told you about Old Mr Bibby?'

'Old Mr Bibby,' says the Bean.

'Yeah, all right,' I say. 'Stop saying his name. No, you haven't told me.'

The Bean's mouth is full so she gestures at Graham.

'When she bought this place, I helped her do it up,' Graham says, gesturing back at the Bean. 'Old Mr Bibby was the gent who had it prior. A farmer. He died in the house. He died in bed. And when we were doing the house up, I was upstairs putting wires in, and I heard the door open – that door right there – and footsteps cross the kitchen. I thought it was Beany. Then they came into the hall. Then the staircase. One step, two steps, three. Then they stopped. I shouted – no answer. I came to the banister and looked down. Nobody there.'

'It wasn't me,' the Bean confirms, shaking her head.

'But he was – Old Mr Bibby – I'm not being funny – he was a big lad. He was old and he just got bigger as he got older. He was—?'

'Ninety-six.'

'Aye, ninety-six. And he'd just kept on getting bigger and bigger. I remember him from when I was a little lad. Him and his brother, wemblin' up the hill from the pub. Road wasn't big enough to hold them, even then. Anyway, Robinsons – y'know, off Corney – were carrying him down the stairs and they dropped him.'

Robinson is the undertaker and he lives on Corney Fell. He's a customer and Graham assures me that sometimes Robinson asks him to help move a coffin or two if the river's getting high. He lives in a grey stone end-terrace with a little yard and a grey stone outhouse, and the coffins are in the cellar of the outhouse, where it's always nice and cool.

But it's Robinson's father that Graham's referring to here, I think. He's going back a bit.

'They were carrying him down after he'd died and they dropped him and he landed on his head and slid down the last three stairs, his head bouncing off the steps. Thump, thump, thump.'

Out of the corner of my eye I'm watching the Bean eat.

'And sometimes you hear his step. Only Old Mr Bibby's big enough to step that heavy. Sometimes he comes in here, and the floor's lino but the step sounds like it's on wood, because it was on wood back then, when it was his, and he walks right through, into the hallway. And then up the stairs. But how we *really* know it's him is because he only ever takes the first three steps.'

I think about the figure I saw the other night. I nearly say something about that, but bite it back. 'Is it his foot on the stair then,' I ask, 'or his head?'

'What?'

'If he was dropped and his head bounced down the three bottom steps, then when you hear the sound maybe you're hearing the ghost's head bounce.'

'But the thumps go up. A body isn't going to bounce *up* the stairs.'

'What's the relationship then, between what happened to his body and what the ghost does? If the ghost's walking around downstairs and you can hear it, why wouldn't you hear it on every step? Or does he only walk up the stairs that his head bounced off after he died? And why would he do that?'

'Oh, he's a smart-arse this one, Bean,' Graham says. 'I dunno how ghosts work, do I? Won't bloody bother you with any more ghost stories then.'

'I like ghost stories,' I say. 'It's just that they have to make sense.'

'It's real though,' Graham says. 'Can't change it just to make sense.'

'Well – okay. I didn't mean to say it wasn't real.'

'When *we* tell ghost stories, we mean them.'

'Okay.' *Who's* '*we*', I wonder. But I don't ask.

The Craggesund Drop

THIS MORNING I'M LATE to Craggesund again. I slept in. I feel like I spent all night only half asleep, listening to the man with the hood and cloak creep around the house. It was a dream though. I'm thinking that my first encounter with him was also a dream. It must have been.

You have to stick to the speed limit on the Craggesund site, which is frustrating if you're late – crawling along at ten miles per hour when you know you're already ten minutes, fifteen minutes, thirty minutes behind. Slowly crawling past the mountains of timber towards the huge blue factory. But if you break the speed limit, they'd ban you and the Bean would lose the contract. Silver metal chimneys that look like giant screws point up at the sky, thick white clouds billowing out. Incredibly elaborate labyrinths of metal pipework cluster around the buildings, all illuminated by orange lights in the autumn morning gloom. You can always hear machine alarms as you approach.

I pull up in the desolate deliveries bay and hop out of the van. I lift an empty trolley out of the van on to the ground, then proceed to shift a load of full crates from the van into the empty trolley. Then through some open double doors into a dirty yellow no-place, where I hit the buttons to call the lift.

The lift is very old-fashioned, with those rickety concertina doors. It judders up and down, and the lights flicker incessantly. Every inch of the lift interior is covered in graffiti. I never see anybody on my way into Craggesund – the lifts and corridors I use are the modern-day factory equivalent of servant passages in an old manor house.

Never see anybody until I get to the canteen, that is. The canteen floor is at the top, and the moment the lift doors open, the noise and the smells hit me. I can see down the corridor, past the empty trolley that the kitchen staff have left out for me, to the canteen. And the canteen is jam-packed full of men in blue overalls, eating from plates piled high with bacon, eggs, sausages, black pudding, beans, mushrooms and toast. They're all drinking from big steaming plain white mugs.

I don't mind Craggesund normally, but something about it today makes me anxious. Being late always makes me anxious, so there's that, but also something else: the canteen is busier than normal. But what does that mean? Why does that matter? It means *something*, but I can't think what. The thought can't get off the ground. It's like a hurt bird.

A door in the corridor swings open and the chef bursts out. He is short and tanned, wears a tall white hat and brandishes a meat cleaver. 'You're late!' he says.

'I know,' I say. 'I'm really sorry.'

'We've run out! They're all drinking their tea black!'

'I am really very sorry,' I say. 'That's the last thing I want.'

'Come on. Just wheel it over, and go and get the other one.'

'I'm sorry?' But then it clicks. The hurt bird takes to the air. Oh no.

'The other one. The other trolley!'

I probably open and close my mouth, like a fish.

'We're on shutdown!' He waves the meat cleaver about. 'You know that, right? There is another trolley, right?'

Sometimes, for reasons that we're never privy to, the Craggesund factory goes on shutdown. This means that although somewhere in the depths machines might continue operating, no work by actual people can be done. But Craggesund cannot send everybody home in this circumstance; they keep them at work and pay them for their time regardless. What this results in is a very busy canteen and for us milkmen, a doubling of the usual delivery quantities.

'I'm sorry,' I say.

'Have you got it at the depot?'

'Yes,' I say. 'I'm sure it's there all ready and waiting.'

I return to the van feeling suitably chastened. The Bean must have forgotten to mention the shutdown to me. But I shouldn't have promised the chef that the milk was at the depot, because I don't know one way or the other. It would be unlike the Bean, but it was possible that she'd forgotten to order the extra milk entirely.

Graham is striding about in his half-mast jeans when I get back to the depot. He stops and waves a big, meaty hand at me as I park up.

'Left the Craggesund milk, eh?'

'Some of it.'

'They're on shutdown.'

'I know that now.'

'What?' he says. 'You've already been up there?' He laughs. 'Bet laddo wasn't too happy.'

43

'No,' I say. I walk off towards the fridge and shout back over my shoulder. 'Can you move your van out into the yard? I need the ramp.'

'Aye,' he says. ''Spose. It'll make me late, like.'

I scowl to myself once I'm out of sight. I don't want to make him late. But he knows a customer like Craggesund is more important than a few individuals down on a domestic round. I hear him move his van and then hear him back my van in.

The trolley is still there in the fridge. It's the only one left. The Bean had obviously ordered it and trolleyed it up the night before with the rest, as usual. And I'd just forgotten, or miscounted. Shit. I wheel it out, and of course it's somehow wobbly and stiff, unbalanced and heavy. I get it out to the bottom of the ramp, take a deep breath and heave it up the slope as fast as I can. But I misjudge; it veers off to the right, its right front wheel slips over the edge and the sudden shift in weight means the whole thing is wrenched from my grip and the trolley is suddenly toppling into the nicely painted van side, denting it, and then it slowly slides forwards and down, its sharp metal corner scoring the van with a great grey arc.

'Fuck.'

Graham sucks air in through his teeth. 'Beany won't like that,' he says.

'Just help me,' I say.

44

The La'al Tattie Shop

O N MY WAY BACK to the depot from Craggesund, I like to swing through Egremont so that I can stop at the La'al Tattie Shop. In today's case it's on my second return from Craggesund that I make the stop. The jacket potatoes there are very, very good. It's usually about half past nine, but that's more or less halfway through my working day. On this occasion, it's about ten forty-five that I park up. It's a small café on the high street, with a black-and-white striped awning and a blackboard outside. In fact it isn't really a café: they just have one little round table inside with a couple of chairs.

I went to school in Egremont and these high street dinner stops are a direct echo of my teenage years. So much is the same: the grey feeling, the iron-ore statues of iron-ore miners outside the school gates, the charity shops, peeling-paint pubs. When I was at school we'd go across the street to Pat-a-Cake, where we bought chips and beans in yellow polystyrene cartons – or sometimes, if we were feeling extravagant, a portion of lasagne or shepherd's pie – and the women there always gave us loads, big portions, huge portions, because we were all growing boys and we were quite friendly, from what I remember, not trouble-makers or thieves like some of the other boys at that school, not at all. The women liked us. Pat-a-Cake is gone now, and the La'al Tattie Shop is in its place.

I hop down from the van. I remember lying on the grassy school grounds on hot days, and I remember the ruins of the castle at the south end of the grey main street, and I remember cross-country running around the muddy edges of the rugby pitch, and I remember kicking around school after badminton club waiting for a lift. The empty canteen, all those little red plastic chairs, all the empty buildings, squeaky-floored corridors, sometimes seeing a distant teacher staying late to monitor those in detention, maybe, or just going about their business. In that dead time between Friday badminton club and being picked up, we would play can-football across the concrete slabs – football, but with a squashed can. The only normal football rule that we enforced was that you couldn't use your hands. The rougher the game, the better: trips, shoves, shoulder-barges – all fine. The can was a difficult thing to catch when you were in goal because it was sharp-edged and it travelled hard and fast. We never wore gloves because we didn't play normal football, so we didn't have any. I always used to be the goalkeeper.

And there were those giant red-headed triplet boys who were our age but never came to school. Sometimes you saw them grinning around the small pathways that circled the edges of the housing estates. They didn't come to school because they didn't want to, and they were too dangerous to try and force. We knew not to get anywhere near them, but we didn't know why.

And I remember the blond-haired boy who sold drugs at the

school wandering around the hallways at break time with a lidless Flora tub full of pills. There was that time as well that he had a big block of resin he was trying to flog but the teachers found out and he hid under the stairs and tried to chew and swallow it all and they found him throwing up everywhere. I saw him about ten years ago crawling around on the uncleaned floor of a toilet cubicle in the Ship Launch, which was a pub in Egremont, a pub we used to go to all the time. But it isn't there any more.

'The usual?' asks Kathryn, as I step inside.

'Yes, please.'

'Nice day for it.'

'It is.'

Kathryn has shoulder-length brown hair, green eyes, a wide nose and freckles. She always wears black, with being in food. I find her very attractive, and the conversation is always a little stilted because of it. I think if we knew each other a little more, I would like her a lot. She's always smiling, but occasionally the smile kind of twists a little and becomes very knowing, almost suggestive, and it awakens something in me. Something I want to let sleep. I want to let it sleep because the truth is, I have very little tolerance for other people. I don't like their attention, or even really their presence, for any length of time. Kathryn is the one exception. But if I were to get to know her at all, or if we were to develop a relationship, then perhaps that would change. I'd be happy to give into the animal arousal if we could act on that and that alone. But obviously that's rarely how things go. And I already feel more for her than simple physical attraction. If I had any sense, I wouldn't come to the La'al Tattie Shop. Every time I leave I resolve not to return. But I always find myself back there, gazing across the counter at her hair and the thin red oven burns on her forearms.

'Here you go,' she says, sliding the paper bag across the formica. 'Two pounds sixty, please.'

I pay up and say thank you. She smiles and I feel it in my stomach. 'And a coffee, please,' I suddenly blurt. 'Strong.'

'Late night?' That smile again.

'Yeah,' I say. 'No sleep.'

'In a bad way, or . . . ?'

I stare at her.

'You milkmen aren't like in the films, huh?'

'What films?'

She laughs sharply and shakes her head.

The First Orders

DANIEL WAS IN AGAIN today. For a handsome man, he's very, very bad at picking up signals. I'm going to send him a dream. Give him a kick. Put some ideas in his head. It's a bit more honest than a charm, at least. Actually, he isn't handsome. He would be properly handsome if he was a bit less *nervous*. As it is, he's just kind of good-looking. He's got a nice face, behind all the beard and the hair. Talk about damning with faint praise. But the nervousness does seem to come with a kindness and to be honest, I haven't even had a 'nice face' in a while, so all things considered, he's not bad. So many of the men around here have those massive, muscly torsos, and wear tight, long T-shirts and skinny jeans. They look like triangles walking around on their points. I don't understand it. But there's no reason why I should, I suppose. Presumably they're just trying to make themselves feel good.

Anyway. My socials are doing pretty well. Lots of new followers from the US, due to me accentuating the old English roots of some of the spells, I think. I feel like I'd do better if I wasn't anonymous, but I'm not ready to drop the anonymity yet. The website's getting a good few views, and I've even had a couple of orders. One was from nearby, weirdly – Wasdale. They wanted a witch bottle. The item description I wrote has the line 'to protect from unwanted spirits', and the buyer repeated that in their order notes. 'Need this to protect from unwanted spirits / unwelcm ghost of family member, long dead. Will send hair as required.' Witch bottles are tricky, because you need the subject to provide some of the raw materials. I'm glad I got the PO box set up; hopefully I'll get enough orders to make it worthwhile. I was thinking of asking Daniel to help me out with deliveries. Let's see how we get on.

Decision Gate

IT WAS AS IF another person – another me, a different version of me – had moved into my body. During that time I honestly felt as if there were three of us living in the flat. And this new me, this third person – they were a more overt and explicit liar than I'd ever been. I told Ellie I'd finished the first draft of the book, but I hadn't. I'd spent all that time on about ten pages. I was way behind schedule and didn't want to admit it. Eventually I pretended that I was sending it out to agents, when I wasn't. She came off the pill and I stopped initiating sex. When she tried to initiate, I either pretended to be asleep – if we were in bed – or, if we were somewhere else (the kitchen, the living room, the park) to be distracted, too tired, busy-minded, stressed out. It wasn't much of a pretence.

One morning she simply presented me with an ultimatum.

'If we're to have a baby, we need to have sex. So either you commit to our decision and to me, and we start fucking again, or you admit that we want different things, and we break up.'

I stood with one hand on the plunger of the cafetière. I wondered which version of me was going to respond. I pressed the plunger down and watched the agitated coffee grounds swirl around inside the glass. I felt similar turmoil behind my eyes; if I closed them, I could see red and black tendrils writhing against each other.

'I want to be with you,' I said. 'It's the truth.' I still wasn't sure which me was in control. 'I'm just— I need to forget what we're trying to do in order to have sex, I think. There's something about it that turns me off. Takes me out of the moment. I need to shut down my brain and let my body drive itself.'

'Well,' she said, and then she stopped herself from saying something. She waited a moment, and then spoke again. 'If you're lying, you're going to end up trapped. I don't want that. I don't want you to feel trapped, I don't want you to resent me and I don't want you to resent our baby.'

I didn't know it at the time, but the way I felt about other people was not entirely normal. I was removed – detached – from every relationship I had, whether it be with family, friends, or my wife. I didn't trust anybody, but I didn't realise that. I wasn't truly present in any interaction or conversation I ever made; I never thought about what I wanted or what I felt, but instead the effect my words or actions might have. As if I were an observer experimenting with my life, instead of a participant. I acted as if the people around me were all the same as me – that is, as if they had no solid core, and no guiding principles, and that they, like me, were either saying or doing whatever was most expeditious for them, or whatever they felt like they should be saying or doing. I never considered actual meaning, or actual feelings. But as I'd considered the prospect of becoming a parent, I'd felt something. In idle moments I'd picture our future selves, happy in a full, busy home. Sharing the books and toys and films and games that we'd loved as kids with our own children. I was prepared to work hard for it – in some kind of job to earn money, yes, but also the work of being a parent. But now here it was: the decision point, on which all of these abstract futures depended. At which point they began to manifest. A *decision gate,* Ellie might have called such a threshold in her profession. And here I was, trying to move forwards through the gate, and something inside me was not cooperating.

It was mostly because of Robert. For a very short while Robert had been my baby brother, but then he'd died. Sudden infant death syndrome. It had left my mother almost catatonic, and damaged my father in ways less overt but, I think, just as severe. Eventually he died too. Robert was the only baby I'd ever really known, and I couldn't shake the grief, fear and loss that I still associated with the idea of babies, the idea of having a baby.

That night I let Ellie tie me up. Once I'd diminished my own agency, things were easier. There were no problems physiologically. I took this as a positive sign, for some reason; deep down, I told myself, I am at peace with this decision. I didn't have to think too much about what I was doing. There was no decision-making into which doubt could creep. Nor were there any moments in which I did not feel entirely absorbed by what she was doing to me. Things felt different. Not only was my body responding positively, but every sense had opened up somehow. My skin was hypersensitive. The room was alive with dark shadows cast by the flickering candlelight. Her skin smelled oily – not that she was wearing any – and tasted sharply of salt. All sounds seemed to originate inside my head, deep within, as opposed to finding their way in through my ears. And later still, when the time came, every time I thought I'd reached my climax, it would instead just climb and grow. It felt stepped, or tiered, as if I was ascending, and with each level up it somehow doubled in intensity. It lifted me out of time and filled me with light. Every muscle grew rigid and every joint locked. Eventually that light burst out of me – it felt like a rupture – and for a period my frozen form was nothing but a conduit for it.

After coming back to myself, I blinked, swallowed, closed my eyes again. I wondered if I'd unwittingly exiled my unwelcome other self. Cast him out through some sort of sex magic. But no. The black and red tentacles were still there inside my head, wrestling.

Only now, years later, do I think back to that period and wonder at how readily I accepted the premise of some kind of magical other, inside me.

The Cat

I SIT CROSS-LEGGED IN AN armchair with a whisky and a book, but I'm not reading the book. I'm not sober enough to read. I'm thinking about my wife. I'm imagining her taking photos, but then, in my head, it becomes Kathryn taking the photos.

River static. Blengdale. Fresh and wet. Kathryn is taking photos of off-putting things. Eruptions of thick, mossy growths. Florid orange gunk settled at the bottom of forest pools. Skullish rocks dripping black slime. Fleshy ferns, unfurling. 'Look at this mess,' she says, huskily. I want her to take her clothes off and step into the frame. Pose obscenely in the mud, in the brown and green. I want to join her in nakedness. I want a walker to spy us between the trees, our bodies entwined like roots, full of blood and turgid, burgeoning, burgeoning, until she's good and arced and sated and I can let the seed spurt violently, like an accident.

Later on, higher up – in this fantasy we're on a walk, ostensibly – where the forest is entirely managed pine, I break from the path and pass between the trees. There are only a few feet between the ground and the lowest branches, so I have to crouch. I want to go deeper so I move on all fours. My hands sink into the ochre carpet of needles.

There's a rustle behind me. And then hands on my arse, sliding up the back of my coat. The woods have been playing on her mind too, then. I take off so that she has to chase me. I raise up from my hands and knees to my hands and feet, running like a misshapen dog. Quiet laughter. All sound falls dead here. It's a soft, dark place. Tiny flies drift through the stagnant air. She catches my ankle, just, but it's enough to bring me down. She's on top of me. I turn my head so that my face isn't pressed into the ground. She kisses and bites my ear. I hear her unzip her waterproof coat. I twist, rolling over between her legs, so that I can look up at her. My hair is full of pine needles. She is smiling, happy. Above us the pine branches cross and layer each other so densely as to form a kind of cocoon. We've stepped out of time here. We're alone in the world, and nobody can find us, and we can do whatever we want.

I wake to the sound of heavy hoofbeats. Something huge barrelling away. I shriek and clutch at Kathryn and we're both breathless, confused, waking in animal panic. I catch the sense of a great beast in motion but night has fallen and here beneath the pines the darkness is thick. The darkness is all I see. The hooves pound into the forest floor, further and further away. How something big enough to make that sound can move so quickly beneath these low branches is a mystery to me.

I'm waking up in the armchair again. The window is at my back again, and I feel certain that if I were to turn around and look, the ragged figure would be out there once more, watching me. It takes every effort not to look. I walk through the dark room towards the top of the stairs and it feels like it takes physical strength, as if there's some force, or some invisible elastic band, trying to pull me back to the window.

I ALMOST CAN'T FACE the embarrassment of going to the La'al Tattie Shop the next morning. But I tell myself that I'm being stupid; Kathryn doesn't know about my dream. She smiles at me as I enter and I will my cheeks not to redden.

'The usual, Daniel?'

'Yes, please.'

I watch her go about the business behind the counter and think about the dream of her. It was so vivid. I become uncomfortable and try to study the menus on the wall. But my eyes keep returning to her. I suddenly want her in a much more direct and immediate way than usual.

'Hey,' I say, 'do you want to go for a drink?'

'Yeah,' she says, without turning around. 'Can do.'

'What time do you finish?'

'About five. Meet me at the Cat, at six?'

'I can do that.'

'Good.' She turns, grinning. She has bright, slightly pointed teeth. Briefly, I see the pink tip of her tongue through them.

LIKE MOST PUBS IN Egremont, or any of these towns, the Cat is an uneasy mix of traditional old-man pub and widescreen TV multiplex. Steroidal young men lounge around the screens in tracksuits, hands down pants, while old men with red faces and pot bellies sit morosely atop barstools. Surround-sound football commentary drowns out speech. Whichever way you look, fruit machines are blinking. The room smells of spilled lager and chips.

I've come by taxi so order a pint. Kathryn isn't here yet. I'm halfway through the drink before she arrives, but that's only because I'm drinking fast. Too fast. Slow down. Slow it down.

'Hi,' she says, from behind.

'Hi,' I say. 'Hello.'

'So what brought this on?' She motions to the barkeeper and taps a pump clip.

'I've been meaning to ask you out for a while,' I manage.

'I'm glad you did,' she says.

It is easier to talk with her than I thought it would be. I realise that it's been a long time since I've had a conversation with somebody outside of work, and I start to enjoy it.

The Young Man

As I bounce down the long lane towards the depot, I note that Ryan's van isn't there. Ryan usually speeds through all his rounds, races back to the depot, unloads, boxes up any orders for the next day and darts – all before I get back. And this suits me, because I don't like him and I don't want to see him. The fact that his van isn't sitting there, dormant, makes my heart sink, because it probably means that he's still out somewhere and has yet to return – and could do so while I'm still here.

So I hurriedly begin to unload the van, wheeling the first jinky trolley across and down the ramp and through the heavy sliding doors and down the concrete corridor into the walk-in fridge. The fridge is always chaos by this point in the day, so I have to have a bit of a sort-out in there – it's like one of those puzzles where there's one square missing, and you have to use that tiny little bit of space to slowly rearrange all of the other squares, piece by piece, until you have a picture or – in the case of the fridge – you've moved the empty space to where you want it. That is, by the door – where it should have been all along, of course, to enable the orderly return of trolleys. I generally put it down to the others always being under too much time pressure to put their trolleys back properly. But on this occasion, my breath misting in the dark temperature-controlled room, I find myself quietly cursing them.

Fridge sorted and first trolley returned, I go back to my van for the others. Ryan still isn't back. Good. Maybe I'll be done before he shows up. There doesn't seem to be anybody else around, either. Four of us work here: the Bean, Graham, Ryan and myself. The Bean is usually around; she tends to stay at base. But the depot is completely still and silent, apart from a few scraps of cardboard blowing about, and the corrugated metal sheeting of the covered area creaking and whistling in the chill wind.

I hear his van approaching as I'm fitting my last trolley into the fridge. I know it's Ryan's because of the way he drives it, in the same way that you can recognise a person from the sound of their footsteps. And there is nobody else here to dilute his attentions. Typical.

It isn't so much that I don't *like* Ryan, I suppose. He just has a very threatening demeanour. I can't honestly say that I know him enough to dislike him. But I know enough not to want to get to know him. Simply the prospect of being alone with him feels like a risk. He's one of those people. On reflection, though, it's unlikely that he'll try to engage me in conversation. I can just nod and grunt and get on with stuff.

His van screeches to a halt, spraying grit and gravel. He flings his door open and jumps out. 'All right, marra,' he drawls, as he sees me.

'All right,' I say.

'Where's that fucking bellend?'

'Who?'

'Queen Bean. The Beanis. Want to give her a flick.' He quickly drops into a boxing stance and throws a fast punch in my direction. I flinch, even though he's a good ten feet away.

He sniggers at me in a way that I don't really like.

'I don't know where the Bean is,' I say. I worry that she's had to go up to Craggesund to do some grovelling. That would be a big contract to lose. 'I'm going to go and listen to the answerphone, see if any orders have come in.'

'Aye, righto.' He turns to his van and walks around the back to open the double doors.

'Wait a minute,' I say. 'What's that?'

'What's what?'

It's not like me to challenge somebody. I frequently feel the urge, and know that I'd get satisfaction from the occasional argument or fight, but usually bite it back. A reputation for violence never helps anybody. Not in real life. But after asking Kathryn out, and having it go well, I'm feeling a little emboldened.

'On your passenger seat. That's my carrier. I've been looking for that. I've been running late all week and I think that was in large part because I did not have my carrier.'

'Aye, well. It was just on the side. Didn't know it was yours.'

'It was *not* just on the side!' I exclaim. 'It was in my van!'

'Listen, mate,' Ryan says, reaching into his van and getting the carrier, 'having your carrier wouldn't have stopped you getting a flat fucking tyre, or forgetting the extra Craggesund trolley. Don't blame me just because you can't fucking drive and hit a sharp rock or some shit.' He throws the carrier at me and I'm not prepared for

61

it. When I try to catch it, it hits the ends of my fingers and falls to the floor. It's made of metal and the impact hurts.

Ryan laughs and shakes his head.

I pick my carrier up, and wave it at him. 'I bought this myself, off the internet!' I shout. Then I throw it into *my* van and storm into the Bean's house to listen to the answerphone. Thankfully, no new orders have come in, so I'm done. I just get on my bike and ride away. Behind me, Ryan drop-kicks empty cardboard boxes and whoops like an excited child. For a brief moment, I wonder where he's been to make himself so late. But the curiosity passes after a second. I just don't really care.

The Beach at Drigg

THE NEXT NIGHT, THE figure is out on the grass again. I stand in the window and stare at it. It doesn't walk, but it isn't motionless. It sways on the spot, and its ragged garments flutter in the wind. It's a clearer night tonight, and I can see more. Its legs are bare and pale in the moonlight. There'll be a frost come morning; if it's a person, it will be painfully cold.

I feel as if – and I don't mean this literally, but it's as close an approximation as I can manage at the moment – there is a parcel in my head. And I know that there is some information about this figure inside the parcel. The parcel is wrapped in brown paper. And I try to unwrap it, but I can't find the seam. I rip open the paper, but there's just more paper underneath. I know that somewhere inside me there is a memory that might help explain what this figure is. But I cannot access that memory.

It holds its arms out to the sides, palms forward, almost beatifically, as if about to offer a blessing. Its head, beneath the black pointed hood, tilts to one side, as if listening.

I snap the curtains shut.

Naturally, I do not sleep properly that night. Nor the next. I research hallucinations on the internet, and order a carbon monoxide detector. I stop drinking whisky. I lay wide awake in bed every night, my bedroom being on the ground floor, imagining the figure slowly prowling – or shambling, or crawling – from the grass around the side to the front of the house, to wait outside my bedroom window. I stare at the thick curtains, certain that it is just on the other side, looking back. So I get up and go upstairs and make some coffee, and then fall asleep in the armchair with the coffee just sitting there on the coffee table, waiting for me to drink it.

A couple of weeks pass. Some nights I manage not to look outside. Some nights, I look outside and it isn't there. I'm happy to get out in the mornings and get to work. I don't tell anybody about it. Between getting home from work and going to bed, I sit at my computer and try to write, but really I'm expending all of my mental energy just resisting the urge to look out of the window.

I get home from a particularly tough day; I'm too tired to be driving, really, and I've been making mistakes. When you make a mistake, the Bean sends you immediately back out to correct it. For example, today I left Mrs Grey semi-skimmed instead of whole, so I had to go back to Gosforth after I'd finished my usual rounds and replace it. I'd forgotten that the Naylors were back from holiday, so I hadn't left them anything, when I should have – so I'd had to go back to Beckermet too. And that's not to mention the bad driving. Pulling out of a junction when I shouldn't have. Doing a three-point turn in a nursery car park and narrowly missing a car behind me, but only by luck; I hadn't seen it at all.

'Just check the bloody File,' the Bean had said, frustrated.

'I'm sorry,' I said.

'What's going on? Yer head's a shed.'

'I know, I'm sorry.'

I can't tell her I'm not sleeping. If I'm not fit to drive, she'll send me home, unpaid.

So it's been a long day, and I feel shaky and nervous. Because of my internet research, I'm hyper aware that stress or anxiety or extreme tiredness can cause hallucinations, so I feel primed to see that figure again, which in turn makes me feel even more anxious and nervy. Because I'm on my own so much, it's difficult to break the cycle of thought. Difficult to get out of my own head. I think about going for a walk.

In the end I go to the beach at Drigg, on my bike. I ride across the level crossing and down the long tarmac approach. You can't see the sea on your way there, because of the row of dunes blocking the sight of it. Except for a little glimmer where the road cut through them. Above is a mass of grey clouds: not that uniform blanket you often get, but a pile-up of different sizes and shapes that conspire to hide the sky. The dunes are covered in long grass that sways. The sun is approaching the horizon, and where the sea and sky meet, orange fire is breaking between the clouds, throwing their uneven surfaces into vivid relief, making them look solid.

I dismount and lock my bike to the insubstantial wire fence that keeps the sheep on the dunes and off the road. Then I open the gate at the end of the road and pass through on to the beach.

Drigg's a sandy beach and really quite beautiful. But Netherhall glowers from the coast to the north, raising all kinds of concerns in the minds of visitors, so it doesn't get the tourist attention it probably deserves. And it's true that the northwest coast is a cold coast, with frequent bitter winds. Tonight the wind is up. Sometimes the sea can be calm and blue, but it often isn't. Tonight it's choppy and dark grey-green. Seagulls cry. I head south, putting Netherhall to my back.

There's nobody else around. I walk aimlessly down the shore. It feels good to be walking without purpose, without that sensation of time pressure urging you to move more quickly, to run a little bit. The sunset becomes more and more beautiful; it looks as if it's burning the clouds away from the western sky. Ships far out at sea put their lights on, which I like to see. It reminds me that everything is connected. I visualise networks of shipping lanes crossing the seven seas. There is a great system of freight, which in turn plugs into other great systems that, despite their flaws, generally all work together to keep the lights on, to keep food on the shelves. I watch the far lights slowly move along the horizon and then disappear. I see car headlights move across the Isle of Man. Beyond the Isle of Man is the dusky blue shoulder of Northern Ireland – a very faint, distant outline against the pink and purple sky.

I find two old wooden chairs standing upright in the sand, facing the water. Flotsam, presumably. I keep walking until I find the old shipwreck, if that's what it is; the rusty metal ribcage of some old vessel, crusted with limpets.

I hear a low rumble and look up. The rumble grows into a scream as two fighter planes tear past. Whether they're destined for the war or not, they remind me of the war. I watch them until they're out of sight, and then turn around and head back to the gate and my bike.

Approaching the gate, I stop. Up to my right, on top of the dunes, is an old World War II lookout hut, a small, concrete building now mostly used by sheep for shelter and teenagers for drinking. This stretch of coastline features various military and Ministry of Defence facilities, most now decommissioned and dismantled. But vestiges remain.

Next to the bunker stands my nocturnal visitor. They strike exactly the same pose as they do when in the grass outside my house, but their cloak or cape or the sheet or whatever it is billows more wildly in this coastal wind. As usual, they're angled so as to face me. I stare up at them. Then I run. I run for the gate, which means I have to move *closer* to the thing, which my body does not want to do. When I'm at the gate, I can see the lookout, just on the dune that rises immediately next to the path, but the figure was on the other side of the lookout, which means I can't see it. I fumble with the latch. It could be descending into the dunes right now. It could appear on the path between me and my bike at any moment. It could have gone down on to the beach, and be coming up behind me.

I get through the gate, struggle to close it again for a moment and then just leave it to clang open. I'm not wearing gloves and suddenly, upon trying to put the code into my bike lock, I realise that the cold has made my fingers numb. I don't look over my shoulder, much as I want to. In the end I get the code in, I shove the lock into my bike bag and I pedal as fast as I can away from the beach.

It's more or less dark by the time I get home. I put all the lights on downstairs and take off my shoes and coat. I'm going to have a whisky. I've gone without for two weeks, and I'm still seeing the damned thing, so it's not the alcohol. I can rule that out as a contributory factor. I go to the bathroom and run my hands under the hot tap to get some feeling back into them. I stare resolutely at the mirror above the sink, ensuring there's no chance of me looking at it, looking away, and then looking back at it and receiving a nasty surprise. I dry my hands, check the front door is locked and stomp upstairs.

I reach out to put the light on, but freeze before my hand hits the switch. The figure is sitting in my armchair, in the gloom. Its hooded head hangs forwards as if it is asleep. Close up, its legs and arms are pale brown, emaciated and horribly bruised. My heart hammers in my chest. I can't breathe. Then it takes a deep breath, its chest rising, and lets out a long, low moan. I nearly fall down the stairs in my haste to get away. Behind me, the moan becomes a sob, and the sobbing sound follows me out of the house, back on to my bike, down the road, all the way to the depot, where I throw my bike down into the gravel, unlock my van and climb gratefully inside. It's as if my brain has recorded that moan and that sobbing sound, and is replaying it on a loop. But I lie down on the wide cab seat, and close my eyes, and drift between full wakefulness and something gentler, and that is as much as I dare hope for.

The Patterns

THE NEXT DAY I'M putting away a delivery from the whole-saler, and the Bean calls me into her kitchen. The kitchen is muddy-floored, with piles of letters, bills and assorted paperwork covering every surface. The door is always open and nobody sits in here without their coat on. Decades-old crockery teeters in open cabinets, and blackened pans hang from hooks. This house used to be a farmhouse and the kitchen still feels like a farmer's kitchen, even though the Bean is by no stretch of the imagination a farmer. She does not grow things, or keep things alive.

'Bloody Craggesund, eh?'

'Yes,' I say.

'Now then. I'm angry. I'm really angry. I'd be angrier with you, but I'm angry with everybody else right now and I'm too bloody tired to act on it. Not just forgetting the trolley, but the bloody van, lad. You put that whacking great scrape in it. Looks like shit now.'

'I'm sorry.'

'You don't know how tight things are. You don't know how small

69

the margins are. Thing is, you shouldn't have to. I shouldn't have to tell you all that. You know what your job is and you know how to do it. It's not hard. It's hard for thickos, but it's not hard for a bright lad like you.' She's getting red in the face and her voice is wavering a little bit. 'You've got to respect it, is all. Maintain focus. Try. Don't get complacent. Don't get clumsy. Don't think you're above it. I can't afford fuck-ups, lad.' She stares hard at me. 'We've still got the contract. But you can't be late again. Understand? No speeding, but you *can't* be late.' She sighs. 'Anyway, that's not what I called you in for. It's that arsehole, Graham. He's leaving. Been offered another pound on the hour by fucking Dawson's. Need somebody new. Know anybody looking for work?'

'I don't think so.'

'Going to have to get somebody new. Don't want a friend of Ryan's. Ryan's been having somebody else in his van. Know anything about that?'

'No.'

'Aye. Could be one way he gets around so fast. He leaves his cab a right dump, so I went in there last night and the passenger-side door pocket is stuffed full of crisp packets. Driver side is empty.'

'I suppose it's a risk,' I ventured, 'if you don't know who they are.'

'Exactly! Could be some reprobate. And that's before we get on to tax and insurance. Anyway, Graham did the Bootle round and Ryan can't do that. You've got all the old biddies down Bootle, they like the craic. Got to be a people person for the Bootle round. Got to be human.' She purses her lips, and then bares her teeth. 'No, Ryan can't do it. On a Friday down Bootle you've got to be the shop. You've got to do maths. Ryan can't do maths. You know where I'm going?

It's got to be you, lad. You're on the Bootle round now. But you've still got to do the others, until I've got somebody else in. And Ryan will pick up Graham's other rounds – Drigg, Seascale. And he'll take Ravenglass off you. You'll still be on the valleys at weekends.'

'When does the pattern change?' I ask.

'Tomorrow. You're on Bootle tomorrow. You'll still be doing Corney, Beckermet, Thornhill, Westlakes and Craggesund. I know you like yer stops at the La'al Tattie Kitchen.'

'Shop,' I say. 'La'al Tattie Shop. What do you mean? No, I don't.'

'Aye, right. Just don't dally. You'll already be hitting Bootle and Waberthwaite much later than they're used to. So tomorrow it's your usual, then back to the depot, then Bootle and Waberthwaite.'

'Okay.'

'Is she pretty? The Tattie Kitchen woman?'

'I don't know who you mean.'

She smiles. 'You don't mind me taking Ravenglass off you, do you? You won't miss Deborah?'

Deborah was the Post Office woman. She would open the shop door with her dressing gown open and nothing underneath it. I always got the impression it was just accidental though. 'No,' I say, 'I don't think so.'

'I saw her once in the Westview Hotel bar, up on the top there? Ski-poling.'

I shake my head. I don't know what she's driving at.

'Y'know?' She mimes the action. 'Two men at once. As brazen as you like.'

'Oh.' I frown. 'Was one of the men Bobby?'

'Oh aye.'

Bobby is the Post Office man. He is irritatingly officious, and has a long scar across his forehead.

'Look. You and Ryan, you're young lads and the women like you, and I know what it's like. Just don't do it until after you've hit Craggesund, don't dally when you *do* do it, and don't do it in the van like Ryan does.'

'I wouldn't.' I shrug. 'I don't do that.'

'Aye, all right.' She eyes me for a moment. 'I'm throwing a lot more hours at you, I know that. But you're paid by the hour. So it's more money, aye?'

'Oh yeah, I understand. It's fine.'

'If you've got something else going on, if you can't do the hours, tell me now.'

I shake my head.

She nods, as if satisfied. 'More hours, more money,' she says.

'Okay,' I say. 'Thank you.'

The Transformation

So it's going all right with Daniel. We've started sleeping together, which I mention only because it's noteworthy. As in – he's a different person in bed. Like an alter-ego being unleashed. In a good way. The rest of the time, he can be very wound up. He's either very wound up, or barely there at all. It sounds like he's not getting a lot of sleep, due to – and this is weird, timing-wise – his own unwanted spirit. I've offered to help him out in that department, though I haven't explained fully what I do beyond the La'al Tattie Shop. I've alluded to a couple of things. I'm not sure if he's picked up on them, though. I want to help him. I want him to relax a bit more, around me at least.

So I'm working up a witch bottle for him. I'll need him to make a contribution or two, mind.

I'm getting a slight increase in requests, despite holding off from advertising on local Facebook groups and that kind of thing. I want to advertise, but I can't physically deliver anything at the moment, even if I'm able to meet the demand. Charms, wards, unguents, candles, various preparations: all apotropaic stuff, which was not the aspect that I expected to take off. I need to expand my back garden a bit and put in some foraging time. And given Daniel's new rounds, he's perfectly placed to deliver some of it – I'm reluctant to send much through the post, due to the potential for damage, or sniffer dogs.

The Witch Bottle

KATHRYN PRESENTS ME WITH two brown paper bags. One of them, I know, contains my usual – a hot, buttery jacket potato, piled high with cheese and coleslaw. The other bag has a tag tied to its handles. I look at the tag and see that she has drawn a milk bottle on it, with a row of three small kisses. She's also written 'For My Milkman'.

'What's this?'

'Have a look.'

I open the bag to find a milk bottle. I remove it and hold it up to my face. It's full of yellowish fluid and contains three long, rusty nails that lean against the inside of the bottle. There's some kind of orange sediment at the bottom with lumps in it, and a dark scum is floating on the top of the liquid.

'What's this?' I say again, and then, suddenly worrying that I sound rude, I add, 'Thank you. I love it.'

She laughs. 'Don't worry,' she says. 'I know it looks horrible. It is horrible, in some ways. It's a witch bottle. I made it for you, to help with your visitor.'

I look at her. 'Thank you,' I say. 'You . . . made it?'

'The bit I haven't told you, the bit you're missing, is that – okay, get ready – I'm a witch.'

'Okay,' I say. I can feel myself frowning. 'As in – a real one?'

'Yes, a real one.'

'It's no stranger than ghosts, I suppose.'

'Well, exactly. And one kind of magic witches' practice is apotopraic magic, which is intended to avert evil influences or deter malign presences. Hence, this witch bottle.'

'Thank you,' I say, more sincerely this time.

'I'd like your help in return, though.'

'Of course.'

'I've got a website, with a blog and that. And I give advice. And people are starting to order things. Things like that bottle. But I have to be careful not to accept too many orders, because I can't deliver products myself – I don't want people to know who I am, and some of this stuff can't go in the post, if you know what I mean.'

I don't really know what she means.

'So I was hoping you could help me out with some deliveries?'

'Of course.'

'Well then!' She claps. 'I'll start advertising properly!' She reaches over the counter and gives me a hug. I put my arms around her, but its awkward with the counter between us. I lower my head and kiss the side of her neck before I know what I'm doing. She sighs and runs a hand up into my hair. And then when I try to straighten up, she doesn't let me go. 'Kiss me there again,' she says. So I do.

'You smell of sweat,' she says.

'I know,' I say. 'I'm sorry.'

'No, it's the good kind. Smells like real work. And you look good in your work clothes, too.'

After a few more moments, a few more kisses, a few more sighs, we disentangle. 'As well as deliveries,' she says, 'maybe you could keep me in bottles?'

'I'll get you some out of the van right now,' I say.

'Look at you,' she says.

'It's nice being able to provide,' I say.

'Listen. Your witch bottle. You need to bury it by the door or hide it in the wall by the door. It protects the threshold. It protects your home. But it needs something of yours to make it work properly.'

'Something important to me?'

'Well, maybe. Or, better, something *of* you. Hair, blood, urine.'

'Oh,' I say. 'Okay.'

She smiles that smile again. 'Let me know if you want any help with that.'

'I want to bury it tonight.'

'Then why don't you go and get me those empty bottles and then come and find me in the kitchen? It's dead between now and dinner.'

'Okay,' I say.

I'M IN AND OUT of a lot of pub and café kitchens all the time in this job. The La'al Tattie Shop's kitchen is the cleanest and most well-ordered one I've ever seen. Kathryn stands in the middle of it wearing all her black, surrounded by the smooth gleam of brushed steel. She slowly peels off her disposable latex gloves and then lifts herself up to sit on a worktop. She beckons me. I carefully deposit the numerous empty milk bottles that I have my fingers in and go to her. She opens her legs and wraps them around me and we kiss again. She stops me from lifting up her T-shirt. 'A customer might come in,' she says, 'and I'd have to go back through.' She doesn't resume the kissing. 'Take them off,' she says, tugging on the waistband of my waterproof trousers. She withdraws the witch bottle from the bag as she watches me roll the trousers down. I unzip my muddy, battered waterproof coat and shrug that off too.

THAT AFTERNOON I LIFT one of the sandstone paving stones outside the door to my house. It's a cold, misty day. The mountains loom out of the banks of white fog and their peaks are disappear into thick, low cloud. This kind of weather warps perspective and the mountains feel gargantuan. Impossibly big.

Underneath the paving stone is sand and mud. I dig out a pit and bury the witch bottle in it.

The Damage

Mʀ sɪssoɴs, ᴡʜo ɪs perhaps the friendliest customer on Corney Fell, is frowning and stubbly. He's not even fully dressed, which is unusual for him – he's wearing an old yellowed vest and some dirty shellsuit bottoms. Normally he'd have been out on the farm for two hours by this point. He waves at the fridge.

'Just stick it in there, lad.'

'Everything okay, Mr Sissons?'

'Aye. No.'

I open the fridge door. The inside is filthy, coated with the mould of old food and spilled fluids. I carefully slot the two-litre bottle on to the shelf.

'I keep seeing her.'

'Who?'

'The old lass. Me wife.'

I don't let him see my eyes widen. Then I say the wrong thing. 'I didn't know you were married.'

He starts to sniffle and covers his eyes with his hand. 'Used to be,' he says. 'Used to be. She died. And now I'm having these dreams. Don't feel like dreams though.'

'Why not? What do you mean?'

'I wake up and she's . . . y'know. Touching me. Like she used to. Long time ago! When we were young. She'd . . . y'know. Wake me up. With her hands.'

'Oh! Okay. You don't need to tell me that.'

'I'm asleep and she's . . . touching me. I can feel her hands in my dreams. And I'm waking up. I'm half asleep. And I can feel her and I forget she's dead, forget that I haven't felt her hands like that for thirty years. They're cold and soft. I open my eyes and look across at her. And she's there! She's really there. But she's messed up from the accident. From when she died. Then I think, it's a dream. It's a nightmare. But I don't wake up. I just lie there and she's touching me. I slide away, out of bed. Run downstairs. Sit here drinking coffee. Check the bed after the sun's come up and she's gone. But the next night, it happens again.'

'Have you tried sleeping on the sofa?'

He looks at me balefully. Then breaks into a harsh laughter. 'Don't think that would make a difference. It's not the bed that's the problem, is it?' He takes a long gulp of his cold coffee. 'It's the ghost.'

OUTSIDE OF THE TOWNS and villages, many of our customers are farmers. Others live in old farmhouses but run them as bed and breakfasts, for walkers. Yet more live in farmhouses that they've inherited, but don't really run as farms any more; land gets sold off as generations pass, until you have somebody living in a big old tumble-down building and a couple of fields, but no business.

On the valley rounds, I feel like Postman Pat, driving my van down the narrow winding roads, up and down small hills, beeping my horn before traversing little humpback bridges, as all around birds chirp in the trees and sheep bleat from the fields. Friendly sheepdogs nip at my tyres and I know everybody's names, even if they don't know mine. Customer names as listed in the File become almost like a mantra or a poem as I memorise them. Branthwaite, Agnew, Osborne, Phizacklea. The Naylors, the Taylors, the Putnams and the Allingtons. Or I make associations between names that follow each other. Race, Pavey, Sissons. The Goodwins and the Badleys. Wood and Stone. Royle and Waters. In a barn conversion down one long lane, a Mrs James lives next door to a Mr Brown.

Sometimes I have to put the handbrake on and sit in idle as shepherds release their flocks of sheep on to the road ahead of me. I bob in and out of beautiful little stone houses with perfect gardens, in and out of working farm kitchens, in and out of mansions with elaborately tiled floors, expensive wallpaper and gleaming dark wood staircases following the curve of the hallway wall. Wherever I go, there's a perfect view of mountains or lakes or rivers or the sea, or combinations thereof. At times, especially when the weather is good, I feel as if I live in some kind of pastoral fantasy. There isn't as much pressure on the valley rounds, because you aren't trying to align with office or factory hours, or even commuters, really. If I didn't have to do the other rounds – and of course if the pay was enough for me to become independent of my uncle's charity – it would have been the perfect job.

So once I've got those pressurised early morning deliveries behind me – and once I've picked up my usual from the La'al Tattie Shop – I relax and enjoy the rest of the day. I enjoy being the friendly local neighbourhood milkman. I provide sustenance for farmers to keep them going; everything hostelry keepers need to feed their guests a hearty breakfast before they head out on to the fells. I drop off litres of whole milk for slightly manic and well-to-do young parents with growing toddlers. I stop by and slide glass bottles and bruised fruit into the fridges of pensioners who like their tea milky and their pears soft. I listen to them talk.

'It's queer as owt,' says Race. 'Every night now. Summat on the landing. There's me in bed, wide-eyed, and summat on the landing, just scratching at the bedroom door, like.'

He looks tired. It's a nice bright day and we're standing in Race's yard, right at the end of the valley. Great grey mountains rear up on either side of us, scraps of white cloud caught on their sharp peaks.

'Mice?' I say.

'Aye,' he says. 'There's nowt in the traps like, but aye. Mice, or rats. I mean, the first couple of times I opened the door and had a look, but there was nothin' there.'

'They run away though, don't they?'

'Except the last time. The last time I opened the door and looked out at the landing like. I was looking all over the landing. But then, just out the corner of my eye, I saw a head at the top of the stairs, like somebody was crawling up the stairs, like. A head and a pair of hands. But it was dark. I put the light on and it was gone. I mean, of course it was.'

'Could still have been mice? Or rats. Looking like something else in the dark.'

'You don't believe in ghosts then, lad?'

'Well,' I say, and I struggle for a moment and then I decide to just tell the truth. 'I do, but I thought it might make you feel better if I persuaded you that it was something else.'

He looks at me and then laughs. 'What would make me feel better, lad, is if it stopped bloody happening. If I could get some bloody sleep again.' He rubs his eyes. 'I know what I need to do. I just don't want to do it.'

I wait for him to elaborate, and when he doesn't, I ask the question. 'What do you need to do?'

'Never mind that,' he says. 'Never mind that.'

'We might be thinking of the same thing,' I say, 'but in case we're not . . .'

I write down Kathryn's web address in my order book, tear off the slip and hand it over. 'Have a look,' I say.

I BROACH THE SUBJECT with old Mrs Goodwin one day, as I deliver her whole milk, bacon, eggs and bananas. She stands in the doorway to her kitchen, slippers on, apron on, thick glasses magnifying her eyes. The warm smell of baking drifts out into the muddy yard. 'Saw the Fallen Stock wagon was here the other day.'

'Oh yes,' she says. 'That's right.'

'They're around a lot recently, it feels like.'

'Do you think so, lad? We don't get them in any more often, I don't think.'

'Is there anything going on? A new disease or something?'

'Oh no, nothing like that. We lost some sheep to a bloody dog. Should've seen the state of them, lad. Ripped right open, they were. Keep 'em on their leads! Dogs! Or better still, shoot the little bastards!'

'I'm sorry,' I say. 'About the sheep, I mean. I don't have a dog.'

'Oh, it's all right. And if you did, you'd keep it on a lead. You're a good lad.'

'What are the Fallen Stock drivers like?'

'Ooh, they're like men used to be!' She laughs, but I can't work out if the laugh is happy or sad. 'Thinking of getting into the business?'

'No,' I say. 'No, I like what I do.'

'Suppose it's all one big business really,' she says. 'Right, bye then.' And she suddenly and firmly shuts the door.

I find that, with our older customers – they suddenly just get tired of talking and shut the door. Even when they'd been the ones that seemed to really want to chat.

It's only when I get back in the van that I think about her final words. *It's all one big business really.* She's right, of course, in a way. But I don't like the idea of it.

The Real Husband

THE BOOTLE ROUND IS unique amongst our runs because of its Friday routine. On a Friday, on the Bootle run, customers will leave little shopping lists out on their doorsteps, usually accompanied by a five-pound or ten-pound note. Or they'll come out to the van to have a browse. This isn't the way we do things anywhere else. Anywhere else, if a customer wants something extra, they have to place an order in advance. In Bootle, those rules just don't apply.

'Why don't customers in Bootle have to place orders like anybody else?' I ask.

'Graham,' mutters the Bean, darkly. 'Graham made that round his own, he did.' If we were outside she would spit on the ground, I'm sure of it. 'And now he's fucking off to Dawson's.'

There are numerous difficulties caused by the Bootle Friday, as I think of it. One is that you frequently have to do maths, often on the spot in front of old people, involving only half-remembered prices. Another is that you never know what people are going to ask for, so you have to load the van up with a bit of everything. Invariably you fail, and you end up without that particular vegetable that the Knightley lot want and they slowly mill about the van, all four of them, parents and daughters, tutting and frowning and complaining that they won't be able to make the big ratatouille that they were planning, and you have to shrug and apologise even though they could have just fucking ordered what they needed if it was so important. Another difficulty is that some customers don't leave enough money out, so you have to keep a note in the File of how many pennies short they are – and then remember to add the difference in the following week. Only to find that they haven't put enough money out, again.

There are other quirks to the Bootle round. One is the weapons range: this is a Ministry of Defence facility on the coast. It feels strange being able to enter it. Not that I can just drive in, or go anywhere once I'm in. The Bean's got me clearance and I have to sign in as I go through the gate, and then I can only drive around the back and go into the kitchen. But it still feels strange, seeing the big signs declaring the national threat level (SEVERE), and knowing that just on the other side of that building, they fire experimental guns and artillery out over the sea.

And there's a little community that lives on a narrow, circular road – really, road is too grand a word for it – that you can only access by passing under the coastal railway. The single lane goes through a very narrow cutting under the line, so narrow that the van can only just get through it. You have to fold the wing mirrors in. And once through, you find yourself in this verdant, overgrown little pocket of bohemia – a cluster of small, low wooden houses with this one lane that goes around it, and weirdly, some big old manor houses on the outside of the lane. And they all have beautiful gardens and wildly successful vegetable patches, and all the kids run around with bare feet and they're all home-schooled in one of the manor houses. I have to interrupt lessons to drop off bread and milk for them all.

But the place makes me uneasy. Not the people – just the access. If the road under the bridge became blocked for any reason, nobody could get in or out.

The Hewitts, who have a long bungalow with a huge vegetable patch, are arguing when I arrive. I hear shouting as I get out of the van. The front door is open and he's leaving the house as I approach with their milk, eggs, bacon and bread. He scowls at me, tears fresh on his cheeks, and walks across the yard into the woods with his wellies on and his dressing gown flapping about his knees. They've got a few pigs that grunt dispassionately from behind the fence as he goes.

'Just ignore him,' says Mrs Hewitt, from inside the kitchen.

'Oh,' I say, 'he didn't say anything.'

'Ignore him anyway. Ignore him all the time. Best way.'

She's been crying too. Her face is drawn. She doesn't say anything else and I don't ask questions.

I'M STANDING AT THE end of Mr Greenley's driveway. Mr Greenley is perusing the stock. I gaze at his yellow bungalow while I wait for him to make his mind up.

'How much does it come to now?' he asks.

I do the maths in my head. 'That's five twenty-five.'

'Excellent! In that case I'll also have two bananas, for Saturday breakfast.'

'Five sixty-five then, please.'

'Ooh, and a loaf of bread.'

I hand over a sliced brown loaf. It's the last loaf I've got and the Bean told me that Mrs Salmon often likes a loaf on a Friday. I hope this time she won't. She's one of those with it in her to get a bit shirty if I can't give her exactly what she wants.

'Any white?' Mr Greenley asks.

'No, sorry,' I say. 'This is the only bread I have left.'

'No problem,' he says, putting the loaf into his bag-for-life. Then he puts the bag down and goes into his pockets. He roots around for a bit and slowly a pained expression crosses his face. 'Ah,' he says. 'Looks like I've only got a fiver.' He holds up a tatty green specimen.

I look at him for a moment. He just holds the note out, waiting. In the end I take it.

'Make the difference up next week?' he suggests.

'Yes, let's.' I nod at his bag. 'Can I carry it in for you?'

'It's okay,' he says, cheerily. 'I'm not dead yet!' With a great grunt he picks the bag up, slowly turns and shuffles back to his yellow home.

Back in the van, I open the File to record Greenley's deficit. When I get to his row, I stare. Greenley's been accruing a deficit of between one and two pounds a week for the past three months. He owes over seventeen pounds! I'll have to speak to the Bean about this.

I'M ON A COUNCIL estate that stretches out from the village towards the sea. In the File, the next customer is named simply as 'Dot', and the following is called 'Fran'.

'Hello?' I call. 'Hello? Dot?'

'In 'ere!' comes a cracked old voice.

I step through the open door into the kitchen. It is perhaps the dirtiest kitchen I've ever seen. Some old people I deliver to in the villages and in the valleys either can't or don't clean very well, and nor do they appear to have family or carers who can clean for them; their kitchens are encrusted with spilled foods and full of rotting leftovers. But this one is the worst I can recall.

Every surface is piled high with unwashed crockery, as is the sink. And what's at the bottom of the piles clearly hasn't been cleaned for years and years. Green fur overflows from stacked bowls and plates. On the tops of the piles are cooked dishes – a baking tray with flapjack in, for example, or a Pyrex dish containing half a lasagne. The cupboards are streaked with thick brown spillage marks. Everything is covered with sugar and crumbs. The floor is sticky with mouldy bits of food cemented to it. It smells of earth. The walls, once white as far as I can tell, are yellow. White powder is scattered liberally around on the floor and worktops. When I look closely, I can see dead ants curled up in it.

Cleaning this kitchen would be a couple of days' work for me, and I'm young and fit and able-bodied. Dot, I predict, is not any of those things.

'You coming through or what?' she rasps.

I go through the kitchen and into the front room. The house is a two-up two-down. She sits on a sofa surrounded by TV magazines, with a metal tray on metal legs in front of her. The heat is stifling. The curtains are drawn. She's watching the TV and the volume is right up. A cigarette burns in her hand. On top of the TV magazines are plates full of half-eaten biscuits. She reminds me a bit of my mother, but she's older.

'You the new lad, eh?'

'I am,' I say.

'Younger than the last one,' she says.

'Well,' I say, thinking of Graham's stooped shoulders and lined face. 'Yes, a bit.'

'Something for me to look at!' she chortles. Behind her, stacked from one end of the wall to the other, and almost to the ceiling, are jigsaw puzzle boxes. She lowers her glasses and peers over the top. 'Aye, you're a handsome lad. Fran'll want you for a new husband.'

'Maybe she's in luck!' I say. I don't know what I mean.

'Ooh!' she says. 'Now then, sometimes I'll be out. Just put the milk in the fridge. On a Friday, whether I'm in or out, I'll leave the money on the side in there.' She points to the kitchen. 'Door's always open.'

I look back into the kitchen and see the change on the side, nestling against a used teabag.

'Listen,' I say. 'Could you use any help? Cleaning? The kitchen?'

'Why?' she asks, lowering her glasses again. 'Is it dirty?'

'Well,' I say.

She bursts out cackling. 'Get out,' she says. 'Go and see Frannie over the road. She'll be wanting her nice soft pears. You're running late!'

FRAN'S EVEN OLDER THAN Dot, and less mobile still. There's a carer with her when I arrive. Fran's house is tidier, but it is similarly hot and the TV is similarly loud. Fran cannot get into or out of her chair, or into and out of bed, without help. Graham had explained this to me; he'd once found her on the floor and had had to help her back into her chair. If the carer wasn't there, I was to make her

90

a cup of tea and slice her fruit and put it in a bowl that she could reach from her seat.

She's buried beneath big fleeces and blankets. Her old face emerges from the top like a bobble on a hat.

'Well, hello,' she says, smiling. Her voice is like the voice of an old woman from a Disney film. 'You're the new fellow, I take it?' Her teeth are perfect pearly dentures.

'I am,' I say.

'I was devastated when my husband told me he was leaving,' she says. 'But you can be my new husband.'

It takes me a moment to realise that she's referring to Graham and not her actual husband. I can see that she was once married; the walls are covered in sepia photographs of a man in military uniform and photos of them together from when they were young. There's a ring on her finger.

She must have caught me looking. 'That's my real husband,' she says, and the sparkle is gone from her voice. 'He was the most wonderful man. He was perfect. He treated me so well. I've never known anybody so kind. He died over twenty years ago. I've been waiting all this time to meet up with him again. And he's been waiting for me, up in heaven. I've been keeping him so long. I've never met anybody so patient. I loved him so much. I love him so much. We met on the bus. We were both in our uniforms. Now look at me in this ridiculous chair. Oh, lad. I'll be happy to die.'

I'm far too hot. 'I'm sorry,' I say.

'Are you married?' she asks.

'Yes,' I say.

'Well, I'm sure your wife's a lucky woman. Just don't tell her.'

91

'Don't tell her what?'

'Don't tell her you're marrying me, as well!'

'Ha,' I say. 'Okay!'

'Now then. Are your pears soft? Because the last one, his were always too hard.'

'Well, I'll choose you some soft ones out of the van,' I say.

'And I'll have three bananas. Not too green, not too brown. And what apples do you have?'

'Gala,' I say. 'And cooking apples.'

'Gala aren't English, are they?'

'I don't think so.'

'Tell her I want some nice sweet little English apples. Tell her to get some. Nobody sells nice apples any more.' She sighs. 'And see how much milk I've got in the fridge. Leave as much as you think I need.'

'Okay.'

I head back out to the van. The carer smiles at me from Fran's bedroom, where she's doing something with a very mechanical bed. I open the back of the van and go through my boxes of assorted fruit. I have a load of pears. I squeeze one. Too hard. The next. Too hard. She won't be able to eat these. Too hard. They're all too damned hard. Oh God. Maybe if I just bruise them a bit. Next time I'll have to pick up some soft ones. I've got some good bananas, at least.

I make her a bag up and return to the house. I drop a couple of pints into her fridge, and then add another, just in case.

'I'll cut the fruit up,' the carer says, taking the bag from me.

'Okay,' I say. 'Thanks.'

Fran calls through from the front room. 'Come back, lad. I need to pay.'

When I go back to her, she's holding an old biscuit tin on her lap. She passes it to me. 'Open that, would you? Just take what you need.'

The tin's full of coppers, notes and wrapped biscuits. I work out the cost of what I've delivered, take a note, root in my own money pouch for change and drop the change into the tin.

'See anything you like?' Fran asks, smiling.

'Sorry?'

'In the tin.'

'Oh. You mean – the biscuits?'

'Yes! Take one. Your wife won't mind, will she? Little presents from another woman?'

'No,' I say. I wink. 'I just won't tell her!'

'Ooh,' she says, swatting. 'You're naughty!'

'Bye then,' I say.

'Will I see you tomorrow?'

'Monday,' I say.

'I'll look forward to it,' she says. 'You're my visitor. I'll look forward to it.'

From the van, I can see Dot's house and Fran's house. I don't want to be like either of them when I'm old. I don't want to be on my own. I don't want to be just waiting to die. I don't even have the comfort of believing in heaven, like Fran does.

And I don't want to be poor. Not that Dot or Fran are, necessarily – but Fran's care must cost a lot of money. And I am poor, by any standard metric. As soon as my uncle decides to withdraw his charity, I'll have nothing but my overdraft and my minimum wage job. It's more than a lot of people have, but it won't buy me a place in a care home, and I'll have no assets to sell. And . . . I think about my wife and our daughter. I once had this idea that I'd leave something behind for them, or for her, at least.

Dot and Fran both seem so lonely. I shiver. I should visit my mother.

The Anxiety

OLD MRS WATERS IS out seeing to the goats as I arrive. She's often outside first thing; for somebody in their seventies, she's pretty sprightly. Except this morning she's not – she's hobbling slowly, bent over, one hand on her hip. When I catch sight of her face I nearly recoil. She looks ghastly. She looks like a different woman. Her lower eyelids are hanging low enough to reveal crescents of red, like a basset hound's. Her cheeks are purple. Her nose is running freely.

'Is everything all right?' I ask.

She looks at me with something like hate in her eyes.

'We're all seeing ghosts, aren't we?' she wheezes. 'What's happening, lad?'

'I don't know,' I say.

'What about yours? What's your ghost? Or do you young folks not have them?'

'I don't know,' I say again. I'm not sure mine is a ghost. I think back to Race's ghost; wonder who or what that was.

'Mine's my boy. He's come back. Back from the river that took him under. I can't bear it. Can't bear his face. So I'm not going to bed.'

'He just comes back at night?'

'Yes.'

Mrs Waters is really struggling to walk.

'I have an idea,' I say. 'I know somebody who can help. She makes wards. She helped me with my visitor.'

Mrs Waters squints. 'A cunning woman? In this day and age?'

'Yes,' I say. 'It's coming back, I think. Witchcraft. That kind of thing.' I scratch under my hat. 'And her prices are quite reasonable.' I look around. 'I thought you had more goats than this,' I say.

'I did, lad,' she says.

OF COURSE NOT ALL of the customers talk to me, and of those that do, not all of them confess that they've started to receive unwelcome nocturnal visitors. However, more and more of them seem more and more tired. There's a general peevishness. More hard stares and sharp words. A few of them explain that they're not sleeping well, but don't elaborate. The older ones are slower. The younger ones are fraught. I start to meet customers I've never met before, because they're getting up earlier. Those who have always been in bed at four, five, six a.m., are now up and awake and waiting impatiently for their delivery. There are more tears. I hear more arguments.

There's a pall hanging over everything, even on the brighter days. I feel it myself. Mr Royle seems particularly despondent one morning. 'The flowers are wrong,' he says. 'The birds are wrong. Wrong time of year for this, wrong time for that. What should be here isn't here, and what shouldn't be here is.' He's wearing a constant frown.

Ms Allington, who's somebody I hadn't met until recently, has taken to watching the news in her kitchen in the early morning. She sits there watching and gnaws at her fingernails. 'Can't believe it,' she'll say, after beckoning me in, or, 'It's just awful.' Or, 'Everything I hear these days just makes me feel ill.'

This is the kind of thing people are more likely to tell me. They don't tell me about the ghosts, but they tell me, 'I have nightmares about flooding,' or, 'I've started to meditate because I, um, I couldn't control my thoughts, and I was thinking about such awful things,' or, 'I always just looked forward to the weekends like, and that were bad enough, wishing the days away. But these days even the weekends are shite.' Or, 'I'm so tired that I'm literally sick, literally vomiting every morning.' Exhaustion loosens tongues, is what I'm finding. So even if they don't talk to me about ghosts, they talk to me about other things.

The Uptick

'THE USUAL?'

'Yes, please.'

'How's it all going? The bottle doing the trick?'

'Yes, thanks. But hey – it sounds like I'm not the only one with a visitor. People are worked up – customers, I mean. Seeing things. Receiving visitors. Like me. A couple said they might have a look at your website.'

'It's certainly getting busier,' Kathryn says, shutting the oven door and turning around. 'You know how you deliver the products for me? Well, could you also collect the ingredients? You know – like I used your semen for yours? I'll need materials provided by the customers.'

'I don't know . . .'

'You could. You leave them bottles all the time, right? Just ask them to put a little something in them before they give them back.'

'I'll have to make sure I don't get them mixed up with the empties.'

'Well,' she says. 'Yes. That's something you would have to manage.'

'Yes,' I say. 'I think I could do that. What's the price? What should I tell them?'

'I don't know. Finger in the air – twenty pounds?'

'How long does it take you to make one?'

'A couple of hours.'

'At least fifty, then.'

'Let's start there.'

I START TO ADVISE customers that we might have a solution to their nightly troubles. Those who've told me about their visitations, that is. I'm met with immediate understanding from some.

'Aye. Hair? Blood's more potent, lad. I could do a finger prick tonight but in a couple of days I'll come on and I can give you some of the good stuff.' Or, 'Stop beating around the bush. You're talking about semen. How fresh? Does it matter?'

Others are completely mystified. 'A witch . . . *bottle*? A *witch* bottle?' Naturally, this latter group are a little more sceptical of the potential efficacy of the wards, and more hesitant. I understand that. Invariably, though, they come around within a few days of me making the offer.

If the customers take their milk in plastic bottles, I switch them to glass. 'Leave the personal element in one of these bottles after you've emptied it,' I tell them, 'and I'll pick it up with the other empties. Just keep it separate somehow. Wrap it in a carrier bag or something and write your name on it.'

Some of them do and some of them don't, meaning that I have to get into the habit of checking. I collect bottles with used condoms inside, used tampons, clumps of hair, yellow cloudy piss, something that *must* be semen, but it's like half a bottle's worth, and I only told him what he needed to do the day before, so I don't know. Sometimes there's blood and it's just too much blood and it makes me feel unwell to look at it. Sometimes I don't know what it is and I avoid looking too closely or for too long.

Kathryn, of course, is unfazed. She takes the raw materials and does her work, returning the bottles full, heavy, nicely packaged and wrapped, with name tags.

One morning when I'm picking up the stock – and my usual – she says, 'If we didn't need personal ingredients, I'd say we should just make them for everybody. You could drop them off at every house on your round. If they help. Do you think they help?'

'They're definitely helping,' I say. 'People have told me. They're delighted. They want to know if you can help with warts, boils, weevils and ague.'

'I was with you there, for a moment. I thought you meant it.'

'I did mean it. But yeah, they don't say warts, boils, weevils and ague. They want help with depression, rheumatoid arthritis, infertility, their partners' libidos and migraines. And warts, actually. They do say warts.'

'They can't get appointments at the doctors.'

'Yes, exactly.'

'God,' she says, 'it's depressing.'

'Good for you, though.'

'It's a good job I'm conscientious. I mean, I can't do anything about depression. Or arthritis. Others might pretend to be able to.' She sighs. 'All of that aside, though, I'm worried about why people need witch bottles in the first place. Something's happening.'

The Radio Signals

B Y THE TIME I'M done I'm exhausted. But when I get home I can't settle. I sit down and then get up again. I stand at the window and look out over the grass for a while. The sun's passed its apex already and the thought of nightfall makes me uneasy. I consider the whisky but decide against it.

I go outside. Big white clouds are turning blue as the wintry sun descends. A cold breeze blows and buffets black birds back towards bare trees. I head towards my own old car; I don't use it often and each time I do, I'm a little apprehensive that it won't start at all. I get into the driver's seat. It feels bizarrely low compared to the delivery van. The car has a faulty seal somewhere and lets in the rain; it smells badly of damp and you've got to keep the blowers on a while before the windows clear.

Once I can see through the windscreen, I pull out of the drive and go to see my mother.

*

THE HOUSE IS STILL the same. It's one reason I find it difficult to come back. My mother's enduring sadness is another reason. She goes to the gym once a day around seven in the morning and rides the exercise bike for about two hours, but otherwise tends to just sit and smoke and *think*. I try to encourage her to do things, but nothing brings her much joy. I can see how it happens – I too like to be by myself – but it does bring with it a risk of excessive introspection. Other people distract you from yourself, which can be a good thing. Especially as more time passes and you acquire more history to reflect upon.

It's raining now, so she's not in the garden. If it's not raining, the garden is where she sits. The back door, which leads into the kitchen, is unlocked. I knock and then open it.

'Mum?' I shout.

'In here,' comes the croak. 'Come through.'

The house is clean but yellowed with cigarette smoke. The colours and general atmosphere remind me of Deckard's apartment in *Blade Runner*. The heavy, stale smoke smell compounds the time-capsule sensibility of the house. She is only just a pensioner and not yet what I think of as 'old', but the house feels like an old person's house.

She's sitting and smoking and drinking tea. A small tower of biscuits balances on the side of the saucer. She's thin and wears thick glasses with rainbow frames. Her iPad is on the sofa next to her, Facebook shining out.

'Daniel,' she says.

'Hi, Mum,' I say. 'You okay?'

'I'm fine, love. Sit down. Sit down.' She only speaks quietly.

'What are you up to?'

'Just a little break. What about you?'

'Working. Just finished work.'

'Going out tonight?'

'No, Mum.'

'You should go out more. Meet somebody else. Don't want to end up like me.' No smiles, no inflection.

'You're not so bad,' I say.

She picks up a biscuit and takes a bite. 'Put the kettle on then.'

Standing by the kettle. On the drive over, twilight fell. The kitchen fills with steam. As I've said, my car is old, and it rattles and growls when it shouldn't. It has a tape deck that doesn't work and I don't bother trying to tune the radio. As I was on the A595, I heard the gathering roar of a fighter jet. Exercises. When I hear the jets I get anxious, as should everybody. Between my house and here, I pass Netherhall – the old nuclear power plant, now no longer operational but well into its hundreds of years of decommissioning. The chimneys, the steam, the lights that colour the night clouds. It's bigger than a town. Time it right on the right day and it burns orange as the sun sets in the sea behind it. It turns to brass. My nanna always had a brass coal scuttle by the fire and I can't disassociate it from Netherhall. She called it *the factory*. You have the factory on one side and then open fields on the other. Owls, foxes, badgers. I just about avoided the Netherhall traffic. Twice a day, the A595 becomes impassable due to it. Netherhall inhales everybody into it, and then it exhales everybody out. The A595 is the only A-road we have. It's arterial. If you need an ambulance, good luck.

I start to wonder if my mother's kettle has broken; the kitchen is filling with steam and it's not clicking off. It's going and going. In the end I click it off myself and fill the pot.

'Don't know if you saw it on Facebook?' she says, as I carry the tray back through. 'New scam going around.'

'No, I didn't,' I say. I've muted my mother on Facebook because she insists on sharing the grimmest, goriest health warnings.

'People pretending to be deaf.'

'Okay.'

'Have a look.' She's started a fresh cigarette. 'Next time you're on Facebook, have a look. Don't see much from you on there any more.'

'No.'

'Did you see that baby that drowned in a bowl of cereal milk?'

'No. Listen—'

'You should pay attention.'

'Never going to have another baby, Mum. And Marianne isn't a baby any more. And . . . you know . . . we're not in touch.'

'I know,' she says. She sucks on the cigarette. I don't know what she thinks about Ellie and me. She was always cold and disinterested towards Ellie, in the same way that she has been towards everybody since Robert died and to be honest, I think that her prevailing emotion when Ellie and I broke up was relief. Relief that she didn't have to have another baby in her life any more. She might feel guilt that she never helped us, or sad, or angry with us for not trying harder. I've no idea. I never asked her, and she never told me. And when I think about it, I don't want to know.

By the time Ellie and I broke up, we had cut ourselves off from almost everybody. A few people reached out, confused more than anything, and I just told them what I wanted the truth to be: that it had been mutual, that Ellie and I would remain amicable and raise Marianne between us. Then, when I realised Ellie and Marianne had left the city, I stopped taking calls from friends. As I understand it, this withdrawal can be a symptom of mental illness; I did everything possible to avoid talking to people, even if it would have been good for me.

I try to remember what I wanted to say to my mother. I have this constant low-level guilt that I don't visit my mother enough, but then when I'm here I feel awkward and unable to speak. I think about that night, the night I'd seen her lying on the floor in the front room, my dad standing over her, saying, 'I can't help you.'

'Is there anything I can do for you?' I ask. 'Anything I can get for you?'

'I've still got my legs, son,' she says. 'I'm not infirm yet. Mrs Parsons though, she's going. She's been going ever since her daughter died. Cancer. She was your age! And three little kids too. Mrs Parsons hasn't been right since. And Willy Graham – his greenhouse fell into a sinkhole.'

'What?'

'Aye, a big hole just opened up in his garden and his greenhouse fell in.'

'The mines?'

'The mines.'

Egremont has been thoroughly mined for iron ore across centuries. I went to school here and there was an experiment the A-level geography students did every year. The brief was to either prove or disprove the rumour that the science block – a sixties tower – was slowly sinking into the mines. Every year they proved it wasn't, but the rumour persisted. And the occasional sinkhole does open up.

'He's not far from you, is he?'

'End of the street. They'll come for me soon.'

'The mines?'

'The mines.'

'I was thinking about when I was little.'

The cigarette stops on the way to her mouth. She hasn't touched the tea I made her. 'What about it? A bad few years.'

'There was one night you were fighting and I woke up.'

'More than one, as I remember it.'

'This time you didn't know I was awake.' I paused. I don't know what I want. 'I came downstairs and you were lying on the floor.'

'Did that a lot. Was this before? Or after?'

'Before. Well – I think it was the very night.'

She nods, lips trembling. 'Oh, son.' She rubs her forehead. 'I'm sorry, son. You shouldn't have had to see all that.'

'What was it about?'

'We just weren't coping. I was sick and your dad was useless. No money. If you've got problems, if you've got cracks in you, then no money's like a weight on top, making everything worse.' She pauses for a moment and then carries on. 'You shouldn't have had to see any of it. All that fighting, all for nothing. We weren't bad. He wasn't bad, I wasn't bad. But it was so horrible. The fights were so horrible. We tore each other to pieces.' As far as I know, she's speaking metaphorically. 'And for what. We didn't know, son. We didn't know how bad things were going to get. We should have spent that time happy. We *could* have. We tried to hide it from you, but we didn't succeed. I know we didn't. Do you think the shouting did something to you?'

I shook my head. 'No. I just thought it was normal.'

'You turned out okay.'

I shrug. 'Jury's out on that.' It's meant to be a joke but I'm not sure it lands.

'Why were you thinking about it?'

'The memory came back to me.' I take a sip of tea. It's more about doing something with my hands than wanting to drink it. 'I don't know why.'

'I know he's dead now,' she says, 'but me and your dad will have our time. I believe that now. We worked too hard for us not to get it. A happy, easy time. After death. It doesn't make any sense that death is the end. By the time you're my age, son, your body's just a prison. You know there's something else inside, waiting to get out. And that thing trying to get out, that's the real you. I think we're like radio signals and our bodies are like radios. The radio might break, but the signal's still out there. We're the signals. The signals, not the radios. Do you see? I saw that on Facebook – I shared it. Did you see it?'

DRIVING HOME. MY MOTHER didn't tell me much she hasn't told me before. When I was married, my wife would ask me why this kind of talk didn't make me angry.

'They had you. They should have been happy with you.'

'She's not well.'

'She is well. She's just sad. She hasn't got depression. She's a wallower. You're not responsible for how sad your bloody mother is.'

I feel that I am responsible for it, though.

It's misty now. Netherhall looks like a sci-fi city. The mist comes in off the sea. By some current forecasts, sea-level rise will be hitting us hard within about fifty years. It won't be fog laying between the various nuclear facilities or pooling in the farmers' fields, but seawater. You like to think that there's a plan, but if there's one thing you learn from paying attention, it's that nobody's really driving the bus any more. Brave people don't have the power to make the changes and powerful people don't have the courage.

One of the decisions I need to make for my book is – what triggered the catastrophic war in the first place? Resource scarcity caused by climate change is the obvious one, but I worry that's just a failure of imagination on my part. It's the track my thinking is stuck in.

But perhaps I don't need to decide at all. Maybe I just start it after the event and leave the past unknown.

It's properly dark by the time I get home. The first thing I do is close all the curtains and walk around the house putting all the lights on. I'm not going to let darkness pool anywhere inside the house; I don't want to be walking past doors that open into dark rooms, or windows that look out into the night. I can't articulate why. There is something happening. Unease is growing within me, and I believe it's growing outside of me too.

I don't sleep.

The Tree from a Long Time Ago

YEARS AGO WE WOULD go away on holiday every year to a hostel on the shore of Derwentwater. Not just my immediate family, but the whole of my mum's side. She was one of many siblings, so some years we got up to about forty people. We always booked out the whole place. And the weather was either good, clean, hot sun, or incredible thunderstorms. The hostel was surrounded by trees, consisted of a couple of buildings and had a wooden balcony that extended right out over the lake's beach, with a view from one end of the lake all the way down to the other, mountains rising up all around.

It was on one of the hot days and I was floating out on the lake in a dinghy. I was alone, on my back. There was no breeze. The heat was like a blanket. No – the air was like glass. I felt at the time as if we were all fixed in glass, as if the air itself was hot and solid and transparent, and we were all just stuck, unmoving. I had this incredible sense of peace. The water beneath me would be clear, if I was to look at it. The sky above was this unreal blue, with high white streaks of cloud kind of tattered to nothing in the upper reaches. All sounds were distant and muted. I could hear my cousins shouting nearer the shore – everyone was in the water. But I couldn't see them. I was just looking up. Further out were islands, the closest of which had a grand old house on it. This lake was the setting for *Swallows and Amazons*, which I took with me every year but never got around to reading. Anyway, I was looking up at the sky and thinking about this book and completely consciously appreciating this stillness that was both eerie and peaceful, and mindful of how strange it was to become aware of some kind of altered state without also ending that state, when I heard a whispered voice, close to my ear.

I fought to sit up. Fought the heat, the heavy air. There was nobody close by. But the whisper came again. I twisted around, rocking the dinghy. The dinghy was a hot yellow. The sense of being set in glass persisted; everything was bright and focused. Whatever I looked at was magnified by the air. The whisper came again and I stared in the direction it came from. The bracken-furred flank of a mountain. There was a lone tree, tiny in the distance. But then suddenly I could see its every leaf, as if it was close to me. My vision was sharp. Its leaves were fluttering, but there was no wind. The bracken did not move. Just the leaves of this tree were rustling and susurrating. This was the whisper. But the whisper was not just a sound; it was words. The tree was talking to me.

Save yourself.

I took that to mean that nobody else – no relationship with another person – would save me. I didn't wonder what I needed saving from. Deep down somewhere, I already knew.

The Family

DANIEL TOLD ME THAT he has a wife and daughter. Ellie and Marianne, they're called, respectively. I asked if they're planning to get divorced and he said that they're not in touch at all, but it's something they would probably arrange if they ever do make contact. It wouldn't bother me at all, except it doesn't feel in keeping with him as I see him. Nor does his reason for leaving them. He said that he was scared he'd hurt them if he stayed. I haven't seen that side to him, though, and I can't imagine it.

Although saying that, I have been feeling a bit as if he's got a carapace of some sort, one that I'm not getting through. We've been seeing each other a while now and I get the impression that he thinks everything is fine. Whereas I feel like we're only engaging on a very superficial level. And maybe that's fine. Some company, some help with the business and some good physical loving . . . that's okay, right? Maybe I shouldn't push for more. Maybe inside the carapace is this violent *other* and I'm better off not releasing it.

He did explain that due to what happened, he finds it difficult to get into new relationships. He doesn't want to hurt anybody else; he doesn't want to get hurt. So maybe that's it. The question for me is how far I want to push it. How important is it to me? I'm not sure.

In perhaps more interesting news, there's been a real surge in orders. Daniel's been putting the word about, but in itself that shouldn't do it: witch bottles and the like are not things people buy unless they have a need. They're hardly ornamental. So the demand is growing. Either that, or there's a large pre-existing demand that's just marrying up with the supply. It feels like there's this . . . I don't know. The words that come to mind are *rising tide*. But that sounds more portentous than I usually like to sound.

The Knees

THE NEW MATERNITY CENTRE was an impressive building. We entered into a gigantic atrium, at the far side of which a long reception desk beckoned. Nice soft light spilled in from the glass ceiling. Screens advertised 3D scanning services and products, such as incredibly detailed pictures of the foetus, or even actual models of it. Ambient music played. Above and to the sides, nurses and midwives hurried along balconies. It felt like a hive of activity. It felt warm and good. It felt safe.

Next to me, Ellie held her stomach. She did not look like she felt warm or safe. Her back hurt, her hips hurt, her breasts hurt, her legs hurt. Walking was difficult. I held her free hand. Suddenly the reception desk seemed a long way away. It felt like a strange decision, to put it so far from the door, when so many people coming into this building would be heavily pregnant.

We were just on time for our appointment. The receptionist bade us take a seat. 'Or you can keep walking about,' she said brightly, to Ellie. Ellie grimaced.

Twenty minutes later we were still sitting there. 'For fuck's sake,' she said. 'What's taking them so long?'

'Maybe they're understaffed,' I said, looking around.

'Oh fuck off,' she said. 'Don't make excuses for them.'

The baby was not due for another three weeks but Ellie was in a lot of pain. Not labour; just extraordinary general pain. This is where we would come to have the baby, but it was also where we came for scans and check-ups, which is what we were there for on this occasion.

I could hear the sounds of the city outside. Traffic and sirens and sometimes snatches of music. We were excited about raising our child in a city. We'd both grown up in the countryside, and as much as we'd loved certain aspects of it, we felt at home in the city in a way neither of us had expected. There were so many different cultures and kinds of people to learn from. The volume of people made it easier to be yourself, and we felt that our child would have a better chance of being themselves, of expressing themselves, of having greater self-confidence, in the city. They would not feel pressure to conform, or to bite their tongues.

I felt totally useless throughout the pregnancy. I wanted to help. I did the obvious, practical things that I could. But just the very fact that she was feeling pain and I wasn't started to drive a wedge between us. It was not fair. And sometimes my very presence was just a reminder, to her, of how unfair it was. Especially when I tried to make her feel better.

'It will be okay,' I said. 'They'll look after us. After you. They'll look after you. They deliver hundreds of babies here every day, probably. It will be okay.'

'I don't think it will,' she said, shaking her head and looking utterly desolate. 'It hurts so much. It's wrong. Something's wrong.'

'I'm sorry,' I said. 'I know it hurts.'

'You don't know,' she whispered, shaking her hand free of mine. 'You don't understand.'

'I know,' I said, 'I know I can't really understand. But—'

'*Stop.*'

'Sorry.'

We didn't get to see a doctor, which is what we thought we were there to do. We saw a midwife. The facility was a new midwifery-led unit, which meant there were not that many doctors around.

'So what's going on?' she asked, cheerfully. She was young and tall, with a long ponytail.

'There's something wrong,' Ellie said. 'It hurts too much.'

'It's quite normal to feel some pain at this stage,' the midwife said.

'Okay,' Ellie said. 'But I think this pain is *ab*normal.'

'This is your first pregnancy, isn't it?' the midwife asked.

'Yes.'

'Okay then.' She did something with her computer, letting the implications percolate for a moment. 'Okay then. Let's have a feel. If you could just get on to the bed, please.'

I helped Ellie on to the bed. Lying on her back was one of the most uncomfortable positions for her and her face communicated her pain.

'See these lumps?' she said, lifting her top up to reveal her bulging abdomen. 'I think these are her knees. And this here, this is her forehead. I think she's the wrong way round. Because her back is meant to be facing out, right?'

'It's very hard to tell like this,' the midwife said. 'Really, we should only go by the scans. And on your last scan, she was the right way round.'

'But she could have moved!'

'That doesn't usually happen at this stage.' The midwife said everything in the same patient, slightly tired tone, with a big smile that didn't quite look genuine.

'But she could have.'

The midwife ran her hands over Ellie's stomach. 'I think they're her elbows,' she said. 'And that's not her forehead, that's her back.'

Ellie was shaking her head. 'Then why does it *hurt* so much?'

The midwife took my wife by the hand. 'It's okay,' she said. 'It's a scary time. But everything's all right. Some pain is to be expected. It could be that you have a lower pain threshold than other women.'

'I suppose we've got nothing to compare it against,' I offered. 'With it being our first pregnancy.'

'Exactly,' the midwife said. 'Now, I'd suggest some paracetemol and lots of walking around to bring it on. And we'll be seeing you very soon!'

BACK IN THE ATRIUM we slowly walked to the door. Coldness radiated from Ellie. She wouldn't hold my hand. I knew that in her pain, she was alone. But I still wanted her to know that I loved her, that I wanted to make things easier for her. Even though I knew I'd pissed her off, and I knew why, I couldn't stop talking.

'They see so many pregnant women every day,' I said. 'They must know what they're talking about, a bit. We have to trust them over our own feelings.'

'*Our* first pregnancy, is it?' she said, quietly. '*Our* own feelings?'

'I know I'm not pregnant myself,' I said through gritted teeth. 'I realise that.'

'I need you to support me,' she said. 'Not just agree with *them*.'

'But they're the experts,' I said.

'Oh,' she said, 'go to hell.'

Soon the pregnancy would be over, I told myself. And we'd have our perfect little baby, and we could share the work out; it wouldn't just all be happening inside her body. I could help properly. And this wedge between us, this distance, would just melt away.

The Stag

KATHRYN HEFTS A LARGE, clinking bag-for-life up on to the counter. 'Here we've got witch bottles, salves, essence, charms and plain old herbal remedies. Each order is wrapped up and has an address on the packaging. They're all on your rounds, more or less.'

I recognise some of the names on the packaging as names of our own customers: Goodwin, Greenley, Brown, Royle, Taylor and Jackson, amongst others.

'Any sign of your ghost?'

'Still none,' I say. She asks me the question every day. 'Thank you,' I add.

What with the extra round and me squeezing Kathryn's deliveries in too, my workdays are getting longer and longer. And as winter draws in, I find myself regularly coming home in the dark, which is not the way things are meant to be for milkmen.

I'm out in beautiful, crisp cold weather, I'm out in fog, in drizzle, in torrential rain, in high winds, in sleet, in frost, in unseasonably warm sunshine. I had my rounds down already, more or less, and I work to incorporate the new drop-offs without too much disruption, making sure to find the most efficient ways to do it – much as the Bean had when working out the original rounds, I imagine. I can't put notes on the actual File, because the Bean would see them then, but I interleave tracing paper with the File and add my notes to that.

Kathryn has customers on the housing estates of Thornhill and in the offices at Westlakes Business Park, where I leave pints of milk on top of desks and brown paper packages under desks. I could be dropping anything off really, but nobody ever stops me. She has customers in the richer villages like Gosforth and Beckermet, and she has them in mansion houses in the valleys. She has customers amongst the farmers and customers amongst the contractors who work at Netherhall. One day I remark upon just how many customers she has.

'I had a few customers who would come into the shop. But I didn't realise how many were out there, waiting. It's always the way that numbers go up in winter – in winter, more people want protective charms. Against the dark and the cold. Against sickness.' She waves her hand. 'And I think given everything in the news, people are losing faith in the institutions that are meant to provide for them.'

I spend more time with her, too. The first night she comes to mine, we go out to the old shed. There's a bitter wind. As decrepit as the shed is, it still offers a little cover. Inside, the walls are lined with shelves that have thin sliding panels fitted, to either contain or hide their contents. I slide open the panels and the things on the shelves resolve themselves out of the murk. At first they're just slimy, organic shapes in sickly tones. Then this pale brown curve becomes a lip, that lichen green blurr a handle, that pink and red swirl the fat belly of a lopsided pot. These are the creations that had been left here when I moved in. Other more wholesome pots and bowls and jugs are left out in plain sight, but the ones behind the sliding panels are those that even the potter presumably felt were bad, or off. They all have the same feel to them – the same fleshy aesthetic – and are badly made in similar ways, with gaps in the clay where the sides meet the bases. But what really makes me uncomfortable is the warped face each one bears. I don't know what the intention was, but the end result is a series of faces that look saggy and pained, like somebody had cut an actual face from a head, pasted it to a rock and used that as a model for piece after piece.

Of course Kathryn loves them. 'They used to make witch bottles out of clay pots like this,' she says, gathering an armful. 'They were meant to look like fat little men.'

'I didn't like this shed before,' I say, 'and now I imagine these shelves full of fat little men, I like it even less.'

'Do you mind me taking some?'

'Take all of them,' I say. 'Please.'

And she invites me to her house, too. She lives in Thornhill herself, in a council house full of books and candles and resin skulls and tarot cards. Her front door has a Green Man scowling out from it. Her next-door neighbour's front yard is small, concrete and jam-packed full of Disney character garden ornaments, most of their colours faded to near-white. She lets me watch her make the witch bottles sometimes. Many of them are full of hair and gunk like the kind of stuff I sometimes pull out of the bath plughole. Sometimes they look to be stuffed full of wire and rust, sometimes full of nothing more than discoloured water with unidentifiable things floating in it.

I never ask for a closer look and she never offers one. Sometimes she grabs me and strips me and *draws forth*, as she puts it, and uses my seed. She always asks my permission and I never see any reason not to give it. On other occasions, we make love for pleasure.

She doesn't work weekends, so one Saturday she comes with me in the van. I pick her up in Thornhill and drop her off on the A595 as I return to the depot, prior to continuing on to the valleys. After reloading, I go back and pick her up on the A595 and we carry on.

She steals a bottle of milk from the back and drinks greedily as I drive through Eskdale. I head down a lane through some woods to a peculiar little row of three terraces that look as if they've been cut and pasted from a mining town out into the lush green valley. Even now, with winter coming on, Eskdale feels alive. They were miners' houses of course, back when Eskdale was being mined for iron ore. Crows shriek out in the woods. After finishing the round, I make a detour to the river I used to swim in and we strip off and jump into the icy water, screaming with delight. I half watch her, half watch the orange leaves falling from the trees. We're in our own private valley here.

Saturday night and the winds are up. Sunday morning it's as if all the leaves fell at once. And now we're in winter properly: a bitter November. A grinding week follows, a week in which I start to feel old. I wear gloves but they slow me down; I take them off but then the bones of my fingers hurt. This week my teeth chatter in a way they never have before. My jaws are clattering unnervingly. I imagine my teeth cracking against each other, shards coming loose and breaking off. I could put them in a witch bottle, maybe.

The following Saturday, and Kathryn comes with me again. On

the way back out of the valleys we find a dead stag on the roadside. Winter! When the deer come down off the cold fells to die beneath the hot wheels of bone-tired shift workers. Kathryn hops out so she can gather some antler chips. I watch her carve away with a small knife and can't help but run a finger across my teeth. She finishes with the antlers and I think she's done, but she takes her knife and suddenly she's sawing away at the corpse's belly. She kneels down on the road in the grey midday mizzle and, using just a penknife, starts to fill a bag-for-life with the stag's internal organs. She scoops things out, reaches further and further inside, lowers her head to see, crawls forwards, until I think maybe she's found her own wardrobe to Narnia and she's going to slip inside and never come back. Afterwards the bag sits heavily in the passenger footwell in the same way that a persistent worry just kind of slouches against the wall of your brain. That's what it reminds me of. A thought you just can't shake.

The Driving Ban

IT'S MID-NOVEMBER WHEN RYAN gets caught speeding again. This time he's been snapped by the police on the long stretch between the Gosforth crossroads and Seascale. And this time, he's lost his licence.

'Absolute bloody lump!' the Bean shouts. She tends to only *really* vent her frustration when Ryan is not around. 'He's an empty bloody vessel, that lad!'

'Why don't you just sack him?' I suggest.

'I can't sack him,' she says, slicing open a bag of grated cheese and scattering shreds of it all around the kitchen. 'It would kill his poor mam.'

'What?' I take a sip of tea. The Bean made it, so I feel like I should drink it in order to be polite, but it's far too milky for my taste. 'How?'

'He only works here as a favour to her. We go way back, her and me. And she's got nowt, believe me. Nowt but that great oaf. And crippling anxiety, she's got that too. And he's got his kid, and another on the way. He lives with his poor mam and what I pay him mostly goes to her.'

'But if he can't drive, then how can he work here?'

The Bean gives a wan smile. 'I'm glad you asked, lad.'

'What do you mean?'

'You can drive.'

'I can.'

'He can do all the running about.'

'What?' Then it clicks. 'Oh. Oh, no. I'm afraid not.'

'You'll have all the rounds to do, but you'll do them together.'

'No. Please.'

'And with you splitting the work like that, it might not even take you any longer.'

'That's not what I'm worried about,' I say.

'Then what are you worried about?'

'He makes me uneasy.'

'Well, it's not your decision, lad.' She assembles one of her weird cheese sandwiches. 'As long as you want to work here, that is.'

I think about it.

'I know you're up to something,' the Bean says. 'I knew you were dallying at the La'al Tattie Cottage already. But the van tracker shows that you take some detours I can't work out.'

'The La'al Tattie Shop,' I say.

'Aye. I won't ask any questions about those other detours of yours if you help me out.'

'Okay then,' I say. 'I don't like it, but I suppose I don't have a choice.'

'That's the spirit.' The phone goes as I'm leaving the room.

I'm breaking up the last of the boxes when I hear the Bean shouting across the yard. She sounds furious. Ryan must have got back without me hearing. I turn around to see what's going on and see that the Bean's rushing towards *me,* spittle flying from her lips as she screams, 'You useless bloody *lump*! Meathead! You know what you've done? What you've gone and done? You can't half fuck up, can you, eh? What a fucking *pillock*.'

'What?' I say.

She lifts her hand to hit me.

I flinch.

She takes a deep breath and lowers her hand. 'Graham hasn't just gone, has he? He's taken Craggesund with him. That's a big fucking contract, lad, and he wouldn't have been able to steal it if you hadn't fucked up during shutdown.'

'Shit,' I say. I feel blood rushing to my face. I feel hot. 'Sorry.' I shift my weight from foot to foot. 'Shit,' I say again. 'I'm so sorry.'

'We were just and so, all right,' she says. 'As a business. But we're not any more. We're in real danger now, lad. With Ryan being a fuckwit and you losing us Craggesund, we're on the wrong side of the line, money-wise.' She opens her mouth, closes it and starts pacing. 'Yeah,' she says, 'I'm going to need you to make it up. Wage cut. I'm taking a pound off the hour. And a pound off the hour for Ryan too. Given that you're going to be out on the road a lot longer now, you'll end up no worse off. But you'll be working longer for it.'

'Okay.'

'This could be it for us. This could be the bloody end of us.'

'I understand.'

'No,' she says. 'Not sure you do. *Shit.*' She pulls at her hair. 'Going to have to go and see the lads next door. Maybe put the rent up.'

'The lads next door?'

'Aye. The whole building belongs to me and I rent t'other half out. The bit over the wall.'

'Oh, right,' I say.

'Get on now,' she says, turning away. 'Out of my sight. Get.'

IT'S OUR FIRST DAY together. Ryan is bigger and stronger than me but I still feel like I'm in a position of authority. Partly because I'm older, partly because it was his misdemeanour that's resulted in this situation – which neither of us is happy about – and partly, I think, because I'm driving.

He's pissed off with me though, because of the pound off the hour, which I understand. And I don't want to test the authority I feel I have. I'm conscious that it maybe only exists in my own head. He might not feel that I hold any authority at all. It distresses me that his default sitting position is with one foot up on the dashboard and his hands down the front of his pants. But I don't say anything about it.

I have to admit that he's speedy on his feet, though. And he's efficient with his movements. He uses the File and my carrier to great effect, constantly filling empty slots with upcoming drops so that it's always at optimum capacity. (I took my tracing-paper sheets from the File before he got into the van.) There's a variety of milks that customers might want: whole, semi, skimmed, organic – and that's just in glass. You've got the same range in plastic, and in plastic, there are different bottle sizes to factor in as well – five hundred mil, one litre and two litre. And of course that's not to mention the cartons – all your soyas, almonds, goat milks, all of that. So there's a bit more to using the carrier than keeping it full of red-top glass bottles. And considering that we started off doing my rounds and not his, he's done well; he has not had the opportunity to memorise everything yet.

None of that is to say I like him being around. I don't.

I bite my tongue when he scratches himself, when he belches, when he breaks wind. Sometimes he just kind of stares at me with a hostile expression on his face. And I'm increasingly worried about how I'm going to make Kathryn's deliveries with him in the van. Well, I can't.

'So,' I say, on a long drag between villages, 'how's your boy doing?'

'Well,' Ryan says, through his chewing gum. 'He's a little twat. And his mum's a bitch. Hope she fucking dies.'

'Okay,' I say.

'Then I could see him, maybe.'

'She doesn't let you see him?'

'No.'

'Why not?'

'She says I battered her, didn't she? Anyway. That's what I'm going to court for. Custody.'

'I didn't know you were going to court.'

'Aye. The Bean not tell you?'

'No.' No, the Bean has not told me that.

Ryan laughs. 'What a fucking cunt, eh.'

I nod.

'You've got a kid too, right?'

'Yeah. Yeah, I have. The Bean tell you that?'

'No. Boy or girl?'

'Girl.'

'And is her mum a bitch too?'

'No. No, in our case it's me. I'm the b— I'm the problem.'

'Oh aye?'

'How did you know I'm a parent?'

'Can just tell. Can *smell* it.'

I don't like that.

'Do you ever wonder if you're the problem in your relationship?' I ask.

'Fuck off,' he says, and his tone suggests that the conversation is over.

THE EXTRA ROUNDS — Ryan's rounds — follow mine, meaning the day will be longer, but Ryan being quick means that we're back at the La'al Tattie Shop before nine o'clock, which is more or less unheard of for me.

'Just stay in the van a minute, please,' I say, opening my door.

'You what?' He throws his head back and laughs, the red of his cheeks darkening. 'Oh aye? The Bean said you liked to stop here. You got a stop-off bird? You're a dark horse, you.'

'I'm not and I haven't,' I say. 'Just – please stay in the van. Just for a minute.'

'All right, Dad.'

I run around the back of the van and retrieve the bag of witch bottles and other things that I picked up from Kathryn yesterday. I'll have to give them back, and I can't pick up any more today either.

'Who's that?' she says, as I burst in.

'That's Ryan,' I say.

'The scary one?'

'Yeah.' I hand her the bag-for-life. 'He's with me now. I won't be able to drop these off, I'm sorry.'

She takes it from me and puts it down behind the counter. 'He's getting out,' she says.

I hear him swagger in behind me.

'All right, lass,' he says, loudly. 'What you got?'

'Just jacket potatoes,' says Kathryn with a big, genuine-looking smile. It isn't the same smile she gives me. 'All the different toppings are on the board there. And you can pick and mix your salad, if you want salad.'

'No salad for me, thanks, love.' He leers at us. 'What's yer man here normally get? I'd go for a bit of what he's having.'

I roll my eyes. 'Don't talk to her like that,' I say.

'I'm only asking about dinner! Fucking hell. You're not offended, are ye, love?' Then to me, in a stage whisper, 'Aye, she's fit her, like. Fair play, marra.'

'Come on,' I mutter. 'Will you get your hands out of your pants at least?'

'Just keeping them warm, pal.'

'Here you go,' Kathryn says to me, handing me my usual. Then she addresses Ryan. 'Do you want anything?'

'Aye, a jacket with cheese and beans, ta.'

'In that order?'

'Yeah.'

He's quiet until she gives him his own brown paper bag. 'Thanks,' he says, grinning. Then, loudly, to me, 'Nice pair of spuds, eh?' as we leave the shop. I look back at Kathryn to see her grinning and waving. 'I'm sorry,' I say.

'What for?' she asks, through a forced grin. 'Just – you go and carry on. You just go.' Ryan's words crawl around in my head as I climb back into the van. *She says I battered her, didn't she.* I feel cold.

Ryan chews noisily, occasionally laughing to himself through his food. He shoves it all in even though it's too hot, and then breathes frantically through his open mouth to cool it down. Deep inside me, flickering sparks of anger grow and steady into a constant flame.

The Passenger

I T's A BIT ANNOYING, to be honest. I understand his situation, and I wouldn't ask him to put his job at risk. His passenger – that Ryan – seems like a massive liability. But we could have talked about it a little more. There's also the slightly awkward fact that the binding exchange I used to make Daniel's witch bottle was one of services and not money: his help with deliveries in return for the bottle. I shouldn't have done that, but I did. The bottle might stop working if he stops the deliveries. I'm starting to get that feeling – you know the one – that something you thought would be simple and good is becoming a bit more complicated. The feeling of regret.

The thing is, I'm getting a lot of orders now. I'm spending all of my evenings on this. But I still need the La'al Tattie Shop; I can't normally take time away from that. I feel the loss if I ever take a day off. So even if I were happy with people knowing who I am, and even if I had a car, I wouldn't be able to make the deliveries myself without taking fewer orders or reducing the Tattie Shop opening hours.

I want to help Daniel with his ghost. I do. But I like to think that he also wants to help me. There'll be a way, I'm sure. I'll talk to him.

The Hostel

W E WERE ON THE shore of Derwentwater, walking. Some of my cousins and I. I can't remember if it was the same summer as when the tree spoke to me, or not. But it was hot; we were in our swimming costumes. A couple of older cousins – Alison and Timothy, siblings – had suggested we go on a walk down the beach, so we were a little way away from the hostel itself and its balcony. We could still see it, and we could be seen from there, so we didn't feel unsafe. There was Alison, Timothy, another cousin called Jane and myself.

Alison and Timothy both played football seriously and they had this kind of endearingly brash physical confidence that was alien to me. I wanted it, I wanted to feel it, but I could only ever imitate it and it always came out unconvincing and wrong. They were also physically big and, being older, comfortable with their bodies in a way that I wasn't.

Anyway, I remember being grumpy on this day because there were two things only that I wanted to do at the hostel: play in the lake, or play board games in the kitchen. And we'd gone on this aimless walk down the shore – most of it stony and hard on our feet – in the blazing sun, Alison and Timothy leading the way. And if they'd been keen walkers, or if we were going somewhere, it would've been fine. But they weren't, and we weren't, and it wasn't. I looked out at the islands in the lake. I was hungry. And the heat was probably making me grouchy too.

'I want to go back,' I said.

'Yeah,' said Jane. Jane was the youngest of us. 'All the lilos are back at the cottage.'

'No,' said Alison and Timothy, in unison. 'Let's just walk a little longer.'

'Where are we going?'

'Just for a walk! Get away from the adults for a bit.'

'I want to go back and get in a dinghy,' I said. 'Let's go and get the dinghies and play pirates.'

'Y'know, that would've worked,' said Alison to Timothy.

'What?' I said.

'Nothing,' she said.

'I want to play chess,' Jane said.

'I'm going,' I said. 'Jane, if you want to come back, now's your chance.' She was only allowed out with us.

'Do you . . . *need* to go?' Timothy asked.

'I *want* to go,' I said. 'Is there something going on?'

'No!'

'Well, I'm going.'

Jane came with me. About halfway back to the hostel, I suddenly began to urgently need the toilet. 'We're going to have to run,' I said to Jane.

'They put something in your drink at dinner time,' she said, her small face serious beneath a bright red headband. 'To make you poo yourself.' She shook her head. 'I don't want that to happen.'

We ran together. We weren't really that far away and I got to the toilet in time. But that wasn't the point. The point was that they'd given me laxatives, and then tried to lead me far enough away from a toilet for me to humiliate myself. At the time, I thought it was just a weird joke that I didn't really get, and I was deeply relieved that it hadn't come off.

It made me feel sad and uneasy. I didn't tell anyone, because I didn't want to acknowledge that it had happened.

Later that night I was playing chess with another cousin, called Philip. We sat at the long table that ran down the centre of the long, thin dining hall. He and I got on well, but he'd been out in Keswick with his parents during the earlier episode. I hadn't told him about it. We were drinking shandy. Daddy-long-legs wiggled through the warm air, drawn in by the light. A couple of aunties played chess further up the table and some uncles were playing liar's dice at the far end. I could hear a car radio on out in the car park; somebody was out there listening to the cricket.

Jane ran in and came and sat next to me. 'I got you these,' she whispered, and slipped a blister pack of small glass vials into my hand.

'What are these?' I asked.

'Stink bombs,' Jane replied. 'My sister got them from the joke shop. They're for you to get back at Alison and Timothy.'

'Thank you,' I said.

Then she ran off again. She was like that; never said hello or goodbye, always running instead of walking.

'What do you need to get back at them for?' Philip asked.

'They put laxatives in my juice at dinner time.'

Philip pulled a face. 'Bloody idiots, mate.'

'Yeah.'

'It's your turn.'

Philip won. Philip always won at chess.

ALISON AND TIMOTHY WERE allowed to drink, so they and the older cousins were out on the beach under the balcony with their small bottles of lager. Philip and I first went to the girls' dormitory and Jane was in there reading a Famous Five book. We pulled Alison's small case out from underneath her bunk. I fumbled to open the packet of stink bombs and Jane snatched it off me. She tore off the plastic and held it out to me. I took the little vials and snapped their necks, emptying the liquid into the case. The smell was immediate and intense. Strong sulphuric fumes rose into the air. Perfect.

'Thanks, Jane,' I whispered. And then the three of us crept into the boys' dormitory and did the same to Timothy's holdall.

We giggled together, and then zipped the bag back up and ran away.

PHILIP AND I WERE there the next morning when Timothy went to get dressed. He was hit by the smell and staggered back, gagging. It was brilliant. 'That's *rank*!' he yelled. 'What scruffy meff's shit theirself?'

'Must've been you,' I said. 'It's your bag.'

But the real trouble came when he and Alison got their clothes out of their bags and they were all stained with white splatter marks, as if the stink bombs had somehow bleached the fabric. Philip and I disappeared from the room at that point, but we caught the fallout. Alison and Timothy were more into their brands than we were, being older than us, and we hadn't anticipated that the stink bombs might damage the clothes or that damaged clothes might somehow be a serious problem. Anyway, we'd ruined some expensive stuff. We didn't admit to it, not even when their mum pulled us up for it. And she was scary.

HALFWAY THROUGH THE HOLIDAY, another uncle arrived from London, bringing with him two more cousins. (This was the uncle I rented from, as an adult.) Excitingly, this time, they brought a PlayStation 3 with them.

It was set up in no time and suddenly a horde of damp, tanned cousins in their swimwear stampeded from the lakeshore into the living room and crowded around the tiny TV. Actually, I remember Philip wasn't shirtless; he was wearing a grey woolly jumper with a shirt underneath it, for some reason. There were only two controllers, so we all had to take it in turns. The living room felt slightly shabby because it opened right on to the balcony, and the doors were always open for people coming up out of the lake to head for the showers. The carpet tiles were always a bit damp.

Alison and Timothy – not our friends by this point – were closest to the London cousins, by virtue of being old enough to have their own mobile phones and social media accounts. So they got to play on it first. They were playing *Street Fighter IV*. Philip and I could tell we were very much at the back of the queue.

It was a winner-stays-on kind of deal. Philip and I gradually moved closer to the TV as cousins were defeated. Nobody was demonstrating any kind of real aptitude. Outside, the heat was incredible. I could hear people splashing in the lake. The London cousins had turned gore on, so fountains of blood lashed across the TV screen. Philip was impatient; he had a PlayStation 3 at home and knew he'd do well.

The time finally came. It was Philip's turn. He reached out to take the controller from the defeated cousin. But Alison snatched it instead.

'Hey,' Philip said. 'It's my turn.'

'I was only on it five minutes,' Alison said. 'I want another go.'

'It's my turn, though.'

Alison waved the controller in the air. 'Come and get it then.'

We were moving very languidly in the heat. Everything felt slow to me. I watched Philip grab for the controller and he managed to knock it out of Alison's hand. It fell to the floor and they both followed it.

'Get off!' I heard Philip shout. 'It's my turn!'

I dived in to help and wrestled the controller from Alison. Philip stood up and took it from me, his usually neat blond bowl cut all tousled. 'There,' he said, smiling, as if it were all resolved.

Timothy, who'd been playing as well, stood up. And then he just punched Philip in the face. Philip's feet left the ground. He wasn't much younger than me, but he was smaller. He left the ground and then came back down, landing on his bum with a thud. He blinked. Blood blossomed from his nose and his eye was darkening already. He started to cry. I think he was about eight years old, I was nine and Timothy was fifteen.

'That Adidas top was the only birthday present my mum could

fucking get me!' Timothy yelled down at Philip. His voice shook. 'And now it's fucking ruined!'

I looked at Philip sitting on the floor with blood dripping down on to his grey woolly jumper, him wearing that jumper in this heat and that red blood getting on his white shirt too, and the tears on his cheeks, and something inside me exploded. I grabbed Timothy's face from behind and pulled him down. I knelt on his arms and started really laying into him. Punch after punch. I aimed for his nose. I broke his nose. I tried to force my fingernails through his cheeks. He was shrieking but I didn't stop. If we'd been on the beach I would've picked up a stone. All of the other cousins ran away screaming.

It was Jane who pulled me off before I hurt him any more. And she took me to my mum and my mum drove us home, both of us sobbing in the car.

The War

I DON'T GET A MOBILE signal at my house, so Kathryn adds me as a Facebook friend and we message that way.

'What are we going to do?' she asks.

'What do you mean?'

'How will you deliver my stuff?'

'I don't think I can, at the moment.'

'Does it really have to be a secret from Ryan?'

'Yes. Don't care if he knows himself, really, but he can't tell the Bean. He can't have that power over me. I've got to be squeaky-clean. I need to do well at this job. I need the money.'

'There's more and more orders coming in, y'know. I feel like there's something going on.' A pause. 'What are you doing?'

'I'm trying to write my book.'

'I'm sorry. I'll let you get back to it.'

'No, it's okay. I'm not getting anywhere with it.'

'What have you got so far?'

I consider lying, but decide against it. 'Nothing. Just ideas. It's fantasy, but really it's about the war. I just . . . I just don't want to be a milkman for ever. And I don't know what else I can do.'

A long pause. And then, 'Is the witch bottle still working?'

'Yes. I think so.'

ON THE VALLEY ROUNDS there's a fair bit of driving between customers, just because of the low population density. One day the silence is too much, so I try to talk with Ryan in a bit more depth than we normally would.

'How long have you worked for the Bean then?' I ask.

'About three years.'

'And what did you do before that?'

'I was in the army.'

'Oh right.' I'd like to hear more, but suddenly catch sight of that boxy metal van. The black block capitals can clearly be read on the back. FALLEN STOCK. It's ahead of us. We're driving along Wastwater, in Wasdale. We'll have to turn right shortly, to call at the campsite and then head down the long lonning from the campsite to the Branthwaite farm on the far side of the lake. I hope the Fallen Stock wagon is not going to the same place. If they turn right for the campsite, it means they are; there's nowhere else for them to go up there.

The day is bright and clear and breezy and the ruffles on the lake sparkle in the sunlight. You can see the patchwork of colour on the mountains, the greens and oranges and purples. Not just the grey-black stone and the white of falling streams, though that's there too. The sound of Herdwick sheep bleating carries across the valley.

'Bloody hell,' I mutter, as the Fallen Stock wagon's right indicator comes on.

'What's your beef with them, then?' Ryan asks.

'Had a run-in a few weeks ago. He was driving too fast and I was parked up on the side of the road. He had to swerve, hit the opposite dyke, burst his nose.'

'They're strange fish, those boys,' Ryan says, quietly.

'You've met them too, then?'

'Aye.'

'What happened there?'

'I saw them at the Higgins farm. Y'know, between Drigg and Seascale.'

'I know it.' Higgins is a grumpy one. He'll give you a telling-off if you're late *or* if you're early. He likes you to arrive just when he's making breakfast, so that he can take everything from you by hand. And he likes his eggs: he buys trays of them, with no apparent consumption pattern, and his ad-hoc egg buys would *always* leave you short for any of the more reasonable requests that might arise on the rest of the round.

'And what happened?' I prompt Ryan.

'Nowt. He was just a strange man. Didn't look dressed for the job. Whistled while he worked.' He scratches himself. 'That fucking Higgins has got a load of Poles working for him now.'

'So?'

'Not right, is it?'

I generally try to avoid political discussions, but I bite. 'Why not?'

He shrugs. 'We're full. Been to a hospital recently? Crap. Can't cope. These refugees'll turn our country into the kind of country they're trying to run from.'

'Refugees don't tend to be Polish,' I say.

'Fuck 'em anyway,' Ryan says. 'And the refugees.'

'You think anybody wants to be a refugee? Wants to get in those leaky boats with their babies and cross the sea? Christ, Ryan. They're only refugees because of that war, and that war only continues because people like you keep on signing up to be given a gun and told who to shoot.'

'Had to fucking do something. Had a kid. Haven't all got rich uncles.'

'What, so – wait. You had your son *before* you joined the army?'

'Yeah.'

'How old is he?'

'Seven.'

'You had him at fifteen?'

'Yeah.'

'How old was his mum?'

'Fifteen.'

'Why didn't you do something like this? The Bean said she knows your mum, you could have got a job from her.'

'Didn't want to be a fucking *milkman*, did I? Still don't. It's not a *career*.'

'Would you work there? For Higgins?'

'No,' Ryan says. 'He's a proper knobhead.'

I pull into the campsite, hoping that we can spend long enough here for the Fallen Stock wagon to do its business and then get back out. The lonning is single lane, so if we meet each other when they're coming out and we're going in, one of us will have a lot of reversing to do. But as I swing round the car park, I see the National Trust man waving his hands from the doorway of the campsite shop and shaking his head, mouthing the words *no*. I look around the car park and it's completely empty. Typical. I wave to the National Trust man and circle back out on to the lonning.

'So. You were in the army? Where did you go?'

'Iraq.' He shifts in his seat. 'Don't want to talk about it.'

The lonning is long and surfaced with pale grey shale. But the shale is either sinking into the icy mud, which is pale like the stone, or is disrupted by uneven rocks from beneath. You have to take it carefully. The shale shines bright in the sun, dazzling me.

We make it to the farm without the Fallen Stock wagon coming the other way. And sure enough, there it is, parked up in the yard. We can see that the back of it is open and the ramp is down, but from our position we cannot see inside it.

Back in the spring, I'd see the occasional dead farm animal laid out in the yard for Fallen Stock to come and collect. One farmyard in particular always seemed to have a pile in the corner; I didn't know what that meant. Maybe some kind of disease. Spring seems to be the time of year for dead livestick though: lots of babies that don't make it, or mothers that die giving birth. But I rarely saw the Fallen Stock wagons – and yet now, in winter, when there aren't often dead animals in the yards, I'm encountering the Fallen Stock wagon more frequently.

The Branthwaite farm is relatively tidy. The yard is a proper yard, not just a mudbath; there's never any black plastic sheeting blowing about. The doors and the window frames of the outhouses are wooden and painted a nice rich green colour. I've never seen dead animals in this farmyard. There's nobody in the wagon cab and I can't see anybody anywhere else, either, apart from some chickens and large black cockerel that in my experience can be quite aggressive.

We sit and watch the wagon for a moment.

'Come on,' I say. 'You're meant to be doing the running around, aren't you?'

Ryan grunts and slouches out of the passenger side in that way he has. I hear the sliding door open as he goes into the back of the van for the Branthwaite order. Like most of the valley farm orders, it consists of a lot of whole milk, a lot of white bread and a lot of bacon. The Branthwaites like their order to be put away in their fridge so that the cats and dogs don't get into it, so Ryan lets himself into the kitchen.

Of course it's now that a nicely painted green outhouse door opens and the Fallen Stock driver strides out. He has a dead animal slung over his shoulders, blood drooling from its mouth. This isn't the same driver that I've encountered before, though.

This one wears the same plus-fours, posh wellingtons and tweed cap, but he's done his torso up differently. He wears a red shirt with a mustard cardigan and a smart tweed jacket over the top. He's thinner than the other one I've met, and his face looks a bit more weathered. He has a similarly wide mouth, but it's downturned, whereas the other's had defaulted into a kind of indulgent smile. And this one has big, heavy pouches under his eyes. When he turns his head, I can see that beneath his tweed cap his hair is neat and grey. Where the other one was pale and wet, this one seems dry and tanned.

He looks at our van, and then our eyes meet. He pauses for a moment and stares, and then makes for the back of their wagon.

I resolve to get out of the van, against my better judgement. And I can't say why. Curiosity, I suppose. Curiosity killing the cat. I try to open my door quietly, and then leave it open so as not to make a sound and alert the Fallen Stock driver that I'm on the move. I slowly creep the distance between the vans, planning to — what? I don't know. Sneak a look in the back of their wagon, I think. Try to square the disconnect between the care and containment that they're meant to ensure and the bloody trail I saw the other wagon leave behind. I'm nearly there when I hear the ramp being raised back up. Then the Fallen Stock driver suddenly pops his head around the back of their wagon and frowns at me.

'Can I help?'

'Hello,' I say. 'I was curious. Just coming to have a look.'

The driver barks a laugh, his mouth briefly cavernous, long, browning teeth suddenly prominent. 'I'm afraid not, sonny Jim.' He pats the side of the wagon. 'This old bird's very secretive.' He sounds like he's from London. His voice is a bit husky. It makes me think of coffee and cigarettes.

I look down at the yard. A trail of blood marks the passage from the outhouse to the wagon.

'We've bumped into you fellows before, I believe?' the driver enquires, looking at my van. 'A colleague had a little run-in with a van like yours.'

'Yes,' I say. 'Yes, that was me.'

'I'll tell you this for nothing,' he says. He even leans in and taps the side of his nose. 'You don't want to get on the wrong side of that one.' He bursts into laughter again, pulling his chin into his neck and opening his mouth way too wide. 'Makes the rest of us seem almost normal!'

I hear Ryan get back into our van.

'Thanks then,' I say, and start to back away. After a few steps I turn around, resisting the urge to run. I shouldn't have got out of the van at all. We leave while the Fallen Stock driver is still sat in his cab, filling out a form or something.

As we go, I recall that the Branthwaites are one of Kathryn's customers that I'd marked up on the tracing paper. One of the customers I'm not currently able to deliver to.

'What were you doing?' Ryan asks suddenly.

'What do you mean?'

'Why were you talking to the Fallen Stock guy?'

'I was just curious. I was hoping for a look inside their wagon.'

'Just a load of dead animals. Not hard to find a load of dead animals if you want a gander.'

I wonder at that, but let it pass. 'When I had that near miss with one of the other Fallen Stock drivers, there were maggots dropping out the back of the wagon,' I say.

'Load of fucking dead meat, marra. Course there were.'

'No,' I say, 'that's not right. Not since foot-and-mouth disease. The whole point is containment. They should have systems in place inside those wagons.'

Ryan doesn't say anything.

'So how come you left the army?' I ask.

'I said I don't want to talk about it.'

'Why not? Was it bad?'

He looks out of the window.

'Did something horrible happen to you, or did you do something horrible to somebody else? Tends to be one or the other, right?'

'Shut the fuck up,' he says.

The Reference

'RIGHT THEN,' THE BEAN says. 'How's everything going with the La'al Tattie Place bird?'

'The La'al Tattie Shop. I don't know what you mean.'

'Aye, right. Listen. I need a favour.'

'Another one?'

'Watch it.' We're in her kitchen again and she's eating another of her low-effort cheese sandwiches. 'There's been a lot of change recently. Graham going, Ryan getting into trouble. And there's something else I haven't even told you about yet. Some developments. I'm expanding.' She takes a bite and then speaks with her mouth full. 'Well, the company is.'

I wait while she chews and swallows.

'Ryan's got a court case coming up.'

'He told me about it.'

'They need an employer reference.'

'You're not going to give him one? He beat somebody up! A woman!'

'It's not like that. I've got to give them one as a matter of proce-dure. Anyway, I want you to do it.' She takes another bite, dropping cheese on to her heavy green raincoat. 'But for his mam's sake, aye, I do want it to be a good one.'

'Unbelievable.'

'It's not like the city round here,' the Bean says. 'Everybody knows each other. You've got to be kind. Grease the wheels.'

'It's wrong.'

'Looks like you've got a decision to make, then.' She laughs. 'Way I see it, it's a development opportunity for yourself. With me – with the *company* expanding, I'm going to need somebody to look after all this delivery side of things.'

I don't say anything.

'You don't want to be a delivery driver for ever. I know that, lad. You could wind up managing the firm. You're bright, you could make more of it than I do. Or you could use it to get a better job somewhere else.'

I still don't speak.

'How's the book coming along?' the Bean asks.

'Really well, thanks,' I say.

I REMEMBER GRAHAM TALKING about his dad. His dad had been a milkman too.

'He did one round, every day. Holmrook. The three roads.' Holmrook was a little hamlet clustered around a junction from the A595. The three roads were two brief stretches of the A595, and then the B road that branched off from it. 'He did from Holmrook Hall up that way, all the way to that house on the end of that row

154

there, just before the bridge. And then on the third road, he did up the Hill Green. And that estate wasn't there then. And that was it. That was what he did, every day. What's that? A hundred drops? And for that, he earned enough to own a house and support a family with three kids. And now here we are. Three vans, over ten rounds, thousands of customers every day, and it's minimum fucking wage. And there's folks still can't afford us! Still cheaper at the supermarket! How does that work? How does that fucking work? Don't know about you, but I can't even cover fucking rent. Tax credits, housing benefit, the works. And I'm sixty-fucking-one. Sixty-fucking-one.'

Graham is now one of the other drivers we see out on the roads. He'll pass by in his Dawson's van. We – Ryan and I – encounter his van in the car park of the Strands Inn, in Wasdale. We have a delivery for the kitchen there, a big one – sacks of vegetables, boxes of salad stuff, multipacks of two-litre milk bottles, trays of eggs. 'Just stay in the van,' I say to Ryan.

I get out and hear Graham's voice coming from out of the back door of the kitchen. I go over and listen in.

'Aye, well. The eggs are fresher and for you we'd knock a few pennies off the pint. Litre. Off the litre! And you know, you could rest easy you weren't being delivered to by that flippin' lunatic. You know how busy these roads get in the summer, and I'm telling you, that one's gone right off the rails.'

'Actually,' I say, popping my head around the door frame, 'Ryan isn't doing any driving any more. It's all me.'

Graham turns around, mouth open, eyebrows up. 'All right, lad! How's it going?'

'All right, thanks,' I say. 'How are you?'

'Good, good.'

'Made the right move, have you?'

'Oh aye. It's much better. Much better rate.'

'As many hours?'

'Aye, well.' He drums his fingers along the stainless steel worktop he's leaning on and then changes the subject. 'She'll have you on the Bootle round now, will she?'

'I'm on all of them,' I said. 'I drive, Ryan does the running about.'

'Oof.' He laughs. 'Rather you than me, pal. All those old biddies are bad enough when you're on your own! Have you had to help Fran back into her chair yet?'

'No,' I say.

'I did once. I could hear her shouting and I went in and I couldn't see her!'

'You've told me this before, I think.'

'So I looked about and then she shouted again and it was coming from the floor! That chair – it was her old one, this is why she's got that new one, see – she'd been trying to lower it or raise it or something and it had had a do and thrown her out.'

I nod.

'She's a little old woman but she's not half heavy,' he muses. 'Anyway, she loved it when I got her under the armpits. It'd been a while since she'd been touched by a man, if you know what I mean.'

'So if everything's good at Dawson's, I mean, if it's *better,* you don't need to steal business from us, do you?'

'No, I'm not! I'm not! I'm just—'

'What about Craggesund? That's proper fucked the Bean over.'

'I didn't do that on me own,' he says. 'You did half of it.'

'Look, guys,' says the chef, who's tall and wide and wears a white hat and holds a meat cleaver and looks thoroughly bored, 'please can you take it outside, maybe? And you,' she says, pointing at me, 'I need that delivery, like, *now*.'

'Of course,' I say. 'I'm sorry.'

I duck back out and see that Ryan is leaning against the passenger-side door.

'Take your hands out your pants, please,' I say, and start unloading the food from the van.

Graham follows me out and starts talking to me. Ryan takes over the unloading.

'There was something else I meant to tell you before I finished,' Graham says.

'Oh yeah?' I say. We stand on the white gravel of the pub car park. The Strands has its own microbrewery; the air smells pleasantly of woodsmoke from the pub and yeast from the shed. Water vapour hazes from the evergreen forests around us. The Strands is a place I could happily live.

'Aye,' Graham says. 'So, y'know the Saltcoats road?'

'What about it? We don't go down there, do we?'

'Not usually. We used to have a customer down there, a regular, but now we – you – only go down there for Jenny.'

'I don't think I know Jenny.'

'No, she just rings an order in now and again. Anyway, I went down there to our old customer once. I mean, I used to go every day, but I want to tell you about this time.'

Ryan still has a few boxes to go, so I let Graham go on.

'I went to him. And he liked us to knock, y'know, and hand his

157

delivery over. It was only ever milk. He was an auld fella, you know what they're like. So anyway. One morning I went and I give him his milk and he paid up, like. And then he closed the door. And that was that.' He rubbed his cheeks. 'The next morning, I goes back with that day's pint. And I knock, but there's no answer. It's not like him. So I open the door. And it won't quite open. And it's because he's lying on the floor behind it. He's dead.'

'You found him?'

'Aye, but that's not the story. I've found a few bodies on my rounds, lad! And you will too. No, the story is – by the way, guess what he had in his hand?'

He's smiling, so I know the answer. 'A milk bottle?' I say, tentatively.

'Aye! He must've dropped down dead as soon as he'd closed the door the day before! He still had the milk in his hand, like! The bottle, at any rate. The milk had gone everywhere. Anyway. I checked his pulse. Definitely dead. I needed to call the ambulance. But this was before mobile phones and I didn't want to go in and use *his* phone. And this is just down the road from here – you know, where the Saltcoats road gets close to the sea, that's where I was – so I thought, y'know, go back to the depot and ring from there. So I goes back to my van. And it won't start. And it was still dark – the auld fella, he was an early riser. This was my first drop of the morning. Summer this was, so just starting to get light, but really still mostly dark. So I'm sitting there in my van, t'auld fella's dead body not ten feet away. And I started to feel real cold. Like I say, it's summer, so it shouldn't be cold, even that time of day. It gets colder and colder. I start to see my breath. The van still won't start. The sun's coming up behind me and it's making everything red.'

Graham likes telling stories. We don't really have time to stop and listen, but it feels as if there might be some kind of important point to it.

Ryan finishes and joins us.

'And that's when I see it, walking towards me. A person. Too tall, though. And dressed strange. It's coming from the direction of the sea, slowly walking, slowly, slowly. I look back t'auld fella's house. Door's still closed. Van still won't start. I take the key out, I put it back in. Still won't start. It's getting closer, whatever it is. I feel like it's bad, right, like it's not right, because everything's gone so cold. And because of the dead body. I felt like – you know those old ghost stories where you see a ghost and it's an omen of death? Or, it means somebody's died? I felt like it was like that. This was something come to take the spirit of t'auld fella.'

'Why'd it wait like a whole day, then?' Ryan asks.

'Shut it, you. Ours is not to wonder why. Anyway, I keep trying the ignition. And then I get it. It takes. The engine's on. But I can't reverse – I'm pulled over at the end of his drive and there's a wall behind me. I've got to go past this thing. And my van's on now, my lights are on. I can see it better. I drive forwards and swerve around it. And – this is the thing – it reaches out. It reaches out for *me*! So I wonder. I wonder if it really was coming to collect t'auld fella's spirit, or I wonder if it'd killed him in the first place. And maybe it would've killed me if I hadn't driven off.'

Ryan spits. 'It was good up until the end.'

'And do you know what it was?' Graham's grinning again.

'A ghost?' Ryan asks.

'Aye, of course it were a bloody ghost! But – it was a Roman centurion.' He nods. 'That's why it looked so tall. It had a big feather.'

'You fucking what?' Ryan starts to laugh. 'Graham, mate, we're gonna miss your stupid fucking stories, like.'

'There used to be Romans here,' Graham says. He sounds a bit hurt.

'Aye, but why'd there be Roman *ghosts*?'

'Thanks for telling us,' I say to Graham. 'But, sorry – you said you meant to tell us before you finished? Why?'

Graham shrugs. 'Just a warning, like. I always refused to go and deliver to Jenny, after that. Thought you should know too.'

'Well,' I say. 'Thanks again.'

AS THE ROUND CONTINUES, I think about the Bean's request. It's true that I don't want to be a delivery driver for ever. But primarily because the pay's not great. It's not enough. I like the work, though. I like the driving, I like the physicality, I like meeting lots of different people. If there's an opportunity to make it a proper job, that's something I'd find quite interesting. I wouldn't admit that to the Bean, not yet. But I'm not prepared to let Graham undermine us in the meantime either. *Save yourself*, I thought. I need the job for now; I need to turn it into something more dependable and lucrative in the future.

Ryan's a different problem. I don't like Ryan, and Graham has a point that his reputation is bad for the company. But I can't simply write him a bad reference and get rid of him that way. The Bean was quite unsubtle in her implications: there might be a good opportunity for me *if* I write Ryan a good reference. Maybe I could do that and then get rid of him somehow later. Maybe I'll wind up in a position where I could simply sack him. But no. I glance down and to my left at his big arms, big legs and big feet. Inside his pants his fists are big too, and hammy. If I'm to act against him, I don't want him to know that I've done so. I don't want him as an enemy.

I wonder what the Bean's new business is. More than simply acquiring new rounds, from the sound of it. Maybe production? Dairy processing? Or even getting into livestock. Or recycling? There are plenty of supply chain functions that she might be thinking of bringing in-house. No doubt it's something to do with that building on the other side of the wall.

Another thought occurs to me. If I'm to gain some authority over the delivery side of the business, it would make it much easier to integrate Kathryn's business with ours. Maybe there's a future in all of this after all.

But that brings me back to the niggle that I can't get rid of. More than a niggle. How to get Kathryn's stuff delivered in the short term? I can't let Ryan know for fear of him reporting back to the Bean and the Bean revising her opinion of me downwards. And yet Kathryn is accumulating quite a backlog of orders back at the La'al Tattie Shop.

At least the ghost hasn't come back.

The Overlap

BACK AT HOME I pull off my boots, shrug off my muddy, milky, waterproof coat, peel down my waterproof trousers, take off my thick, damp woollen socks, unbutton my jeans, get rid of the rest of my sweaty clothes and jump in the shower. It's a dirty job, in a sense. Even though Ryan's doing all the running about, I still dress for the weather, which means being encased in a rubbery outer layer and getting incredibly sweaty inside. Now I'm just driving, I could perhaps dress a little more smartly. I'll ask Kathryn what she thinks. Ask her how she likes me.

I get out of the shower, take the nice warm towel from the radiator and wrap myself in it. I leave the bathroom to go to my room and get changed. In my room I put the light on, and then pause. I walk backwards, back out into the hallway, and look to my left into the spare bedroom.

My uncle had advertised the house as having three bedrooms, but in reality one of those isn't even big enough to fit a bed into. So there are two: mine, and the spare.

The door to the spare bedroom is open and beyond it the room is dark. It's a rear-facing room so doesn't get much sun, and by this point, at this time of year, it's getting dark outside anyway. And of course the light is off. But I thought I saw something as I passed, something that didn't immediately register. And I had seen it. I was right.

At the back of the room, the hooded man sits on the bed. Although I'd already caught a glimpse out of the corner of my eye, the moment I fully acknowledge his presence, that awful, thin chest rises again, and that rattly moan comes out, and then that horrible, horrible sobbing follows.

I scream, recoiling from the open doorway, trying to cover myself. It's the first time he's driven me to noise and dimly, somewhere, I'm trying to explain my response. *It's because this time I'm naked*. I grab the clothes I've just discarded and leave the house. It isn't raining outside but it's cold, it's clear-night-in-late-November cold and there's a low-lying mist down over the moonlit river and the stars are coming out and I drop the towel as I try to get my clothes on. My clothes feel disgusting and wet now that all the sweat in them has chilled.

I've got my car keys in my jeans pocket, thankfully. I think about going back and locking the house up, but then – would that thing be locked inside? I don't know. I stare at the door for a moment. I see some movement within and that makes my mind up for me. I'm going to leave it. I get in the car and turn the key in the ignition. It doesn't start. I look back at the front door. I try the car again. It still doesn't start. I get out and run to the shed for my bike. Once mounted I tear away, scattering gravel and mud.

After a few seconds I know where to go. I'll go to Kathryn's place.

*

'HELLO!' SAYS KATHRYN, OPENING her door to find me shivering on the doorstep. 'I wasn't expecting you?'

'Hi,' I say.

There's a moment's silence.

'Can I come in?' I say.

'Yes, sorry. Yes, of course. It's just – I was working, and it's a surprise. I didn't mean to be rude.'

'I didn't think you were being rude.'

She lets me past and closes the door and we go through into her front room and just look at each other for a moment. She has candles burning and her laptop glows bluely from the dining table, surrounded by open books. She sits back down behind the screen, and then gets up and goes to the shelf where she keeps her glassware assembled. She checks a few labels on jars and then returns to the laptop. She flashes me a brief smile.

'Is everything all right?' I say.

'It's fine. It's fine! Well.' She shrugs. 'You don't seem very happy yourself.'

'No! That's what I've come to tell you about.' I sit down.

'Hang on,' she says. 'I've got quite a lot to do tonight.'

'Oh,' I say, standing back up. 'Okay then.'

'All right, I'll admit it,' she says, 'I'm a bit disappointed about this Ryan situation. I've scaled up operations a bit based on our arrangement and, well . . . maybe I shouldn't have, but I have. And now I'm worried it'll all fall apart.' She looks up from the screen. 'I know it's not your fault.'

'I'm sorry,' I say. 'Listen. I'll find a way. I'll try to be subtle about it.' Not easy, I think, given that Ryan's the one that's meant to do all the running around.

'That's good. Because there's another aspect to it. Something I feel really bad about.' She sighs. 'You can stay here tonight, but I do need to work.'

'What are you working on?'

'There are still a lot of orders coming in,' she says. 'Some of it's for stuff I haven't done before.' She reads from her emails. 'This old guy wants a "spider necklace, for the ague". Like, literally, a necklace made of spiders. Living spiders! I've told him I can thread them, but they won't be living by the time they arrive at his.'

I pull a face.

'A lot of people want wards, y'know. Like you. People seeing things.'

'I worked with a guy who'd tell a few ghost stories,' I say. 'It's weird. We had friends in the city who loved ghost stories, but the point there was the telling; it was about being together and scaring each other, and it was about the ideas. But here, people tell ghost stories and it just sounds like they straight-up believe them.'

'Well, yeah.' She frowns at me. 'I mean, you believe yours, right?'

'Yes, I do. But partly I wonder if that's because I'm *here*. And I know I could tell people and they'd just believe me. If I still lived in the city, I'd probably be going to the doctor. But I live here, and instead of the doctor, I've gone to a witch.'

'I believe. And I believe I can help people. And more and more people are wanting my help, which is good. Sometimes it's just . . . demand is higher than I expected.'

'Where are they?' I ask.

'On my website I offer delivery to all the places you deliver milk to. And I do get orders from all those areas. But most of them come from your most southern rounds – Eskdale and Wasdale, Ravenglass, Waberthwaite, Bootle. And that's where demand is growing.'

'I have a tentative theory,' I say. 'I've noticed some overlap between the names of your customers and the Fallen Stock customers.'

She raises an eyebrow. 'Yeah?' she says, after a moment. 'Tell me about them.'

'Well, they're the ones who pick up any dead animals from farmers or smallholdings. I don't know what they do with them after that. But I see them around so much more now than I used to. As in, there are more dead animals about. But there's nothing in the news about new diseases or epidemics or anything. And they're all arseholes – the drivers, I mean. They drive too fast, they don't stop to let people past, they block people in. One of them nearly crashed into my van, and swerved into the dyke instead. I went to help him, but he was a creep. He seemed angry instead of sorry – he grabbed my hand and dug his nails into the back of it, scratching me, and he said something – what did he say? "I just want to walk this world like it is mine again."'

'Do your customers dislike them?'

'No, they don't seem to. To be honest, they don't mention them. I have asked a couple why there are more dead animals than there used to be, and there's always an answer, but . . .' I frown. 'Now that I think about it, maybe the customers are a bit evasive when it comes to this stuff. Maybe there's a pattern there.'

'You haven't made a point of asking Fallen Stock customers if they're being visited by ghosts? Or people being visited by ghosts if they're Fallen Stock customers?'

'No, and I don't think I would.'

'No, I agree.'

I watch her as she rubs her eyes.

'How did you get here?' I ask.

'What do you mean?'

'Tell me everything about yourself,' I say. 'I want us to know each other. I want to know you.'

The Witch at Netherhall

I WAS A LUCKY, HAPPY kid. My parents were kind and clever and somehow both earned well *and* had time to spend with my brother and me. We lived in that intensely manufactured kind of zone that you get between middling northern towns; it's all A-roads and shopping centres, roundabouts and blue-neon Indian restaurants. Cut grass and neat red brick. We weren't near either my mother's parents or my father's parents and so we'd do a lot of travelling during school holidays. Either upcountry or downcountry. I have vivid memories of being in the back seat of the car – falling asleep, waking up, city lights passing by as we sped along the motorway. My dad turning round to look at us, to check on us, my mum asleep in the passenger seat. 'Hey. *Hey!* Who wants a McDonalds? Shall we get a McDonalds?' Service stations, sliproads, clothes in a backpack.

My mum's parents lived up here, West Cumbria, in a two-up two-down in Aspatria. My mum's mum did astrology and tarot. I didn't think anything of it. I thought it was just something she did to occupy herself . . . a hobby. The house was always full of these huge rolls of paper covered in thin straight lines and spidery writing, and there'd be decks of cards everywhere, and crystals hanging in the windows, and she'd sit in the kitchen smoking weird roll-ups – not weed, but just strong, sweet tobacco – and drinking sherry all day. She'd sit there at this small, round, wobbly kitchen table with the fridge behind her, and their fridge was like . . . it sounded like a chainsaw. They had loads of fridge magnets from Blackpool, and the walls and ceiling were yellow. My granddad would sit in the recliner in the other room, watching football with his feet up, until it came time to cook. Then he'd get busy in the kitchen. He was an incredible cook, though it was difficult to work out how. Walk in on him and you'd find him just standing with the back door open, smoking out the doorway, pans boiling over on the hob. He did basic food but he made it magical. It was him who taught me how to do a good jacket potato.

I loved it there but it would get pretty cramped pretty quickly with four of us staying. We'd all have to sleep on airbeds in the front room and inevitably we'd have to wake my granddad and get him out of his recliner before we could blow the beds up and lie down.

Anyway. I went to university to study creative writing. One of our main lecturers was good with his male students, but not us girls. He spent time one to one with the boys, actually helping them. But whenever us girls had tutorials, he'd start making jokes about how he could get into trouble for being on his own with such attractive students, and how he'd better be careful about what he said. He'd recommend novels featuring lots of explicit sex to particular female students, and then joke about how maybe he shouldn't be doing that. I gave him the benefit of the doubt until one day I had a tutorial with him and he asked me for my personal response to a sex scene in a novel he'd told me to read. That was what he called it. 'The sex scene on page such and such.' I told him that it was not really a sex scene and he shrugged and said, 'The rape scene, then.' He'd known what it was. I told him I didn't want to talk about it and it wasn't relevant to the piece of work I'd submitted. He frowned and said that he was surprised that I thought that. But the piece I'd submitted had neither sex nor rape in it, I explained. He smirked and told me that sometimes our subconscious preoccupations come out in our writing without us realising it. I told him that he was making me uncomfortable. He gave me some flannel about how art *should* be challenging, how it *should* make us uncomfortable. I told him I didn't mind art being challenging and that my problem was with *him*. He apologised and then put his hand on my knee and offered me a drink to cheer me up. I walked out and went straight to the course leader and told him that the lecturer was sleeping with an MA student, which was true. Then I left the course. The lecturer was married and because of my complaint he got sacked and his wife left him, which I was glad about. The MA student got in touch with me and told me I'd ruined his life. I told her that he'd ruined his own life. It's something you learn in writing: there's the event, and there's the revelation of the event. Often, the controlled revelation of events is what a story *is*. Without the revelation, there is no story, there is no event, there is no truth. But in real life there is a truth, whether or not there is revelation. That man was an adulterer and an abuser, and that was the truth, regardless of if or how the revelation came about. And it's the truth that deep down ruined his life.

So I didn't get a degree. But I did feel confident about my writing.

I started looking for writing work – work I felt like I could do – all over. I think all that time in the car as a kid meant I was comfortable with the thought of moving. I don't know. As it happened, I found a technical writing job up here, at Netherhall. So my parents bought my mum's parents a sofa-bed, and I moved in with them. It was only after that that I realised my grandma was a proper businesswoman. She didn't just do astrology and tarot readings as a hobby, but as a job. She had people placing orders all the time. People visiting for consultations. And she did more than I'd realised. She placed charms and lifted curses. She offered advice on all subjects – how to turn a failing allotment around, how to rid your street of an aggressive dog without raising suspicion, how to apply for unemployment benefits. This was before the last crash. Some of the work she charged for and some she didn't. She took strong painkillers all day long because she had severe toothache. I think she was addicted. I asked why she didn't go to the dentist. She explained that their dentist had retired over twenty years ago; no other nearby practice had had capacity. So both my grandparents had just stopped going.

My job was frustrating at first. Nuclear decommissioning is another world. Netherhall is not only undergoing its own centuries-long dismantling, but supports other nuclear sites all over the country with theirs. I had to write instructions: documents detailing precisely how to inspect, maintain and repair special containers used for moving waste. Maybe nuclear waste, or maybe other hazardous materials. I'd be translating, in effect – taking documents written by engineers and turning them into plain-English sequences, formatted differently, branded properly, internal style guides accounted for, that kind of thing. The approvals process was incredibly arduous, as you might expect. I'd have to hold stakeholder meetings with about fifteen different people – maintainers, checkers, asset owners, operators, document controllers, the designers, the radiological monitors, on and on it went – just for a document that told people how to replace a flask seal, for example. Then they'd all submit notes and I'd rewrite, but I'd have to hold another stakeholder meeting to get them to check each other's notes. Then they'd all disagree. Because of the nature of the work, it had to be right, and the culture was to take the time required to get it right – challenging each other was encouraged. But these guys were the experts and I was just the author, so I had to wait for them to agree with each other. It was the Forth Bridge. It was Sisyphean. Once I accepted that each task was essentially endless, that that was the nature of the work, it was okay. I'd take a document to the experts, update it accordingly and then take it back, update it some more, and on and on. Meanwhile the flask – or drum, or box, or freight container – would be sitting somewhere in some facility, not being used. And the waste that this thing had been designed and engineered and constructed to move would be sitting in another facility, costing the state hundreds of thousands of pounds because the facility had to be guarded by men with guns or whatever, and it couldn't be shut down because the waste couldn't be moved. Of course, this wasn't *wrong*. Better to take a long time getting the seal replacement document right than ship dangerous materials in a faulty flask, leaking who knows what along our national arteries. And progress would be made; each document would inch closer to approval, to publication. I'd start another document and take it through the same process. And that became the job. Documents upon documents, all at different stages of the circle. The place felt like an accretion of procedures and legacy arrangements and cultural habits, as much as it felt like an accretion of buildings, and they all interacted with each other in weird ways. I had expected work to feel productive, or at least measurable. But instead I just started to feel as if I was making a nest deep within a gargantuan, gnarled carbuncle of paper and people and computers.

I had a manager who was widely regarded as a bit of a bellend. He was tall and broad-shouldered, with black hair that he slicked backwards. Always tanned. A bit older, nearly fifty, always going to the gym. His arms and chest were kind of muscly and swollen. He'd bulk-order chicken breasts off this body-building website and just eat a dry one for his dinner every day. He had this stiff walk. He could be all right but he had various habits that marked him: always asking me or another woman on the team to print things for the men, or to make tea and coffee for the guests. Calling us 'the girls'. 'Ask one of the girls to do it for you.'

The work changed a little when I started to write documents for other sites. I'd go and visit because they were knocking a building down and needed some kind of special container to move the rubble. It would turn out that another site across the country was building a building especially to keep the rubble in. So they were knocking one building down, only to build another building to put the ruins in. And new packaging to move the rubble. I loved it. I found it funny, even though I knew that it only *appeared* farcical. All of this stuff was optimised at a deep national level, not just with regards to cost, but safety. It was work I could do well, and once I'd got used to the circularity, it was work I could do easily.

Meanwhile, I was learning from my grandma. Plants and flowers, trees and birds, how to name the time of year or the phase of the moon. We'd go down to the beach and she'd collect stones with holes in them. There were some spirits she put out small bowls of milk for, and others that she'd ward away with rusty nails scattered around the house. She held her consultations at the kitchen table, and when people came for their readings or their horoscopes, I'd sit out of sight on the staircase, quiet and still, and listen in. She knew I was there – she asked me to hide and absorb it all. It was another method of teaching. The horoscopes she gave were serious: not a few platitudinal lines of guff, but full-on, hours-long discussions around the huge charts she'd drawn. Her customers were old, young, rich and poor. But mostly old and poor. Her voice was low and croaky. Sometimes we'd go to Appleby and feed the wild ponies. I paid my grandparents some keep, and started looking for my own place to rent.

One night I was woken up by my phone vibrating. I'd received a photo from an unknown number. A photo of a penis. Hanging through the flies of some smart trousers, long and fat. The photo was taken from above and to the side. There were no hands in it, nothing but penis and trousers and, blurry at the bottom, some dark shoes.

It wasn't the first time I'd received a dick pic, but previous dick pics had been from men over social media, usually not even anonymised in any way, so I'd been able to reassure myself that the senders weren't close to me or important to me at all. But this unknown number in the middle of the night felt different, more threatening. Partly it was because I saw the penis and immediately thought of my manager. That was in itself disconcerting, but more importantly, he was somebody who knew me in real life and had power over me. I still think it was the trousers that put me in mind of him somehow, or the shoes just caught in frame at the bottom of the picture. There was just something that suggested to me that the penis was his, even though there was no evidence in it that I could show to other people. I blocked the number and tried to go back to sleep, but couldn't.

The next day at work things were different. I caught myself being over-eager to please my manager, and I felt that he was being over-friendly, where usually he was rude and brusque. We were encouraging each other, in that I was being nicer than I wanted to be because I was afraid of him, and he was wearing a new smile and speaking with oil in his voice because I was being nicer, and that made me more scared. At some point mid-afternoon I was suddenly sickened by the extent of my own obsequiousness and had to pick up a couple of forms and leave the office for a little walk before the disgust erupted out of me.

But he didn't notice, or if he did notice he didn't stop. I tried to work out if I was imagining the change in his behaviour – if I'd wrongly attributed the photo to him and was reading him in a different way as a result. It was possible. Whatever the truth, I was desperate to leave work.

When I got home, my grandma was lying on the sofa, clutching her face and moaning. My granddad had shifted his recliner over so he could stroke her head. He wasn't speaking much by the time I got back. He looked distressed and a bit zoned out. She sounded like an injured animal and he looked like a scared one. He'd turned the TV off, so you knew it was serious. He'd squeezed the can in his hand so that it was all dented and the lager in it was warm. Neither of them could drive.

'I'm taking you to the hospital,' I said.

'No,' she said, 'no bloody way. Bloody useless. Jammed in with the drunks for hours. Queues. Infections. Hospitals are for when you've given up. Don't get old or sick, lass.'

I actually picked her up and carried her out to the car. It was like picking up one of those baby birds you find dead on the ground near their nests, having tried and failed to fly. Her short grey hair was greasy and stuck up messily like the fine feathers of a chick. And her old hands were hard and clawed, her fingers yellow. I gently placed her down in the passenger seat of my car and fastened the seat belt. Granddad had shuffled out behind us in his slippers and he got into the back.

This was before the hospitals got as bad as they are now, but it was pretty bad all the same. Grandma had been right. Queues, drunks, standing-room only, everything dirty, every appointment late, every nurse harassed, every doctor fraught and ill-looking. The sense of everything just about hanging together. The sense of everybody depending on a healthy dose of good fortune as much as anything else. And those who'd probably caused the whole fucking crash with their pig-headed votes were the loudest and most aggressive patients, pink-faced, spittle-lipped. Blaming the staff, primarily for not being numerous enough. My grandparents both seemed even smaller than usual, and more scared. Still and overwhelmed in the middle of a crush of sick, worried and bedraggled people.

Eventually my grandma was seen. The doctor, old and pale, probed her teeth with a spike on a stick, occasionally hissing in disgust. He nearly had his whole hand in her mouth, stretching the soft, near-translucent skin of her lips and cheeks. Then he got in there with one of those little mirrors. In the end he sighed despairingly.

'I'll book you in to get them all out.'

'What?' I said.

'I was talking to her,' he said, gesturing at my grandma.

My grandma was bent over, holding her mouth with her eyes squeezed shut.

'She can't talk,' I said. 'I think you've hurt her jaw.'

'Well,' the doctor said, 'her teeth are shot. Quickest and easiest will be to get them all out and stick some dentures in there.'

'You're sure it's not just one tooth?'

'Even if it is, next month it'll be another one.'

I looked at my grandma. She was standing up and nodding.

'Okay,' I said.

'You,' the doctor said, pointing at my granddad with his little mirror. 'May as well have a look at yours too. When did you last go to the dentist? About the last time she did, I'll warrant? Too long ago. We're all about prevention now, the way things are. If yours are half as bad as hers, we'll get yours out as well.'

My granddad looked at me.

'You don't have to,' I said.

'We're running two hours late, but I'm offering you the last three minutes of her appointment,' the doctor said. 'Take it or leave it.'

My granddad got in the chair.

By the time we left, they both had appointments for full mouth extractions.

That night I received another picture of a penis. The same one as in the previous photo, I think, but this time it was erect. Still sticking out through the plain smart trousers, but pointing up. The number it came from was not recognised by my phone, but it was different to the one that the other photo had been sent from. I blocked this one, too.

The next night, a fuller erection against a flat, hard stomach. The photo was taken from beneath and this time the owner of the penis was not wearing trousers, so the picture also included his small, walnutty ballsack. Free of clothing and, weirdly, mostly free of hair. The skin around it was stubbly.

I could see my manager being the kind of guy to shave his pubic region. He was definitely the kind of guy who'd be proud of his abs.

Every night a new picture from a new number. Every day I felt nervous around my boss, nervous and skittish. I couldn't help but think about what lay inside his pants. At work he'd look at me when I wasn't looking. I could see his face turned towards me in my peripheral vision, and I'd slowly move, as if about to look at him properly, and he'd jerk his gaze away. It was evidence enough for me, at that point. But I didn't know what I could do about it. I had nothing to prove it.

At home, my grandma was powering through the toothache. Knowing there was an end in sight enabled her to get on with things in the interim. She struggled to talk, though. She kept a milk bottle instead of giving it back to the milkman and insisted on putting it under my bed. I asked her why but she waved my question away and pointed at her mouth, in order to remind me that she couldn't answer questions.

The penis in the pictures got redder, redder than I've seen a penis get before. Redder than looked healthy. It was just such an angry-looking dick. I didn't want to look at the pictures but I looked at them anyway. There were a couple of close-ups showing it oozing and, finally, a video. I started watching it with the volume way down, and he was stroking himself and grunting. I turned it off immediately, but I expect it was a video of him ejaculating all over himself.

I wondered – who would go to the effort of having all those different phone numbers? And what for? What did they think was going to happen? It wasn't even as if he was trying to proposition me. There was never a name or a face attached. Maybe he thought he'd get a response, but I didn't respond, and he kept going anyway. There's a magic to sex, there's a power, but that wasn't sex. It wasn't arousing, but I doubt it was ever meant to be – not for me, anyway. It was non-consensual, and it was a performance, and it was all for self-satisfaction. I was just a convenient vessel for his output.

The day after the video, he asked me if we could have a catch-up. I said yes. I didn't know what else to say. He asked me to book a meeting room. I lied and said they were all booked, so we'd have to use the canteen. He agreed to that.

It was gone dinner time so the canteen was quiet; there were a few other meetings happening at other tables, but everybody was spread out enough for conversations to remain private, unfortunately.

'So how're you doing? You all right?'

'I am, thank you.'

'Any news? Any news in your world?'

I smiled and shook my head. I didn't really know what he was asking.

'Thought we could do with a catch-up, because there's some new work on the way and it feels like a you job. What's your capacity?'

'I haven't really got any.'

'But some of that should be coming to an end, right? You gave a delivery date of the end of the month for the IF30 document suite. That's a lot of work gone.'

'Well, it depends on approvals.'

'Yeah, well. It's bounced around long enough, to be honest. If you don't get it through this time, I'll be concerned.'

I didn't say anything.

'But I'm sure you will. You're doing well. You're doing well. Everybody says it.'

'Thanks,' I said.

'So then. This new work. There's a site on the south coast ramping up their decommissioning. Once it kicks off, they're going to be moving material as fast as they can. But they need help. They want a whole fleet of containers, but without some real good thinking, they won't be able to load them, ship them and get them back in time to reload again – at least not as fast as they need to, because they're shipping it up here, and our stores are pretty maxed out themselves. For them to ship at the rate they want, we've got to be unloading and shipping empties back *fast*. Faster than we're used to. So we need to work together. To optimise. It's a project. Project work. You up for it?'

'Okay,' I said.

'We'll need to travel down together, so I can introduce you.'

'Okay,' I said.

I WENT STRAIGHT FROM that meeting to HR. The woman in HR nodded slowly as I told her what I'd been receiving, why I thought the pictures were coming from my manager, how his behaviour towards me had changed, and now this invitation.

'I'm sorry,' she said, afterwards. 'I'm not clear on why you think it's him.'

I ran through it again.

'Do you *know* it's him?' she said.

'I *believe* it's him,' I said.

She smiled smugly. 'Not quite the same thing, is it?'

'No,' I said. 'I'm aware of that. I chose my words very deliberately.'

'And he's quite a handsome man, isn't he? Don't think he'd have to do all that stuff to get a bit of action.'

I didn't say anything.

'He was a really lovely fella before his climbing accident, y'know. He fell head-first onto a rock. The way I heard it, it was the only rock at the foot of the crag – lovely long soft grass everywhere, apart from this one big stone sticking up out of the ground, like it had popped up just to meet him. I remember him like he used to be. He was as sweet as anything. His head injury changed him. Made him a bit more abrupt, a bit more aggressive. He swears a lot more. It made him a bit more like men *used* to be, if you know what I mean. He's like a *real* man, now. I liked him before, but now I think he's *hot*. It's different, isn't it? You know what I mean.'

I didn't say anything.

WHEN I GOT HOME that day there was a small glass pot full of black powder on my pillow. It was from my grandma. It was accompanied by a letter. The letter explained how to use it in order to 'afflict the flesh'. I hadn't told her about the pictures I'd been receiving. But the letter advised to mix it into a drink in order to cause 'intense discomfort to the nethers', so I gathered that she knew, somehow.

A couple of days later, I seized my opportunity. My manager's gym bag was under his desk and there was a team meeting in the calendar. About half an hour into the meeting I left to go to the toilet, but returned to our now empty office, donned a pair of Marigolds borrowed from under my grandparents' sink and emptied the glass pot into the tub of protein powder on my manager's desk. I stirred it in and the colours blended perfectly. He made up his protein shakes about twice a day. Sure enough, after the meeting he made one up. I watched him drink it, feeling gleeful.

But he did come into work the next morning. And the next. I was disappointed. It hadn't worked. Though he did look pained after visiting the toilet. And he was walking slightly gingerly. The third day, he came in looking unwell. Pale and sweaty, his stomach distended. About mid-afternoon he started throwing up at his desk. But it wasn't just normal sick: in amongst the regurgitated lunch was a bunch of thick, sausage-like things. We all stared, stunned, and then one of the sausages started wriggling. He screamed – we all did – and then he pissed himself and that made him scream even more. But in pain this time.

He wasn't in the next morning. Word came through he'd called in sick. Later that afternoon, we heard he'd be off sick for two weeks. I was delighted. I was happy and relieved.

That was the same day as my grandparents' operation. Because it was pre-booked, they'd arranged taxis so that I didn't have to take time off work. I got home to find them both sitting on the sofa eating fish and chips with no teeth. Their lips and chins were slick with blood from their surgery and saliva, and they were each giggling at the way the other looked. When they saw my horrified face, my grandma burst out laughing and spat chewed-up cod across the tiny room. I think they were on some serious drugs.

'Did you get him?' she mumbled, after she'd finished laughing.

'I did,' I said, 'thanks to you.'

'Good lass,' she said. 'Present in your room.'

This time, there was a milk bottle on my pillow. It was about a quarter-full of bloody teeth and there were some rusty nuts and bolts in there too. Green leaves crushed up and turning dark, long strands of grey hair, and fluids that I didn't want to identify. The neck of it was stopped with wax. I hid it under my bed. This time, the note read:

A WITCH BOTTLE, TO KEEP THEM OUT OF YOUR HEAD

I didn't know what she meant until later, when she was going to bed. She was full of sherry, which she probably shouldn't have been, and I think it was interacting with the drugs in a weird way.

'Get the note?' she hissed, gripping my wrist. 'Get the bottle?'

'I did, Grandma,' I said. 'I did. Who's "them"?'

'Not *who*,' she said through her still-bleeding gums. '*What*. The astral reachings of evil men. Not lust, lass. A bit of desire's got its place. I'm talking about something else. Sickness, projected. That's what. We're swimming in the evil's shit. We're drowning in their filth. The air's full of their intent. It leaps from eyes to brain, from screen to screen. It courses from root to branch. Poison. Poison! It's in every system. It hatches from blood spilled centuries ago and it grows limbs and stalks across the fields at night. It flies invisibly through the skies. Sometimes it arrives as something hateful on your phone, sometimes a hand on your knee, and at other times it's something unwelcome trying to get in through the door. And you need to listen to me. Listen to me. Learn your wards. Learn what's important. Learn how to pay attention, and learn what to block out. Let the good into your head and keep the bad out of it.'

When my manager came back into work, he was a changed man. Not in a good way. He was uncomfortable sitting, he could only walk slowly and gingerly, and he certainly couldn't work out. He'd stare openly at the women in the office, letting his gaze linger on their bodies. He sneered and leered and after a while got disciplined for groping an agency worker. Shortly after that he applied for home-working and eventually ended up on long-term sick leave. I never received another mysterious penis picture. I dread to think what his penis would have looked like after my grandma's preparation had finished with him.

I don't know what it was, but after my grandparents' operations something changed. They slowed down, lost some vitality. I worried that they'd caught some kind of infection, but they didn't really seem ill. If you took each day in isolation, nothing about their behaviour was concerning. Even if you compared each day to the day before, there was really nothing you could put your finger on. But gradually, over time, from that operation onwards, their vigour slowly drained away. Maybe it was the anaesthetic, or the painkillers. Maybe the operation had nothing to do with it and it was a coincidence. I don't know. About six months later, my grandma died in her sleep. My granddad woke up in the morning, found her and had an aneurysm. He went into hospital, spent three months in a coma and then died.

My grandma had saved enough from her business for me to inherit a little. I left my job and set up the La'al Tattie Shop. But to honour her as she deserves, I need to do more. I need to use the magic she taught me to provide what she used to provide. People are struggling. Old truths turn out to be lies. Every way you turn, you find things falling over, things sliding away. It's a gradual coming apart. People are scared and are looking to strange places for comfort and solidarity. But there's something to worship in magic, in nature, and I can show people that. I can direct people that way. That's what I'm hoping to do.

The Subterfuge

IN THE MORNING I take a backpack of Kathryn's orders to the depot with me. Thankfully the night is dry. I've had my first good sleep in weeks thanks to a tea of Kathryn's own invention and the confidence that I would not be visited in the night by the hooded man. And I feel better for it, even if I'm wearing clothes that need a wash. I feel more capable.

I'll just have to do some of the running about with Ryan, instead of letting him do it all. It'll probably slow us down a bit, but that can't be helped. Kathryn told me that the witch bottle is bound to the agreement I made to help with deliveries. That was what she felt really bad about. So, if I don't manage to keep the deliveries going then the bottle will stop working, and I do not want that thing coming back. And if we take a bit longer, we'll both get paid a bit more, too.

I'M AT THE DEPOT early, before the Bean is out of bed. Normally, if we get there before the Bean is awake, we're meant to take a long pole custom-built for the purpose and tap on the Bean's bedroom window until she turns her light on. I don't on this occasion, though. I look at those customers who I've got witchcraft deliveries for, and I start boxing up their File orders as if they're Order orders. That is, even if they just get milk and eggs and an orange juice – produce normally controlled through the File – I put it all in a nice little box from out of the pile of empty boxes and I bury the witchcraft product in there with it, well hidden where possible. Sometimes even inside the egg box or, depending, underneath a milk bottle. It helps that all of Kathryn's products are wrapped in brown paper, meaning they blend in nicely with the cardboard boxes.

I can pass it off as a small efficiency I don't mind getting there early for. Given how little I'm sleeping recently, I could probably sustain even earlier starts, especially if it means my visitor would leave me alone. Overall, I'd still be getting more sleep.

Some products cannot be managed in this way. Things like witch bottles are too big to hide. So I take an empty milk bottle crate and put it in the corner of the back of the van and put all of these larger products into that crate. I then stack lots of full milk bottle crates around it, hiding it from view. I can't make it inaccessible, so I cover it with discarded plastic wrap from two-litre multipacks and cardboard scraps from around the depot, making it look like I've just been chucking rubbish into the corner while I've been loading up.

I'm done by the time the Bean is up, and by the time Ryan arrives.

'Come on then,' I say, slapping the side of the van as Ryan sidles over from his car. 'Let's get away. And please get your hands out of your pants. We're handling food here.'

'All right, Dad,' he mutters. 'Hope you give your hands a good wash after you've been fiddling yer bird at the La'al Tattie Hole.'

'It's the La'al Tattie *Shop*,' I say. 'And I don't fiddle anybody.'

'Aye, right.'

I HAVE TO OPERATE from memory, because using my tracing-paper system would give the game away. I make it look like I'm just randomly helping out here and there. But Ryan isn't stupid. He watches without saying anything until we've done all the northern villages, until we've been to the La'al Tattie Shop, and until we're back in the valleys.

'What are you up to?' he asks, after I'd insisted on carrying Mr Jackson's box myself. We're both standing at the sliding door. 'Why've you made all these shitty little boxes up? There's nothing fucking in 'em.'

'I was in early,' I say. 'Thought it would speed things up. It's taking too long. You think it's taking too long too, I know you do.'

'Aye,' he says. 'It's because you drive like an old woman, and you run about like – well, you don't run about. You walk like Bobby from Ravenglass.' He does an impression of Bobby from the Post Office – bending his knees, hunching his back, making claws of his hands and then walking in slow motion. 'That's you, that is. You and Big Bob. We'd be quicker if you just let me do it like you're meant to.'

'All right,' I say, walking off down Mr Jackson's driveway. 'All right! I'll do this one, and then leave it.' I put the Jackson order down inside the porch and then turn back to the van. Ryan does his Bobby impression again as I walk back. I don't give him the satisfaction of running.

'Big Bob, like,' Ryan says, as we got back in the van. 'What a guy. Getting ski-poled by auld Deborah in the Westview. My kind of night out!' He looks slyly across at me. 'So what's your bird like in the sack? In the potato sack?'

I shake my head.

'Come on. We're all friends here. We're all lads here. Come on!'

'No. I don't talk like that. I don't talk about that.'

'You know what it is,' he says, turning to the window. 'We're not out here that long. It just *feels* so bloody long because you're so *fucking* boring.'

We drive in silence for a while. 'I don't mind people thinking I'm boring,' I say, eventually.

The Warning

A S WE APPROACH THE Atman lonning, I notice something in the road and put the brakes on. As always seems to be the way, Corney Fell is a bit misty and visibility is low.

'What the fuck?' Ryan says.

I open the door and jump out. The thing in the road is a cow's head. A head from a big cow, too. It lies there in a pool of dark blood. It has been severed from the body very neatly, except for a long section of spine that extends from the head to lie naked on the tarmac.

In its mouth is an empty milk bottle containing a rolled-up piece of paper. I reach down to extract the bottle from the mouth of the cow, but then stop myself. I take a photo of it on my phone. Then I extract the bottle, half expecting to feel that hot animal breath on my hand as I do so. I take the note from the bottle and unroll it.

WE KNOW

'WE KNOW WHAT?' RYAN asks, reading it over my shoulder.

'I don't know,' I say.

'They know,' Ryan says, 'but we don't.'

'It's a message for us, isn't it?'

'How do you know?'

'The milk bottle.'

'Maybe they just had one handy, like.'

I shake my head. 'I don't think so.'

'They've cut its fucking ears off!' Ryan suddenly exclaims.

'So that it can't be identified,' I say. 'Cattle have tags in their ears.'

We stare at it for a while. Then Ryan shakes himself. 'Come on,' he says. 'Went for a dump back at the depot and got a witch's kiss. I want a shower.'

I transfer my stare to him. 'Sorry, what?' I say.

'I went for a dump back—'

'What's a witch's kiss?'

'It's when you sit on a toilet to take a shit and your dick touches the inside of the toilet bowl.'

I nod, slowly. 'And that toilet bowl is a particularly grim specimen.'

'Yeah, exactly. Need to give the old helmet a real good scrub.'

'Which is the witch?' I ask.

'What?'

'Which is the witch? The penis, or the porcelain?'

'The *toilet*, obviously. For fuck's sake, come on. It's all itchy.'

'That toilet bowl is absolutely caked,' I say. I put the empty milk bottle back in the van.

'Tell me about it.'

We drag the cow's head to the side of the road and just leave it there. We can't put it in the back of the van, for hygiene reasons. But I resolve to tell Mrs Atman about it; she's the nearest farmer. That's what people usually do when they find an animal, living or dead, on the roads: contact the nearest farmer. And then I presume their course of action would be to report it to Fallen Stock.

I try to remember if Mrs Atman is on Kathryn's customer list. She doesn't seem to be around. I tear a sheet of paper from the back of the File and write her a note. WE FOUND A COW HEAD ON THE ROAD. MAYBE YOURS? LEFT IT AT END OF LONNING. I think about leaving my name, or the name of the company, but in the end decide against it. I drop the note in the bin with her delivery and she can put two and two together. And then if we don't want to accept responsibility – for example, if there was something else we should have done – we can deny all knowledge.

I SEND KATHRYN THE picture of the cow's head with the milk bottle in its mouth, and then ring her up.

'What did the note say?' she asks.

'It says "we know".'

'Well, what does that mean?'

'Exactly! That's what I'd like to know.' I pause, and then say 'they know, but we don't.'

'Ha! Yes.'

'But I think it was meant for us. As in, Ryan and me.'

'Because of the milk bottle?'

'Yes.'

'And what do you think the cow's head means?'

'I took that to be just something they had to hand.'

'Who?'

'The Fallen Stock men.'

'It could just have been a farmer. Or somebody else.'

'It didn't occur to me that it might have been somebody else. My thinking is—'

'It's okay, I get it. If there's an overlap between people being haunted and people being visited by the Fallen Stock men, then the Fallen Stock men might view our helping the . . . customers – targets? – as interference. The suggestion is that the Fallen Stock men *want* people to suffer the hauntings.'

'Yes, exactly.'

'Are they all men, by the way?'

'The Fallen Stock men?'

'Yes.'

'I don't know.'

'What did that one say? The one who clawed your hand?'

'"I just want to walk this world like it is mine again."'

'Yeah,' she says. 'He sounds like a charmer.'

'They all give me the creeps,' I say. 'You'll know what I mean if you ever meet one in person.'

'He took some of your blood?' she asks.

'Well, not – not in a deliberate way. He would have had some under his fingernails.'

'It might have been deliberate. The haunting only started after that, right? He might have taken it so that he'd have something to use to bind the spirit to you.'

'Yeah,' I say. 'Yeah, it did. But how would they harvest . . . blood or whatever from the farmers? From the targets?'

'It would be easy for them to gather some hair from door trims, or used condoms from the bins. And I use other things too. Like the organs I took from that stag. Think about all the dead bodies they have access too – all the fluids, all the organs, all the bones and skin and hair and teeth.' She pauses. 'I see what you're saying.'

'I've got no evidence,' I say, 'but it's what I think. What I can't work out is what they're doing.'

'Well,' says Kathryn. 'Quite. Are you scared?'

'Yeah, a bit. What do you think they want?'

'If it is them?'

'If it is them.'

'I don't know.'

The Head Injury

'I HAD A GOOD THOUGHT,' Ryan slurs, grinning at me from the passenger seat. He stinks of alcohol and looks as if he hasn't been to bed. 'Now I don't drive, I don't have to be sober.'

'Oh yes,' I say. 'That's a great thought. The customers will love it.'

He laughs sloppily.

It's a properly frosty morning. The yard is as hard as iron underfoot. I step up into the van and shut the door. The Bean's been out before we arrived – before I arrived, even – and turned the van on and got its blowers going, so the windscreen is just about clear. There's no sign of the sun yet.

'All right then,' I say. 'Let's go.'

'All right, Dad.'

'Stop saying that.'

'All right, Dad.'

His eyes are closing. He's not even going to bother staying awake. Actually, that could work to my advantage. It will make it easier to sneak Kathryn's products out if he's asleep. It would take me literally all day, though. So no, that wouldn't work. If I tried in effect to do it all myself, we would be running so late we'd start to lose customers – probably to Dawson's.

'Ryan,' I say. 'Wake up, Ryan.'

'I'm awake.' His voice is thick. His head is resting against the window and his eyes are closed.

'For fuck's sake.' I use the controls in the driver-side door to lower his window. He doesn't notice until the support goes and his head falls out into the freezing winter morning.

'Fuck you!' he says.

'The window's staying open.'

We go to the ESSO garage so he can get a coffee, but he buys some kind of canned concentrated caffeine drink instead. I don't care. I just want him sober enough to do the work.

I *am* going to use this, though.

'So what got you kicked out of the army?'

'What the fuck?' He sits up and scowls at me. 'Who told you that?'

'Nobody told me,' I say. 'I was just guessing.'

I can tell that he's regretting his decision to come in hungover. He's pale and sweaty.

'Fuck you,' he says. 'I didn't get kicked out.' He stamps on the dashboard. 'Got hurt. Our truck got blown up. I was sitting on the back. Went twenty feet up into the air, landed on my head. Head injury. I was unconscious. My helmet was cracked. My skull was cracked. Brain bleed, the fucking lot. They thought I was dying. But I didn't die. Just got sent home. What a fucking joke.'

He falls silent. His breathing has grown rapid and shallow.

*

IT MIGHT BE THE hangover, or it might be my reckless prodding, but Ryan is in a bad mood for the rest of the day. One benefit of that is that when I pull in outside the La'al Tattie Shop, he doesn't want to get out.

'Nah,' he says, when I ask if he wants anything. 'The jackets aren't all that. Tell your bird I said so. Tell her the Potato Palace is not for me.'

'It's the La'al Tattie—'

'I know what it's fucking called, dickhead.'

I go in happy. 'Hello,' I say.

'Hello,' says Kathryn. 'Your charming friend not joining us today?'

'No, thankfully,' I say. 'He said he's not a fan. But I think he's just being spiteful.'

'Poor boy,' she says.

'I think he's the way he is because of a head injury,' I say. 'Like your manager at Netherhall.'

'The usual?'

'Yes, please.' I look back at the van. Ryan has slumped down and closed his eyes. 'Look,' I say. 'I could take some more of your orders and put them in the back of the van while he's having a little rest.'

'Excellent. We're getting back on it, now!' She passes me over a bag-for-life. I take it outside and put it in the back of the van. As before, I cover it up with all of the various bits of rubbish we end up with after a few hours on the rounds – disposable plastic packaging, empty cardboard boxes, empty plastic crates. Then I return to the shop, glancing surreptitiously back up at Ryan. His eyes are still closed.

'Here you are,' she says, handing me the brown paper bag with my potato in it.

'Lovely,' I say. 'Thank you.'

'How's the witch bottle doing?'

'It seems to be working again.'

'Good.' She frowns. 'I feel like I've got to say something, though.'

'What?' My heart sinks. 'What is it?'

'Obviously, the bottle is working and that's good. I'm glad. If it's working, it will keep the thing away. But . . .'

'What?' I search her face for a clue as to her concern.

'There shouldn't be a *thing* in the first place. What is it? Why is it coming to you? Why now? Does your experience have the same root as all of the others – the farmers and everybody?'

'Yeah.' I sag. 'I don't know. I wonder the same things. What it is . . . it feels familiar to me, but I don't know where from. I feel like the answer is inside me, somewhere. I just can't access it. But as for the other questions, I'm stumped.'

'You need to think about them. The witch bottle is just like a . . . it's like an ibuprofen. It gets rid of the headache. But you should still try to understand why you have a headache, yeah?'

'Yeah.' I nod. 'Yeah. Thank you.' I hold up the paper bag. 'And thanks for this, too.'

RYAN GROWS INCREASINGLY FRACTIOUS as the day progresses, and he was pretty fractious to begin with.

'Just stay in the van for these ones,' I instruct, somewhere in Bootle. 'You don't need to get out.' I slip down from my seat as I'm talking, nip round the back and quickly secrete a few brown paper packages from the hidden bag-for-life into my carrier. I'm away along the terraces before Ryan catches up with me.

'What the hell are you playing at?' he demands. 'What are you doing?'

'Nothing! You're hungover, and I get bored sitting in the cab all day.'

'It's like this, though.' He looks around. Then he slams his open palm against my chest and pushes my back into the hedge. 'I just don't fucking believe you, right? I don't trust you. I know you're lying to me, and that pisses me off.'

'I'm not lying. And why do you care so much? It saves you a job, is all.'

'I care, because it makes the days last longer!' He's right in my face now. His deep eyes are narrow and bloodshot, his cheeks are burning red and spittle flecks his lips. His lower jaw juts out like that of a piranha. 'I don't want to be stuck in this fucking van with *you*! I want to get home and see me auld mam! I want to go round and see me lass and give her belly a rub!'

'I thought you weren't allowed?'

'Nah. That's the other one.' He grabs the carrier from me. Pulls it right out of my hands. It's as easy for him as plucking a petal from a flower.

'No,' I say, as he turns away.

'Or what?'

'Or I'll write you a bad reference for your court case!' I almost reach out to grab the words and pull them back as soon as they've left my mouth.

He slowly turns back to face me. 'You fucking what?'

'It's true,' I say.

'Why the hell are you writing my reference?'

'Because the Bean asked me to. Because I'm working more closely with you than anybody else is.'

'But she won't want you to make a call. She wouldn't want to hurt me mam. She wants it to say good stuff about me, but she wants your words because you talk like a posh person. And you know what we do all day.'

I'm sure the Bean can write well. The whole thing is probably a test. That's what she meant when she said I had a decision to make. That was the only reason to give me the task – to see how I'd decide. Would I do what I thought was best for myself, Ryan and his mother, or what was best for the poor woman he'd beaten up? And any other poor person that might cross his brutish path.

I use the moment of calm to snatch my carrier back. 'Let's just try and remain civil,' I snap.

'You're still lying about something,' he murmurs.

I don't respond. I go and make my deliveries.

The Spaceship in Alien

'OH GOD,' SHE SAID. 'Oh God, oh God, oh God. They shouldn't have sent us home. They shouldn't have done that. It's wrong. It's wrong. It's going wrong.'

Ellie was sat on a big bouncy yoga ball in the middle of the front room. This was our flat in the city. The flat was ideal. Big, light, spacious, clean and warm. It was the first place we'd lived in that really felt like home — and we'd lived in a few places by this point. I mean, we knew the city felt like home, but none of our previous actual accommodations had been quite right. But this one was. The flat was perfect for us and for the baby on the way. We'd done out the second bedroom as a nursery. It had been a study for us both — for her to use as a studio, and for me to write in. But we'd decided to stay in the flat and make that room a nursery, instead of finding a three-bedroomed place. It would be a squeeze, but we'd make it work.

It was about four in the morning and the midwifery unit had told Ellie that she was still in the early stages of labour and so they'd sent us home. 'Paracetamol,' they'd said, after measuring the dilation of her cervix. 'You've barely started. Paracetamol is all we'd be giving you at this point anyway. Take some painkillers and stay on your feet to bring it on a bit.'

Ellie could barely stand, and paracetamol didn't seem to be making a difference. I was on my knees in front of her, holding her hands. Tears streamed down her face and spotted the big grey sweater she was wearing. She hated that sweater.

'Are the contractions any closer together?' I asked. But she couldn't really tell.

'It just hurts so much,' she said, when her breathing allowed. 'It's constant.'

I had thought it would be like they told us in the antenatal classes: regular waves of pain that you could prepare for, and measure. But it didn't seem to be like that at all.

'We've got to go back. Ring them up and tell them we're going back.'

'Okay,' I said.

In the car she really started to cry. 'It's going to be okay,' I said. She just shook her head and sobbed.

When we got there we had to wait for triage again. The waiting area was full. There were other pregnant women there, and even a couple who seemed to be having contractions. But none seemed as distressed as Ellie.

Eventually they got her back in and up on a bed and they were measuring her cervix again. 'No further dilation,' they said sympathetically, peeling off their latex gloves. Their voices were slightly insincere and wheedling, even to my ears.

'Don't send me home again,' she said.

'I don't think there are any rooms for you at the moment, though.'

I stood up. 'We're not going home again,' I said.

'Well, you can stay here and just walk around until there's a room available.' They smiled down at Ellie's tear-stained face. 'Might help bring it on.'

'Yes,' I said. 'Thank you.' I spoke to Ellie. 'At least then we'll be in the right place for when things do progress a bit.'

I THINK ELLIE BLANKED out most of her memories of the next three days, and mine are quite patchy.

Eventually they got us in a room. It was on a long corridor and I remember the light in the corridor was yellow. The room had a very high ceiling. The room felt dark, and not in a cosy way, despite my best efforts to brighten it up. This is something that Ellie also recollected, later on. The rooms and the corridors were gloomy. Though apparently, that can be a symptom of trauma: memories of traumatising events are altered in significant ways, and one thing that frequently crops up in the reporting of traumatising events is that they occurred in darkness, or bad light – even when that cannot have been the case.

We were alone. We'd call for midwives, but they wouldn't come. On the rare occasion that they did come and check on us, they'd advise that she was still in the early stages, and suggest walking around. Ellie did do this, but it didn't help.

I sat or stood or walked beside her, holding her hand. I'd say things like, 'If there was a problem, they'd be doing something about it,' and, 'They're just really busy.'

She tried the gas and air. All of the tubes were yellow. The systems made a breathing sound. We both became convinced that the breathing sound continued even when she wasn't using the gas and air.

'It sounds like the spaceship in *Alien*,' she said. 'The *Nostromo*.'

'No,' I said, although it sounded exactly like the spaceship in *Alien*. 'No, it doesn't.' I thought that denying the similarities to a horror film would be reassuring; of course, all I was doing was arguing with her when she least needed it.

We'd sit and listen to this loud, laboured breathing, but it wasn't her, and it wasn't me. We thought it was the system, but now I don't know. Part of me now wonders if there was something else in the room there with us. Eventually she was just screaming. We'd ring the midwife bell and they wouldn't come. I'd run and look for them. 'I'm sorry,' I remember one saying as she ran past me. 'Somebody's critical.' Later on, it was, 'I'm sorry – got to get a body into surgery.'

We asked for an epidural. They said they'd get the anaesthetist. Six hours passed before we saw anybody. At least, before anybody came to the room. In between clutching at her hand and telling her that everything was going to be okay, I wandered the corridors looking for help, telling the midwives that Ellie was in a lot of pain. But really all the midwives offered was a kind of conspiratorial sympathy. They reassured me that everything was okay, that it was normal, and in turn, I passed this information on to Ellie. And, as I told myself, and told Ellie, they simply knew more about all of this than we did.

The next person who came to the room was a midwife coming to introduce herself, as she'd just come on shift. She asked if I wanted any toast.

'Yes, please,' I said, trying to sound jovial. 'And when's the anaesthetist coming?'

She frowned. 'I'll just go and find out.'

'Why the fuck are you being so nice to them?' Ellie growled, after the midwife had left the room.

'I don't want to piss them off. There's nobody else around, and if we piss them off, they might come and see us even less.'

About half an hour later, the midwife was back. 'The anaesthetist's in surgery at the moment, and then there's another patient requiring surgery after that. And we've only got the one currently. So they could be a few hours yet. I'm sorry. Tell you what.' She smiled at Ellie. 'When the pool's free, I'll help get you in the pool.'

A few hours later, they came and measured her again. There was lots of silence and slight frowns. 'Not much dilation,' one of them said. They both turned away to confer. 'Wait,' Ellie panted. She grabbed one of their hands and put it on her stomach. 'Those are knees, right? Her knees? Pointing out?'

'Hm,' said the midwife, vaguely. 'They could be.' Then they both left the room. One of them came back in again. 'Come on,' she said. 'The pool's free now.'

Out in the corridor we could hear other women screaming. The midwife held Ellie under one arm, I held her under the other. I felt as if we were almost dragging her along. This wasn't how I'd imagined it at all. But it was precisely what Ellie had been dreading.

Ellie could not get in the birthing pool. The midwife and I ended up trying to lift her. 'Is this right?' I said.

'It'll help,' the midwife said.

'I mean, that she can't use her legs.'

'She can use her legs. Come on, Mum. Use your legs!'

Ellie was crying. 'I can't,' she said, but the words were just a whisper.

Eventually we managed to lift her in.

The pool did not help at all. The midwife left us, and more hours passed. Ellie needed the toilet but couldn't get out of the pool. We rang for the midwife but nobody came. I tried to help, but the sides were slippery and because she couldn't really use her legs, we decided it was too dangerous. She urinated in the water. At that moment the midwife came back, and wrinkled her nose.

'Time to get out, then?'

'Any word on the epidural?' I asked.

'We'll need to measure her,' the midwife said. 'If she's beyond a certain dilation, she can't have an epidural.'

'But it was requested hours ago. We were just waiting for the anaesthetist.'

'Past a certain point it's not safe.'

I couldn't tell the midwives apart. We went back to our room and Ellie lay on the bed and sobbed and screamed. I would find myself crying and shaking, but I didn't let her see. I didn't want her to know I was scared, and I didn't want to distress her. I wanted to try and reassure her that everything was okay. I thought that might make it easier.

They came to measure her a couple of hours later. This time there were a few of them, with a doctor. The doctor looked her over.

'This baby is the wrong way round,' she said. 'These here' – she put two hands on Ellie's stomach – 'these are the baby's knees. This is why the labour is not progressing. The baby's back is against the mother's back.' A few of the others started taking notes.

'Who are they?' Ellie gasped. 'Who the fuck are they?'

'They are students,' said the doctor.

'It's okay,' I said. 'They're not important. Everything's going to be okay.'

'Now then,' the doctor said. 'You'll probably need a top up on the epidural. We'll see about booking you in.'

'No!' she screamed. 'I haven't fucking had one! It's booked in! We've been waiting for – for—'

'Eighteen hours,' I said.

'Okay, okay,' the doctor said. 'You also need the baby turning around. The midwife will be with you shortly.'

After the doctor and the students left, one of the midwives started to measure Ellie's dilation. 'Do you still need to do that?' I asked.

'If she still wants an epidural?'

'Oh right,' I said. 'She does, I think. Yes.'

'I'm going to get a more senior midwife,' the midwife said. 'To see about the turning.'

Eventually a more senior midwife came. She had a good look at Ellie, did a lot of frowning and put on a latex glove. She covered the glove in some kind of lubricant. 'I'm going to have to do this manually,' she said.

She forced her hand up into Ellie and grabbed hold of the baby's head. Ellie screamed in a new way. The midwife grunted and grimaced and twisted her arm for about five minutes, all the while Ellie screamed. 'It's no good,' she said, eventually. 'I don't think I can do it. Phew. No wonder she's taking her time!'

After she'd gone, I squeezed Ellie's hand. I felt sick. 'The way they talk,' I said, 'makes it sound like this is all quite normal.' I was scared at how ill Ellie was, how brutal the care was and how power-less I felt. I kept finding midwives and asking for help and being told the same things. And I realised that there was nobody else to ask. The only people I could turn to for help were the same people who were slowly inspiring a great terror in me. It became obvious that we were entirely in the hands of these people, and for some reason we couldn't convince them that things were badly wrong.

The next thing I remember is the epidural: Ellie lying on her side on the bed, with the anaesthetist crouched behind. I was holding Ellie's hand and a midwife was holding her down by her shoulders so that she couldn't move, which was difficult for her because of the intense pain. I feel as if multiple attempts were required, but at this point things do get hazy.

There's a gap then. The next thing I remember is an old midwife with a cruel face coming into the room. But it was a different room. 'Do you want any toast?' she asked me.

'No, thanks,' I said.

'You can't have any,' she said to Ellie. 'Might need surgery yet.'

This was the first we'd heard of any surgery.

'Cup of tea?' she asked me.

'No.'

'When they've got the room, we're going to take you through to the hospital,' she said.

'I can't walk,' Ellie said.

'Yes, you can.'

'I can't.'

'It's not that bad,' the midwife snapped. 'You can do it.'

'I'll need a chair,' Ellie said.

The midwife looked at Ellie like she had just grown a pair of horns.

'A *wheel*chair?!'

Ellie nodded.

'You're pregnant, you're not disabled! You're not injured!'

'She needs a chair,' I said.

'Oh, okay then,' the midwife said.

She came back a few minutes later with a wheelchair and a stack of toast, and then disappeared. I offered it to Ellie, but she shook her head.

'Right,' the cruel-faced midwife said, reappearing some time later. 'They can take you now. Come on. Get in the chair.'

'I can't.'

'You can.'

Ellie was sitting on the edge of the bed, as white as a sheet, her whole body trembling. 'There's nothing to my legs. I can't stand up.'

'You wanted this chair and now you won't even get in it? Stop being pathetic.'

'I *can't*.'

'We'll lift you,' I said. I wheeled the chair around. 'Come on,' I said, taking her under the arm.

The midwife just stood and watched.

'I can't,' Ellie said.

Eventually the midwife took her by the other arm. We lifted her off the side of the bed. I accidentally kicked the chair as we tried to move her and it rolled away. The midwife was struggling. Ellie was not big but what with the late pregnancy, she was heavy. 'You'll have to use your legs,' the midwife said, wheezing. 'Just get in the damned chair!'

Ellie drew her breath. 'I can't!' she shouted.

'Come on,' I said. 'You can do it.' I held her up with one hand and pulled the chair back towards her.

She couldn't stand up, but she was also scared to sit down. I could see it. We had to be conscious of the epidural as she sat in the chair. And she couldn't bend her legs to enable the midwife and me to sit her down.

I'd been trying to mask how worried I was, and suddenly I couldn't hide it any more. 'Listen,' I said, voice breaking, 'get in the fucking chair.'

She looked at me with a cold fury, and then gingerly, painfully lowered herself down. I pulled her hospital gown together at the back, and we wheeled her down the corridor, through some swinging double doors, and into – I was informed – the hospital. It looked and felt much the same as the midwifery centre. We passed a room with an open door and in the room a breeze blew through the window and moved blue curtains and brought with it the sound of sirens.

ANOTHER ROOM. ELLIE HAD her epidural topped up and was given morphine. We watched the monitor that relayed our baby's heartbeat. Ellie became peaceful, if not lucid. She would not hold my hand. Every now and again they'd come and measure her cervix. 'Another centimetre,' one of them said. 'It's awful, isn't it?' After a few hours, our baby's heartbeat started to slow. I pressed a button. Ellie sat up. 'Oh no,' she whispered, and shook her head. I pressed the button again. I went out into the corridor. 'We need some help!' I shouted. A nurse ran towards me. She burst through into the room and took one look at the monitor. 'She's stuck,' she said. 'She's struggling now. Poor little thing. We need to get her out of there.'

Over the next few minutes, Ellie and I watched her heartbeat drop still further as doctors and nurses suddenly swarmed about the room. One of them handed me some scrubs. Another wheeled Ellie back out into the corridor, and to theatre.

IN THEATRE IT FELT as if, finally, the medical staff had realised that there was a problem here. They moved with urgency and did not try to hide the criticality of the situation. A doctor explained to Ellie and me what they were going to do.

'Forceps,' she said, 'and if that doesn't work, we'll go to emergency C-section. We can't leave her in there any longer.' They gave Ellie some forms to fill out, to authorise further anaesthetisation. She was hooked up to another monitor somewhere, beeping out our baby's heartbeat. It sounded slow. She was covered in tubes and wires, and I didn't understand what they were. They hung out of her arms and trailed down over the side of the bed. They lay across her body and beside her body. They shook as she shook. I didn't know if it was the anaesthetic or pain or fear or all three, but she was shaking violently. She held my hand then and I stroked her hair. I don't think even she had anticipated this.

'I can feel it,' she said, as the doctor inserted the forceps. She could feel the physical sensation of the forceps entering her and opening inside her and twisting around. The doctor managed to do with the forceps what the midwife had not been able to do with her hand – turn the baby round. Ellie felt that. And then, with Ellie pushing, they pulled the baby out. We heard her cry. I caught a glimpse of a dark and bloody little thing. They cut the cord and rushed her into an adjacent room.

'Where is she?' Ellie asked.

Meanwhile, a surgeon was examining Ellie. It wasn't over, for her.

They brought our baby back into the theatre, now all wrapped up. 'Had to clean some meconium from her mouth and throat,' explained the doctor. She conferred with the surgeon. 'We'll have to give her to Dad now,' she said. They put the baby into my arms. She was tiny and soft and smelled sweet. She had a straight black bruise right across her face from the forceps. I wanted Ellie to hold her; she'd made her. It was her body that hurt. I gave her to Ellie. Ellie held her and stroked her and smiled and cried. 'Marianne,' she said.

'Your wife needs further surgery,' somebody said. 'You need to take your daughter and leave. Now.'

I looked at Ellie. She nodded. She didn't want to let go of our child and I didn't want her to have to. I stood and she passed the baby over and I took her. I could see blood, more blood than was right, flowing blood, out of the corner of my eye.

'I love you,' I said. 'See you in a bit. Look, she loves you too.' I held our daughter up. 'I love you,' I said again. I didn't want her to know that I thought she was dying.

I sat in the corridor outside the theatre and held our daughter. She was whimpering, looking for a breast. I don't know how long we were out there.

The Work We Do

THE FALLEN STOCK WAGON arrives in Taylor's yard behind us and blocks us in. Ryan is walking back to our van with a couple of empty cardboard boxes that previous orders had been delivered in. I look around from the cab. I can't see any dead animals. I get out of the van as Ryan slings the empty boxes in and then stand and watch as the Fallen Stock driver descends from his cab. This is one I haven't met before.

Like the other two, he wears expensive wellingtons and plus-fours. He also wears a white shirt and tweed waistcoat. He has a walking stick slung over his arm for some reason.

'Good afternoon,' he says, cheerfully. He has no chin to speak of and his mouth is very small and red. 'Lovely day for it!'

'You all dress very smartly, considering the work you do,' I say.

'The work we do? Ha! You don't know the half of it, my good man.'

'Tell me about it, then.'

'I'd really better not.'

'I just can't work out why there's so much fallen stock, all of a sudden.'

'I don't think there's been a marked increase,' he says. 'It might just be that you're growing more aware of it all, as you become increasingly enmeshed.'

'Pardon?'

'Well, I'd better be getting on. Now, if you'll excuse me.'

He strides past and makes his way to the end of a low block of cowsheds. He disappears into the last one and, a few minutes later, emerges carrying a dead body over his shoulders. Blood runs from its mouth, spotting his white shirt and leaving a trail behind. It's a big one and must be heavy, but he carries it as if it's nothing.

'Still here?' he queries, as he reaches us.

'Well, yes. You blocked us in.'

'Ah yes. How very inconsiderate of me. I apologise.' He walks to the back of his wagon, and unceremoniously dumps the body on the ground. Then he lowers the back of the wagon.

'Can we come and have a look in the back of the wagon?' I shout.

'Aha. Most certainly not!'

'Oh,' I say. 'Okay then.'

'Why did you ask, you idiot?' Ryan hisses.

'Because I really want to see inside.'

'No,' Ryan says, rolling his eyes. 'I meant . . . oh, forget it.'

The Fallen Stock driver picks the body back up and walks into the wagon.

'He's not in a rush, is he?' I say.

'He's taking the bloody piss,' Ryan says.

The Deal

FRAN IS TALKING ABOUT her husband again. The soldier. I want to listen properly, but I'm running late and sweat is rolling down my neck. It's so hot in here. So, so hot. And she's got all of those blankets on top of her. The carers have reassured me that this is how she wants it, but it feels intolerable.

I'd found some good ripe pears when loading the van this morning and put them in especially for Fran. My heart had been in my mouth earlier, when the Knightley lot were milling about the van, groping all of the goods and hemming and hawing about whether or not anything I was carrying was good enough. They kept picking the pears up and putting them back. I should have kept them separate and hidden, but to be honest there's normally so little interest in pears that I hadn't thought to. In the end they didn't take them, thankfully.

'I'm just waiting to go and see him,' she says. 'I wish he'd come and see me. You're my pal, aren't you? I can tell you a secret?'

'You can tell me anything,' I say.

'It's not very Christian of me, but I'd love him to pay me a visit.

My daughter, she married a farmer and she said that all the farmers are seeing ghosties. Loved ones coming back, or other things. A lot of them are scared, but I'd just be glad to see him again, even if he doesn't look quite the same. He was such a handsome man, with the kindest eyes. He'd still be kind. I know that . . .'

'Sorry,' I say, 'ghosties?'

'That's right.'

'Did your daughter say anything else about this?'

'You know the Fallen Stock men. They collect the dead animals, from the farmyards.'

'I know,' I say. I feel breathless.

'Well, these ones demand *more* dead animals. Not just the ones they'd normally collect. And if they don't receive these offerings, they send the ghosties. Do you see?'

'They expect the farmers to just . . . *kill* animals for them?'

'That's it.'

'Or they send the farmers ghosts?'

She slowly untangles one tremulous old hand from beneath the blankets and extends an index finger towards me. 'Precisely,' she says, eyes bright. 'And so the farmers are trying to provide the animals, or find a way around it. Some say there's a witch abroad, who can help.'

'Really?' I say.

'Don't be so coy,' she says. 'Some reckon it's you.'

'*Really?*'

'I won't be looking for any help though. I *want* mine to come back.'

'I don't think you'd like it,' I say. 'These ghosts aren't nice to have around.'

'So you do know a bit about it?'

'I know about the ghosts, but not that the Fallen Stock men were involved. I'm not the witch. I don't know about that.' I pause briefly. 'I have to go,' I say. 'I'm falling behind. I've left you some extra ripe pears, on the house.'

'You'll be back to see me, won't you?' she says, as I leave. 'You'll come back, at least. My pal. My husband.'

'Of course, Fran,' I say. 'I'll be seeing you soon.'

Dawson's Van

THE VAN'S JUST OFF the road, straddling a hedge, wrapped in police tape. I slow down to look at it and then stop. It's a Dawson's van. It's Graham's Dawson's van.

I just stop in the road – it's not like there's any traffic up on Corney now the Netherhall rush has passed – and stare. I don't really know what I'm looking for. The driver side of the van is badly dented and scraped.

'That's Graham's van,' Ryan says, leaning forwards.

'Yeah,' I say. 'It's been run off the road. Look at that damage.'

'Aye,' Ryan says. 'That's a bad scrape.'

I stare a moment longer.

'Come on,' Ryan says. 'It's not like he's there. Let's get going.'

'Hope he's all right,' I say.

'He must be,' Ryan says. 'The police don't leave cars behind like that if there's been a casualty. If they've left it, it just means it's been abandoned.'

'Well,' I say, 'that's good then. That must be a good thing.'

*

I ASK THE BEAN about it later. 'Aye,' she says, 'Dawson's have been on the phone.'

'Asking if we ran him off the road?'

'What?' The Bean laughs, spraying weak tea. 'No! To ask if we've seen him. He just didn't come back in one morning. Then somebody reported the van. They haven't seen him since he set off with it.'

'I hope he's all right.'

'He will be. He's not as tough as an old boot; he *is* an old boot.'

'Tell me if you hear anything?'

'Aye, I will. And likewise, right? If you see him out and about.'

'Yeah,' I say. 'Sure.'

'One thing, Dawson said. They don't have a driver for Craggesund any more. So you've got it back.'

'Oh,' I say. 'That's good, then. That's why you're in a good mood!'

'Won't lie, lad,' the Bean says, 'it'll make a difference. We're on a knife's edge here.' She puts her mug down on the table and wipes her lips and chin. 'You fuck it up again, we're sunk,' she says. 'You understand?'

'Yes,' I say. 'Yes, I understand.'

The Towel

AFTER THE SURGERY, THEY wheeled Ellie through to a maternity room, shared with three other women. The room was light and breezy and long white curtains billowed. Two of the women were holding their babies and chatting.

'Three hours,' one said. 'She just popped out!'

The third woman had a screen around her bed and sobbed quietly to herself. There was a trail of blood leading from under the screen to the shared bathroom.

Ellie held our baby and I sat by her bed and held her hand. It hadn't gone how we'd expected. Even Ellie had not expected it to go so badly. We felt an intense and overwhelming love for the tiny creature curled up like a frog on her chest, but we also felt sad and tired and scared. We had planned celebrations, but that seemed hopelessly naïve now.

Every now and again we'd put our baby in the cot and I'd help Ellie to the toilet. She could use her legs now that the baby's spine was not exerting a huge pressure on her own. The bathroom was covered in splattered blood.

After a few hours, the nurse came and checked the pad on Ellie's bed. 'This is a lot of blood,' she remarked. 'We'll have to keep changing these.'

At least three people came round trying to sell subscription services for baby products. A paediatrician came round to take blood samples from our daughter. I kept helping Ellie to the toilet and back. A nurse came and showed us how to bathe the baby. Another nurse came and changed Ellie's bedding again. Eventually a nurse came and told me to leave.

'What?'

'Visiting hours are over now. You have to leave.'

'My wife needs help, though.'

'That's what *we're* here for.'

Outside, it was pouring down. We'd been in the hospital three days. I realised that I hadn't slept. I was shaky. I got in our car and started to drive. Some time passed, and I realised that I didn't know where in the city I was. I started to cry at the wheel. I felt angry with myself for crying. It wasn't me that had been hurt, or whose pain had been ignored. In fact I'd been one of those making it worse for Ellie. I pulled over into a bus lane. Rain ran down the windshield and beyond it blurry traffic lights changed from green to amber to red and back again. The sound of cars. People shouting. I used my phone to find out where I was, and mapped the way back to our flat. I took off again.

ONCE HOME, I ORDERED a pizza. I rang Ellie and we spoke for a while. She said our daughter was crying a lot and she was struggling to breastfeed. Because she was hungry, she wasn't sleeping. But she was lovely, Ellie said. She was perfect.

Ellie said the towels they'd given her didn't look clean and could I bring her a clean towel in the morning. Of course, I said. We spoke for a long time. There had been a generally frantic tone to her voice that made her sound unlike herself. The pizza arrived and went cold. I found myself reassuring her that everything was okay, that everything was going to be okay. The relief I'd felt momentarily in the hospital dissipated. Our baby had been born and Ellie had undergone surgery to recover from the delivery, and they were both alive, but maybe things were still not all right. Maybe Ellie's bleeding would not slow down. Maybe the forceps had hurt our baby's head and brain. Eventually she started drifting off while we were on the phone, and we ended the call. I turned the TV on and ate my pizza. The pizza didn't taste of anything, and I couldn't hear the TV. I turned the TV up. I still couldn't hear it. I realised I couldn't hear traffic from outside, either. All I could hear was a rising tide of white noise, drowning everything else out. I decided it was time to go to bed. I went and put a clean towel on the table so that I'd remember to take it with me to the hospital the next day.

The next morning I got ready and left the flat, forgetting the towel.

The Threat

IT'S ANOTHER DRIZZLY MORNING and the wet murk in the air blurs the transition from night into day. Ryan is dripping and a bit shivery, whereas I am nice and warm and dry. I've got the blowers on max to combat the condensation trying to build on the inside of the windscreen.

After running back to the van down a long muddy lonning too narrow to drive down, Ryan slams the door and swears.

'This is fucking bollocks,' he says.

'You'd be getting just as wet if you were on your own,' I say.

'Yeah, but I wouldn't have you all cosy sitting next to me. Makes it worse.'

I check the road and pull away from the lane end. 'Shouldn't speed then,' I say, after a moment. 'You're lucky you've still got a job at all.'

'Oh, fuck off.'

'No,' I say. 'Do what you want without thought. Even do what you want and then act all aggrieved and mystified at the consequences, if you must, as if they were somehow unpredictable. But don't get angry with me, as if *I've* done something wrong, just because you've made your life a bit shittier. I don't want you in this van, Ryan. I'd rather be on my own, even if it meant getting wet in the rain.'

He looks over at me, scowling, and then punches my upper arm hard enough to send a wave of numbness rolling through it. I gasp.

'Just fucking shut up,' he says.

I shouldn't have said anything to him. I'm ashamed to feel tears gather behind my eyes. I swallow. Suddenly I'm uncomfortably hot, dangerously hot. I turn the blowers off and inadvertently show him my hands are shaking. The numbness in my left arm makes changing gear to accommodate the twists and straights of the road feel a little bit risky. Chaos inside. The urge to retaliate builds and builds but has nowhere to go, because I'm driving, because I know it's wrong, because I am afraid of him.

Something's in the road. I slam the brakes on, unclip myself and get out of the van as quickly as possible. The cold rain on my face is good. The pre-dawn darkness is giving way to the dreamy blue haze of mist. The hedgerows and the road and the thing in the road are all just colour and shapes.

I hear Ryan's door behind me and turn in case he's running for me, fists swinging. But he's not. He's slowly walking, hands in pockets. He must've made his point. I turn back to the thing.

I know what it is before I'm close enough to make out the detail. It's another severed head. Another cow's head, stump set flat against the road surface. It looks as if it's swimming through the tarmac. Something is wedged in between its teeth, but it's not a milk bottle this time. A length of intestine is tied around its neck like a leash, its other end disappearing into the mist. I move past the head and follow it, until I do find a milk bottle, this one with its mouth smashed open and the intestine emerging from it, from a big bloody knot of guts squashed up inside what remains of the bottle.

The thing in the cow's mouth shines dully. I prize it free and it crinkles in my grasp. It feels warm. It's something wrapped in tin foil. I know what it is. I peel away the foil, my hands still shaking, to reveal a fat baked potato. Still warm enough to drool yellow butter through my fingers. There's a note stuck to the skin, ink blotting with the grease.

STOP THE BOTTLES

SO THEY KNOW. THEY know who produces them, and who delivers them.

I shove the head to the side of the road, and the bottle too. After a moment I chuck them over the hedge.

'A fucking potato?' Ryan says, breaking the silence. 'What did the note say?'

'Couldn't read it,' I say. 'Just the scribbles of a madman.'

'They're mad, all right,' Ryan grunts. 'Fucking potatoes.'

The Blood

WE'RE IN THE BEAN'S kitchen, drinking cups of tea.

'Mrs Lindon never got her carrots,' the Bean says suddenly.

'She did,' I say. 'I definitely went to Mrs Lindon's. She's the only one up that lane, and she only has carrots. I've definitely been up there today.'

'Maybe you just drove up the lane, forgot to leave the carrots and came back again.'

'Why would I do that?'

'It happens,' the Bean says. 'You know it can happen. Autopilot. Anyway, she's a customer. If the customer says she didn't, she didn't.'

'She did, though.'

'Well, she needs some more then. After that cup.'

It's as if she's just had this information beamed into her head or something.

'Okay,' I say. 'Okay.'

'Don't fight me. Not in the mood really.'

'I'm sorry.'

'Things are fragile, lad. Losing Craggesund really showed me. I mean, we've got it back now, but it showed me. Another month and I'd have lost the house.'

'What?'

'The house and the business too. Should be all right as long as we keep things turning over. But I can't start dropping customers. Can't afford it.'

'No.'

'It's not that I love the work. I'd happily retire. But I need the house and the land and the business. Need to leave something behind. The assets, or the money.' She looks at me as if expecting me to ask why. But I know she'll just tell me anyway. 'I've got a daughter, lad. Did you know?'

'No.'

'She can't work. She's in care. And the care's bloody expensive. Kind of thing you used to be able to get on the NHS, but not any more. If I wasn't paying an arm and a leg, she'd be out of care and she'd die. And she's not catatonic – she's not in a coma. She's a happy la'al thing. She can enjoy a nice long life, long as I keep paying for it. And once I'm gone, this business can pay for it. As long as we don't go under. Understood?'

'Yes.'

'It's the only reason I do any of this shit,' she says. 'Don't forget that. Okay?'

'All right.'

'All right. All right, lad. Happy customer's worth more'n a sack of carrots. Get on with you.'

*

MRS LINDON LIVES IN an old farmhouse down a long lane in Eskdale. The farmhouse sits on a loop at the end of the lane. Once you're in the lane, the only ways out are to reverse – unappealing, due to all the twists and turns – or to go all the way up and around the loop. It's too narrow to turn around in.

I drop off the sack of carrots, noting a couple of dead pigs lying in the doorway of an outhouse, and then pet Mrs Lindon's ancient Irish wolfhound a little bit. It's lying in the sun and dreaming, I think. I don't see Mrs Lindon anywhere. Lots of birdfeeders hang from the trees overlooking the yard and bright tiny little birds flit about, singing happily. I can smell wild garlic and hear running water; it's a small, delicate sound, a little stream, as opposed to a river.

Eventually I get back in the van and drive around the rest of the loop. I'm back into the lane proper when a Fallen Stock wagon rounds a corner and appears in front of me.

'What a fucker,' I whisper. I consider being an arsehole and refusing to reverse, but I have much less distance to cover back to the loop, so I start to back up, only to see a second Fallen Stock wagon appear in my side mirror. It must have entered the loop while I was still on it. Weirdly, it's reversing towards me. It must have reversed into the lane and then all the way along it.

It doesn't take two wagons to collect a couple of dead pigs.

I fight down rising panic. It's silly to be scared of them; this was obviously some kind of mistake. They'd both independently picked up the message to collect the pigs, or something.

I wait for one of them to move, because I can't do anything to get out of the way. But they both just sit there. The panic – never fully extinguished, if I'm being honest – starts to come back.

I'm not going to initiate any kind of conversation. Not after the previous encounters and the cows' heads. I'm not opening the van door. I close the window.

Eventually, the one in front of me gets out. It's one that I've met before. He's lumbering over with that big almost-smile, blond hair flopping out from beneath his hat. He walks right up to my door and opens it.

There's just enough space between the van and the tall, mossy drystone wall for him to do this.

'Come on, then,' he says. 'Get out.'

'No,' I say.

'Get out, my good man.'

'What's this about?'

He grabs my beard and pulls with a strength I wasn't expecting. He pulls me right from my seat and I end up hanging over the lane, suspended by my seat belt, yelling.

'Now put a sock in it and unclip yourself. There's a dear boy.'

I do as he says and gracelessly descend to the ground. I hear another van door open and close, the sound coming from the second Fallen Stock truck. Before I can get to my feet, the driver that pulled me from the cab drags me along the lane towards that second truck. As soon as I get a chance I grab at his legs and trip him. He stacks it, falling forwards and twisting sideways to land on his elbow, which cracks. I stand up and plant a boot in his midriff. It feels like kicking a big ball of dough.

'What the hell are you doing?' I shout. 'What's wrong with you?'

He just laughs, and then sits up. He stands, kind of bonelessly, and seems to be in no pain at all. Then he clouts me on the back of the head hard enough to make my vision swim, and the fight goes out of me. Especially when I see his friend emerge from the side of the second truck. It's the Londoner with the mustard cardigan.

Between them, they haul me over to the rear door of the second van. Dark blood is spilling from beneath the door and trickling down on to the ground.

'Drink it,' says the Londoner.

'Fuck off,' I say.

'Drink it or I'll cut your fucking throat and cart you off and all,' he says. Looking up, I can see a long knife in his hand.

'No,' I moan.

'Just do it,' says the plummy blond one. 'Get it over with. And you'll have learned your lesson.'

'I've learned my lesson already.' I want to be sick and I haven't even touched the blood yet.

One of them grabs my hair and pushes my face on to the bloody back step of the truck. 'There you go,' says the Londoner. 'Lick it up.'

The ferrous stink of it fills my nostrils. Hesitantly, I stick out my tongue and lick at the blood, making sure my eyes are closed. I fill my mouth with blood and grit from the step. The blood tastes like bad meat. They scrape my face along the step and then force me further down, on to the ground. I can feel the trickle of blood splashing on to my cheek. 'Open your mouth,' says the Londoner. 'Open wide. Catch it in your mouth.'

I do it. It's warm and thick and has an intensity to it – like spirits or an espresso or chilli, but awful and rancid. I try to swallow without breathing. After what feels like minutes, but can only have been seconds, I gag, and then roll over and vomit.

'Has he had enough, do you think?' asks the blond one, peering down at me. I feel like they're looking down from a great height.

'Should think so,' says the Londoner. Then he sniffs, throws back his head and makes a smoky cackling sound. 'What's the lesson, then?'

I try to speak and taste the blood again and a fresh wave of retching prevents me.

'Stop making the bloody fucking bottles,' he says, and then he kicks me for good measure. 'And don't think we'll kill you. We won't. At least, not first. We'll go for the potato bitch first. And really hurt her. Think on it. Don't get her mixed up in your magic.'

They think it's *my* magic. So maybe the potato in the cow's head was just intended to threaten somebody close to me.

'You're a bit mixed up in our magic, now,' says the plummy one. 'You've got a foot in both worlds. Enjoy it.'

The next thing I know, they're both driving away.

Back to Craggesund

THIS MORNING I CHECKED and rechecked I had everything for Craggesund. I'm not feeling well after yesterday's run-in with the Fallen Stock men, but I don't know who to tell about it. I don't want to tell Kathryn. It sounds stupid. It sounds shameful. And when I say not feeling well, I don't just mean sick – though I do mean that – I mean, everything feels different. I can't get the rich, deep voice out of my head. *A foot in both worlds.*

At Craggesund, all of the external pipework seems more twisted and labyrinthine. Flames spout from chimneys. As I drive down the long road between the gate and the access elevator, I look out over the yards of piled timber, and see distant figures swinging axes, but I can't get a sense of how far away they are; they are a long way away, but look bigger than human.

The elevator doors squeal and creak as they open, which is new. The lights inside the elevator flicker, which is not. I wheel both the trolleys in and press the button. The rickety concertina doors scrape shut again and the lift begins to move. It goes up, but it feels like it's going down. I try to read the graffiti to distract myself from the confusion and nausea, but I can't find any that's legible. Normally I can. I squint, trying to make out letters I recognise, but can't. I begin to feel very, very uneasy.

The lift takes a long, long time to arrive. After the doors open I wheel the trolleys out into the corridor. The lights are flickering out here, too, and I don't think they did last time I was here. But then I'm not sure I'm in the right corridor; this one is much longer than I remember. I can see a little man at the end of it. I think he's running towards me. The corridor is way too long. The man, I realise, is the chef I usually deal with, except he seems shorter than he usually does. He's waving an almost comically oversized meat cleaver in his hand, and his hat is long and cartoonish. I want to turn around and run away.

'You're *late*!' he screams, finally meeting as I progress towards him.

I look at my phone. I'm not late, but I don't want to argue with him. 'Sorry,' I say.

He raises the cleaver up as if he's going to hit me with it; as if he's actually going to hit me. But then he seems to have second thoughts, buries it into the green wall with a solid *thunk* and screams again. No words this time, just sound. He takes the first trolley and pushes it away, receding at speed.

I think the words *pint* and *glass*.

I follow the chef. By the time I get to the kitchen, which is on the left-hand side, they've just about emptied the first trolley. I look through an open door to the right and see into the canteen.

The people in the canteen are almost hidden behind the mountains of sausages and bacon and eggs and beans and mushrooms and toast that they're eating from. There are no words being spoken, but there's an awful industrial chewing sound. When I catch glimpses of their faces, they're all red-raw and streaked with crusty bits of sauce and shining grease. I see that they're just using their hands and not knives and forks.

I feel that this is all wrong, that it is all imaginary. But I know that it is not. It's another layer of reality – either beneath or above the one I usually experience – that I am now, against my will, aware of.

The chef screams at me from the kitchen. I turn around to face him, gladly. 'All done!' he screams. 'Take your empty bloody trolleys! You remembered everything this time! Well done, dipshit!'

'Thanks,' I mumble.

The Hunger

I CAN HEAR THIS MUFFLED wordless shouting, coming from somewhere else, from the other side of something. From the other side of this wall. I lay my hands on the wall; it's some kind of natural, uneven stone. The wall trembles slightly. There's a grey door in the wall. I edge towards it. The door jumps in its frame as the shouting increases in volume. I put my hand on the handle, turn it and open the door, and step through.

The stink of rotting meat rolls over me. I'm in the room with the giant. I'm looking up at it, at its back. Its chair is facing away from me. The chamber is huge and dark and dank. Sweat runs down my back. I can look up past the broken, scarred grey flesh, the thin, lank hair, at the ceiling, and there's this monstrous, organic-looking sphincterish arsehole centred directly above the giant's table. The giant is staring up at it too. As I watch, the arsehole puckers and flexes, as if about to deposit something, and the giant grunts; but then, nothing comes. And the giant shouts. Just an inarticulate howl of rage. He raises his fists and slams them down on to the table, and it shakes the floor. I fall to one knee. He roars again. The roar itself is enough to shake the walls, to send tremors out through the ground.

I can't see the top of the table – it's too high up. But the giant is sweeping his hands across it, sluicing droplets of filth from the tabletop on to the floor. I remember the last time I saw the giant; the tabletop was piled high with matter that it was eating. This time, the table is empty.

The giant starts to make this sound that I kind of recognise, but can't immediately identify. I can't identify it because of the volume and the tone. But then it comes to me: it's sobbing. It's this cavernous, guttural, eardrum-hurting sob. It vibrates my own ribcage and I feel revulsion at myself. I put my hands over my ears and crouch down, trying to make myself smaller. Then the giant throws its head back and opens its weird mouth wide, and forces out a scream. It sounds like it's shredding its own throat. Even with my hands over my ears, I feel a sharp stabbing pain deep inside them. Everything shakes. I hear cracking and groaning and the pitter-pattering of light debris falling to the floor. The giant takes a deep breath, and then screams again. It's crying. It's wailing. It's hungry. With its head back, I can see blood spraying from its lips. I'm reminded of my daughter.

Everything is shaking. My vision is a blur. The giant starts to stamp. I shuffle backwards, towards the door. It hasn't seen me. The shaking feels like an earthquake. I imagine the ground loosening, fragmenting, everything coming apart, everything turning non-solid, everything becoming intermingled.

The giant screams and screams and screams. The screaming of something in pain. Screaming like a baby.

The Uncle

IT IS AN UNSEASONABLY warm morning following an unseasonably warm night. Every month is the hottest of its name on record. This November has had its cold nights and frosty mornings, but not as many as last November, or the one before that. We know the world is heating up. Unprecedented drought and the ensuing resource shortage was one of the contributory factors to the war in Syria, if you read enough of the analysis. But who has the time? Now there is drought in more countries. Drought in some, deep, cold brown floods in others, wildfires like a vision of hell in yet more. These things are never the end; they're always the beginning. The beginnings of crises that haven't hit yet, but will no doubt lead to more boats full of refugees sinking in the Mediterranean, or more internment camps along the borders of the richer, safer nations.

But the warm morning gives us a stunning view of mist rising from the green valley fields. The mist wraps around the trunks of leafless trees like cotton wool and is piled up between the hills and mountains in drifts. Golden light spills from behind the mountains.

I don't feel good after the ordeal at Craggesund yesterday and my nightmare of the giant. It was just a nightmare, I think. It *was* just a nightmare. But it's been two days since the Fallen Stock men made me drink the blood, and I still feel as if I've got bits of rotten flesh stuck between my teeth and maggots in my belly. That wasn't a nightmare. The world is different now.

My phone rings, which makes me jump. I pull over. Ryan groans.

'Just fucking leave it.'

'No,' I say. I don't recognise the number. 'Hello?' I say, opening the van door and stepping down. We're on the little road between Bootle and Waberthwaite, between two tall hedgerows.

'It's your mother.' My uncle's cockney twang. I freeze.

'What about her?' I ask.

'She's dead.'

'Oh God,' I say. 'Oh no.' I sit down on the road. 'Oh shit.'

'I'm sorry.' A pause. 'Come up.'

'You're at her house?'

'Yeah.'

'What happened? How did she die?'

'Big hole opened up, and she fell in it.'

'What?'

THE HOLE HAS SWALLOWED half the garden. It isn't a proper hole, with an open black space in the middle leading through to some unknown subterranean realm; it's just a great muddy basin. My mother lies in a weird angle at the bottom of it, her upper body submerged in the earth. I'm remembering my dream from last night. The giant deep underground, shaking the ground with his screams.

I'm tasting the blood from the Fallen Stock wagon. Things squirm in my gut. There's my foot, and there's the other foot. My uncle stands at the edge of the pit. He wears a trilby and an overcoat over a suit and tie, and he smokes a cigarette.

It was clearly an undignified, horrible death.

'Where's the ambulance?' I ask. 'Where are the police?'

'On their way, I presume. I rang them before I rang you.' He inhales and blew out a great cloud of smoke. 'In the capital, they'd have been here in three minutes flat!' He flicks some ash from the end of his cigarette. 'But then, in the capital, this wouldn't have happened at all.'

'How come you're here? How come it was you who found her?'

'Why wasn't it you, you mean? Maybe because you never bloody visit!'

'But why are you *here*?'

'She was worried about local subsidence, wasn't she? And you know me. I know houses. I know land! So she gave me a call. And I said, well. We've had a wet summer. A very wet summer. Way too hot, and way too wet. Earth turning to slop beneath our very feet! Trees can't stand up any more! I thought, well, it could happen. It could. And I thought, well, it's nearly Christmas! Why not make the trip and have a look for myself? Get away from all the bloody foreigners. All the bloody illegals. Drop off some gifts while I'm at it.' He gestures past the fence to his big expensive car. The back seat is piled high with beautifully wrapped Christmas presents. I've never had a Christmas present from my uncle. But this isn't the time to dwell on old grievances like that.

The sound of sirens now fades in. I look back at my mother's corpse and have to put my hand over my mouth. I look away again.

THERE'S A POWERFUL, AUTHORITATIVE knock at the door. Kathryn, who is staying with me tonight, looks over. 'Who will that be?'

'It will be my uncle,' I say. 'Or the police. From the sound of the knock, it could be either. I'd better get it.'

I go downstairs. Since my last encounter with the ghost, I keep all the lights on all the time, even though the witch bottle seems to be reactivated now. I look through the tiny window and see a pale face hovering. 'It's my uncle,' I say. I open the door.

'Come in,' I say.

'Thank you,' he says. He takes a small tin from his overcoat pocket, opens it and puts out his cigarette in it. Then he puts the tin away, takes out the cigarette packet and puts the unsmoked bit of cigarette back in the packet. He steps inside the house, takes off his trilby and overcoat and hangs them up. He runs a hand through his thick white hair. 'Right then,' he says. 'We need to talk.'

I lead him upstairs. Kathryn is standing, ready to introduce herself. She holds out her hand. 'I'm so sorry,' she says.

'Who're you?' my uncle says to her. 'Who's she?' he says to me. 'Wait a minute. I recognise you. Did I buy a jacket potato from you this morning?'

'You did,' she confirms, lowering her hand.

'The La'al Tattie Hut, was it?'

'The La'al Tattie Shop.'

'It was a very good potato. Well done. How about a nice cup of tea?' He sits down in the armchair, and returns his attention to me. 'Have you remarried, then?'

'No,' I say.

'She shouldn't be living here, then! Not in *my* house.'

Kathryn crosses her arms.

'I just came to offer him some support,' she says. 'He needs a friend.'

'She doesn't live here,' I say. 'Nobody lives in the house but me.'

'Well, that's what I came to talk about. The house. Now that your dear old mum – my beloved sister – now that she's very sadly passed, I intend to evict you and put this property out to let for its full, proper rental value.'

'Oh,' I say, after a moment. 'Okay then.'

'Now then. The funeral. Something simple.' He takes a handkerchief from a pocket and dabs at his eyes. 'Now then.' He pauses, and puts the handkerchief back in his pocket. He clasps his hands together and sits entirely still, as if suddenly frozen. The silence stretches out.

'I'll arrange it,' I say.

'Ha!' he barks. Then, 'I think not. Leave it to me.' He stands up. 'I felt for your mother, I really did,' he says. The sadness he seemed to feel a moment ago has gone; his voice is now sharp and angry. 'Ever since the baby died, I've wanted her to feel peace. I wanted to help her feel peace by taking you off her hands. I didn't want her to have to worry about *you*. Hence.' He holds his palms up and looks around the room. 'I don't think it ever did the trick, though. She was not a happy woman. And now she's dead.' He claps his hands. 'Ah well. I tried. And the simple fact is, the simple maths of it is, I could rent this out for three times as much as what you pay me. So, young man, consider this your notice.' He looks at Kathryn. 'How's that nice cup of tea coming along?'

'Fuck off,' she says.

He points at her. 'Young people today,' he says, 'have got no respect for their elders. And that's a problem, that is.' He points at me. 'You've got one month. And in that time I'm going to find some-body else. There'll be no sign, no viewings that you can sabotage. I'll be finding my own tenants, privately. Make sure I don't end up with any foreigners. Or gays. Or disableds. One month. Got it?'

'Yes, Uncle,' I say.

'YOU COULD MOVE IN with me,' Kathryn says.

'I think you're only saying that because you're here right now,' I say. 'And you feel like you've got to.'

'Maybe.'

'I don't think we're at that stage of our relationship yet.'

'I agree. Yes. But, if it's that or the streets, you're coming to mine.' She holds up a finger as I try to interrupt. 'Not as the next stage in our relationship. Just as a friend. I've got a sofa bed. It's fine.'

'Thank you,' I say. 'That's very kind.'

And it is, and I appreciate her kindness. I do not want to become dependent on kindness though. I want to be able to save myself.

I don't tell her about the blood.

The Fucking Moron

I KNEW THAT BABIES CRIED. But I hadn't realised how much they cried, or how loudly, or how terrifying the crying was. Our daughter had two primary cries: there was this constant, despairing sob, that sounded so sad and hopeless that it hurt to hear, and then there was the kind where her whole body would turn bright red and her eyes would bulge, and she'd scream her thoat raw. She'd make herself sick crying like this, and frequently I'd wonder how she could make the sounds she made without bringing up blood. It was the sound you might expect a baby to make if it had been dropped on its head or if it had kneeled on a drawing pin while crawling, or something. But she cried like this when she was tired, which she always was because she didn't sleep. Or when she was hungry, which she always was because she didn't seem to want to feed. She cried when we put her down, so we didn't put her down. And this wasn't just the first few weeks; this was the first few months. The first year. The first eighteen months.

But before that first year elapsed, there was a moment that I think back to again and again. The flat was hot. We were concerned about the heat of our flat and whether or not our newborn daughter would be okay in it. We'd bought several standing fans to help cool her down. We wondered if the amount she cried was normal – we didn't know. But at this point we thought maybe she was crying because of the heat. Or maybe it was because we were crying all the time. Or because of all of our fighting, or because she was always hungry, or because she was always tired. But maybe the lack of sleeping and eating was because of the heat, we thought. We were struggling with cause and effect. Or maybe she was in pain because the forceps had hurt her head, and that prevented her from sleeping, and her tiredness made her unwilling to feed. Maybe my wife and I fought so much because we were so exhausted. Whichever way we turned there was a downward spiral.

We were not happy. None of the three of us. But I'm not sure I'd realised how unhappy I was.

It was the middle of the night and I was pacing around the flat holding Marianne in my arms, singing 'Twinkle Twinkle Little Star' again and again in this quiet, slow way that I thought might be soothing but in retrospect was just a horrible dirge. On one occasion it had appeared to make a difference, and every night since then I'd repeated it, the singing, scared that if I stopped then she would become even more wakeful and her crying would become louder and more desperate. It was a ritual by this point. The slow pace, the slow sway of her in my arms, the awful singing. The drone of the standing fans. The moon was full and bright outside, shining in through the gaps around the blinds. I walked from her room to the living room, round in a circle for a bit, then back to her room, where I walked in a circle, and then back to the living room. I kept that up for hours every night. She would stop crying, but if I tried to put her to bed, tried to sit down, or even stopped walking, she would start again.

I would feel like I was starting to fall asleep while walking around the flat. My eyes would start to close, and it would be difficult to stop them. My feet would barely leave the laminate floor. I'd jerk back to wakefulness because my shoulder had bumped against the magnolia walls. And every time, I'd see that boiling red and black behind my eyes, and remember the other me who shared my body.

On this one particular occasion, I felt like I was going to drop, baby in arms. So I slowly collapsed on to the sofa, knowing full well that she was going to erupt into fury – but it was that or risk falling with her. I let my eyes close as the screams burst from her tiny throat.

The next thing I knew I was sitting there, watching myself – another me, the other me – carry her around the darkened room. I looked haggard. My hair was too long and I needed a shave. The skin under my eyes was purple and baggy and the rest of my face was sickly pale. My shoulders were hunched, my arms bony, my legs skeletal, and yet my mid-section was paunchy. My toenails were long and yellow, as were my teeth when I smiled. I was smiling down at our little daughter, who was still screaming. No wonder, with that horrible monster grinning down. But that horrible monster did look just like me, and I like it. I watched silently as the other me continued the slow pace around the front room. I thought about getting up and taking my daughter back, but part of me was just glad of the sit-down. Now, I thought, if only the other me could stop her crying . . .

The crying changed from the pained wail back to the despairing sob, which was something. My eyes started to close. I watched as the other me carefully laid the baby down on the sofa next to me.

'Don't,' I said. 'She'll start up again.'

The other me took a cushion and put it on top of our daughter's face.

I reached out, took the cushion and threw it to the floor. My gorge was suddenly high and I wanted to be sick. I picked our girl up and held her close. I held her so that her furry cheek was pressed against mine and she stopped crying for a moment. I stroked her hair and my stomach settled. A few minutes later she was sobbing again, but then, so was I.

MY MOTHER STOOD IN the doorway of our beautiful flat. It was a summer's day. Sunlight flooded in through the big wall-to-wall windows. The blinds cast shadows across the wooden floors. She'd travelled down to meet her granddaughter.

Ellie and I had been fighting when my mother had pressed the buzzer, and between releasing the lock on the door to the building and her coming up the stairs and knocking on the door to our flat, neither Ellie nor I had said a word to each other. We hadn't known what to say. We'd just kind of wilted in this thick, poisonous air. Now my mother stood in the doorway and looked across the room at Ellie – well, at Marianne really, at our daughter, bundled up in Ellie's arms – with a horrified expression on her face. Marianne was screaming, her little face almost purple, the big brown forceps bruise still right across it. Her screaming made Ellie and I sweat and so we were both permanently damp and uncomfortable.

I stood by the door, my hand still on the handle. I wiped my forehead. 'Are you coming in?' I said.

My mother just stood there.

'What's wrong?' Ellie asked. She had stood to welcome my mother, but standing was painful for her. There was an edge to her voice.

'I can't do this,' my mother said.

'Why not?' Ellie asked.

'I can't do this,' my mother said. 'I'm sorry. I can't do it.' She shook her head. She lifted her glasses and wiped away a tear. 'I'm sorry. I've got to go. Call me a taxi back to the station.'

'Mum?' I said. 'Don't go.'

'Goodbye,' she said. And then she walked back out into the stairwell.

'Well, what did she expect?' Ellie said, after we'd heard the outside door shut. 'She's a baby. Of course she's going to look a bit like Robert. Does that mean she's not going to see her, ever? Is she ever going to be able to help us?'

'I don't know.' I still held the door handle. 'Should I drive her to the station?'

'I need to sit down. Take her off me.' I took Marianne from her and held her close as Ellie slowly eased herself down on to the sofa. 'Oh God,' she breathed. Gently she lay down. 'I really needed a rest. I need some time. Fucking useless,' she whispered.

'Hey,' I said. 'She lost a baby. She'll come round.'

'That was nearly twenty years ago. Why do you always defend her?'

'I'm not defending her.'

253

'You always stick up for her.'

'I just think — I mean, I think I can understand why it might be difficult for her.'

'You're her only child and we've just had a baby and it didn't go well and we need some help and she can't do it! She can't even say a word to me! She wouldn't even hold her! Why aren't you angry?'

I shrugged. 'It's not her job to help us.'

'But *we need help*, and if somebody you love needs help, you fucking help them! My parents help us more than she does, and they live fucking miles away!'

Ellie was from East Anglia and that's where her family lived; it was true they were much more willing to help than my mother, but due to the distance between them and us, they couldn't be around all the time.

'Yeah, but—'

She sat up. 'Why are you arguing with *me* to stick up for *her*?'

'I don't know!'

'You always take their side. Whoever it is. Your mother. The fucking midwives. You always take *their* side and argue with me. You never stick up for me. You never defend me.'

She started getting to her feet again. I knew that hurt her. The delivery had fucked her back. And the stitches in her perineum had ruptured twice already. She was on antibiotics for an infection there, and the antibiotics made her feel sick. On the rare occasions she was able to sleep, she had nightmares about hands reaching up around the end of the bed and forcing themselves inside her. She was trying to breastfeed but had severe mastitis and cracked nipples. She suffered from bursts of intense abdominal pain. We'd been to the GP the day before because of vaginal bleeding, and he'd said that she might have a womb infection because of all the manual manipulation that had been required over the course of her labour.

'You don't have to get up,' I said.

'I remember you in the hospital,' she said. 'You and the midwives. Ganging up on me.'

'What?'

'When that awful woman wanted me to get in the chair.'

'But you had to get in. I was agreeing that you had to get in the chair.'

'She told me I was being pathetic. You should have stuck up for me.'

'But I wanted you to get in the chair!' I was shouting now. 'Nothing else mattered!'

'You *always* take *their* side,' she said.

'I thought you were going to die,' I said.

'And yet you were arguing with me, and laughing with her.'

The important thing is that there were various well-worn runnels that all our fights eventually fell into, and the runnels always led to this accusation from her that I was too selfish and preoccupied to really care for her when she needed care. And in turn I'd deny it, and strenuously declare that I tried, but I couldn't get everything right all of the time. And that caring for her didn't mean I would always *agree* with her – sometimes the opposite in fact, as with the wheelchair in the hospital. And it always felt like the stakes were too high to let things slide. Everything felt like the final straw. I couldn't back down. I felt like if I didn't convince her that I *did* care, then she might actually leave me. It got to the point where our only conversations were arguments, and when we weren't arguing we were both giving off anger like radiation. Somehow we both had plenty of time to identify each other's shortcomings, and yet neither of us had the headspace for introspection. And it became impossible for either of us to suggest help or action to the other without the context making it an attack, an accusation of weakness. Of brokenness. Our home became toxic, and it warped our perceptions of each other and of everybody else in our lives. Our deep unhappiness made the everyday enquiries of friends and family feel accusatory, and difficult to respond to. Ellie and I had almost completely isolated ourselves from friends by this point. We'd had a couple of visits, but they'd been so painful and awkward – Ellie and I both desperately trying to pretend that we were okay, that we were, in fact, celebratory – that neither of us had arranged any more. Even if that had not been the case, we were both pretty paranoid and wouldn't have let any friends look after Marianne in order to help us anyway. None of our close friends had children of their own and so we just didn't trust them to deal with the potential disasters that paraded endlessly through our minds.

Increasingly, I wasn't sure how much I trusted myself.

The End of the Tether

'OH, HERE WE ARE,' Ryan says, shaking his head as I indicate right at the Egremont roundabout. Torrential rain sheets down. 'Here we are. Time to hit the La'al Spud Bucket.'

'The La'al Tattie Shop.'

'The Tiny Tattie Hole.'

'All right.'

'Potato Heaven.'

'*All right.*'

I'm not in the mood for his humour. I'm not in the mood for Ryan at all. I'm worrying about the arrangements for my mother's funeral. I've never had to think about a funeral before. My dad had died when I was still quite young, and I'd stayed with my cousin Philip and his parents for a while while my mum had sorted it all out. Last night I tried to ring the Bean to ask for some time off, but I couldn't get hold of her. Nor was I able to find her at the depot this morning. So I'm trying to do the responsible thing and work, but it's difficult. Especially with Ryan being alternatively sullen and crude. And with the taste of that blood still in my mouth.

'How are you doing?' Kathryn asks, as we enter.

'All right, thanks,' I say.

'Really?'

'He's fucking in one,' Ryan says to her, nodding his head at me. 'He's got a proper cob on today, like.'

Kathryn raises her eyebrow at me, surmising that I haven't told Ryan about my mother.

'The usual?' she asks.

'Yes, please,' I say.

'What is your usual, anyway?' Ryan asks.

'Do you want anything or not?' I ask him.

'From her?' he mutters quietly. 'I can think of a few things.'

'Not today,' I say.

'Why not?' he says. 'Why should I do what you want?'

Kathryn has gone to the kitchen to refill her topping trays.

I stare at him.

'You don't have power over me,' he says, getting in close. His hands are still down his pants. I look up, maintaining eye contact as he moves in, until his chest presses against my chin. 'The reference? You think you can control me because of the reference? How about this: how about, you write me a good reference or I knock seven shades of shite out of you. How about that?'

'That won't look very good for your court case, will it?' I murmur.

Kathryn comes back through, stopping when she sees us.

'Everything all right?' she asks.

'It's fine,' I say.

258

'Do you want anything, or not?' she asks Ryan.

'Not right now, babe,' he says. 'But maybe I'll come back later.'

WE CONTINUE IN SILENCE. How can I get Ryan out of my life, and out of Kathryn's life?

We do Ravenglass, Bootle and Waberthwaite without speaking. Thunder rolls around the sky. Ryan is wet through in his thin coat and jogging bottoms. Water runs from his heavy jaw. I make sure I deliver to those customers that are expecting goods from Kathryn, and Ryan doesn't question me. He just watches through narrow eyes. He might even see some of the brown paper packages as I drop them off. I don't try that hard to hide them from him any more, because the situation has developed past those early concerns. The Bean has been much happier since we got Craggesund back.

We return to the depot. The Bean still isn't around, but some new orders have been written out and left on the side – the Woolpack in Eskdale and the Strands in Wasdale both want deliveries.

'I'll take these on my own,' I say. 'I'll drop you at yours on the way if you want.'

'Mm,' Ryan says. 'Aye, go on then. I'll see if Peter wants to go for a la'al drive out. Feeling a bit peckish, like. Could really go for a couple of hot potatoes.'

'Don't,' I say. Peter is his brother. The flame in my chest flares. It isn't a flame, I realise. It's a snake, waking up. 'Just don't joke about it.'

'I'm just hungry,' he says, shrugging and grinning. 'I'm not making a joke about anything.'

I feel as if he's just trying to provoke me. I turn to the orders and pick up a couple of empty boxes from the pile. I slide open the heavy door to the storeroom. 'Are you going to help or not?' I ask.

'Nah,' he says. He spits on to the floor and then goes and gets back into the van. I make up the orders and put them in the back. I go and get all of the milk multipacks from the refrigerator. I heft sacks of potatoes and carrots through the pouring rain. Then I get in the driver's seat. We're both dripping wet and the windows are steaming up. The van rocks slightly in the high winds.

'Listen,' I say. 'I'm going to give you a bad reference.'

'You fucking what?'

'I'm going to give you a bad reference because you're violent and dangerous and probably not a good father, and it's the right thing to do.' I look square at him. 'Hit me,' I say. 'Come on. Knock seven shades out of me, like you said you would.'

'You want to get me sacked.'

'What? No, I don't.'

'I'm not stupid, pal.'

'I know,' I say.

'Here's you strutting about like a dog with two dicks because the fucking Bean's told you to write my fucking reference and you think you've got a tiny bit of power for once in your pathetic, shitty little fucking life, and you want to use it to get rid of me somehow, and then what?'

'Come on,' I say. 'Let's go.'

'No, wait.' He takes a hand from out of his pants and puts it on the wheel. 'You'd stop me seeing my kid? For ever?'

'I just feel like I should tell the truth.'

'The truth about me?' he asks.

'Yes.'

'What about the truth about you?'

'What about it?' I ask. 'I'm not going to court.'

'Where's your kid? I don't think you ever even see her.'

'I'm not taking parenthood lessons from you, Ryan.'

He backhands me across the face. Pain explodes in my nose as my head bounces off the seat behind me. He does it again. Suddenly he's crowding into the driver's seat, all hot animal breath and massive hands and red face and drool. He punches me in the stomach, he punches me in the face. It makes me dizzy. I think I'm lying down but then realise I'm just leaning against the door. My arms are trapped, either under myself or under him. His knee is in my groin and it makes me sick. His meaty fists just keep coming down. I manage to wiggle some fingers into the door release handle and pull it, and the door opens and we both fall sideways into the wet mud with a heavy thump. I start to crawl away, but he grabs me by the legs and gets back on top of me. I'm on my front now. He's punching me in the back.

Save yourself.

In front of me is a crate of empty milk bottles. I get a hold of it and pull it closer. I take a milk bottle from the crate. I take a deep breath and then forcefully twist round between his legs, so that I'm facing up. I smash the bottle against his head and he falls backwards. He starts screaming.

'Shut up,' I say. I've got the whole crate now. I advance and get him with another one. He wriggles backwards in the muck, one hand on his scalp. Blood bubbles out of it and runs down his face with the rainwater. I try to get up but there's a pain in my lower

261

back and I can't and I fall back down, but I fall on to my knees on top of him and drop the crate. I grab his hands and kneel on them. I put my hands over his mouth. 'Shut up,' I say. 'Stop screaming. Stop screaming. Stop screaming.'

The Brother

I'D BEEN WOKEN UP by my parents fighting. Screaming at each other. We lived in a little terrace and when they fought you could not escape it. And they were always fighting. I was five. Normally I'd try to get as far away from the fight as was possible in that small house and hide until it stopped. On this occasion I pulled the covers up over my head – a soft, bobbled *Transformers* cartoon sleeping bag, unzipped – and put my hands over my ears. But it got worse and worse. I started to feel like I had a snake in my chest. It was anger, though I didn't know it then. Slowly twisting around and around. Eventually I crept downstairs. I was going to shout at them to *stop it*. Fill up my tiny lungs and yell. If they could scream and shout, then I could too. The stairs had this horrible murky green carpet. Between her sobs, my mother was shouting something about not getting any sleep. My father was telling her to go to the doctors. As I peered around the door frame, I saw her lying on the floor, sobbing, and him standing over her, arms folded. He had his back to me. I didn't understand why he wasn't just giving her a hug and saying sorry. He was saying, 'I can't help you.' He was muttering it again and again.

Beyond them, the TV was on. A small square of light. My eyes flickered from them to the TV and back.

The argument went on and on. I was frozen, waiting to interrupt them and *stop it*, bring it to a close, but not able to get the courage, not able to get the breath. And then a piercing shriek blasted down from upstairs. My baby brother. His shriek was matched by one from my mother; a despairing wail. I darted back on to the staircase. I ran up the stairs, the snake in my chest churning.

My baby brother was *screaming the house down*, as my father would put it. I could hear my mother crying downstairs, and a kind of ominous silence from my dad. I went into my brother's room. 'Stop it,' I said. 'Stop screaming, Robert.' In my memory the light is on, but the room feels dim all the same. My little baby brother was cute when he wasn't screaming, but he screamed so much. 'Give Mummy five minutes' peace!' I instructed him. That was the name of a book my father read to me sometimes. And then my parents' fighting resumed downstairs. They probably only fought so much because my little brother never stopped crying. If one of them started – usually my brother, sometimes my mother, sometimes my father – it would set them all off. Fighting and crying and screaming. It never stopped. I couldn't stop my mum and dad, but maybe I could stop my brother. I reached in between the bars of the cot and put my little hands over his mouth. 'Shhh,' I said. 'Stop it! Stop screaming!' I held my hands like that until he went to sleep, and then I went back to my own room feeling like I'd done something good.

The Man From The TV

I JERK BACKWARDS FROM RYAN as the memory floods back, my hands coming away from his mouth. That was the night. That was the night he'd died. I'd blocked it out. I'd blocked my hands out. The fight. Him, screaming. My mum on the floor. My dad saying, 'I can't help.' The TV. I'd blocked the TV out too. The soldier in green camouflage on the TV screen, walking a huge dog past a low, scary building. Something about it had made five-year-old me feel sick. And then the image had changed and drawn my eyes back to the TV.

On the screen there was a person wearing a black pointed hood and ragged black cloak. They were standing against a white wall with their arms outstretched. Their arms and ankles were brown. Wires dangled from their body. The image was not moving; it was a photograph. I heard the newsreader, but only intermittent words. *Iraq . . . stripped . . . torture . . . electricity*. More photos followed – men with blurred-out faces lying naked on the ground or in piles, naked men with leashes around their necks, rows of men standing with bags on their heads and their genitals blurred out. More words. *Raped . . . dogs . . . stimulated.*

I stare helplessly at Ryan. He stares back at me. We both sit in the mud. 'That's it,' I say. 'That's where it came from.'

He's picking bits of glass out of his hair. His hands shake. Water runs over everything.

'Ryan,' I say, standing up. 'Find another job.'

He doesn't say anything.

I get back into the van. I watch as Ryan stumbles away down the lane looking like something that has drowned and then come back.

Maybe this is it, I think. Maybe I have exorcised something. Maybe the red tentacles, or the black; maybe now I'm only in one world, or the other. Maybe the blood has done its work. I don't know. I don't know.

I hadn't wanted to kill my brother. That hadn't been my intention at all. But that's what I'd done.

I didn't remember my brother, though. Not until right now. Not until I'd had my hands over Ryan's mouth. I didn't remember him or my hands or the cot. What had been seared into my memory was the torture victim on TV. The person in the hood and cloak – that was what I remember from that night. That's what's come back to me now, in this time of anxiety and ghosts and other unwelcome visitors. But then, it's connected. It's all connected.

I turn the key in the ignition and set off to the valleys. When I catch up with Ryan shambling along the roadside, I give him a wide swerve.

The Job Hunt

I KEEP MY MOUTH SHUT while the Bean frantically calls around looking for Ryan. I watch from the doorway. Ryan disappeared while at work, while working for the Bean. 'Bloody lump!' the Bean shouts, slamming the phone down. 'His poor auld mam's having kittens. And guess who's going to have to get in the van today. That's right. Yours truly. It's not like I haven't got enough of my own work to do. Bloody hell. Here, lad. You just do the northern way today, and the valleys, and I'll do Gosforth, Seascale and Bootle and that.'

'What other work are you busy with?' I ask.

'Expansion!' the Bean says.

'I've been meaning to ask about that.'

'Aye, well. Sorry. But now's not the time.'

The rain is still coming down. I wonder where Ryan has gone, if he hasn't gone home.

THE JOB FEELS SUDDENLY simple in a way that it hasn't for weeks. I'm on my own, I don't have to try to hide anything, I don't have to endure the constant needling or the constant threat. I can just get on with the work.

Of course, everything else has become quite complicated.

My mother is dead. I turn Radio 4 up loud, way too loud, but it doesn't distract me from the deep-down drums of the grief I'm trying to bury. Every few minutes I feel it in my stomach, trying to bubble up to the surface, and I squash it down, stamp on it, turn the radio up a bit louder. Frequently it ambushes me and I burst into tears while thinking I'm thinking about other things. As I work, I become increasingly worried that Ryan is going to suddenly appear and take his vengeance on me. I start to look both ways before getting out of the van, or before coming back out of a front yard. I don't get too close to hedgerows in case he's hiding on the other side, waiting to grab me. By the time I get to Craggesund, I'm quite nervy.

I wait for the rickety old elevator, wiping some tears from my eyes that I don't remember crying, ready to run if the doors open to reveal Ryan waiting inside. Thankfully they don't. I wheel the trolley in. It occurs to me that it would make more sense for him to wait at the top, because then I wouldn't have anywhere to run when the doors open. Thankfully he isn't up there either.

On the way back, I swing into Egremont for my usual from the La'al Tattie Shop. I feel suddenly sick. What if Ryan has fulfilled his threat to Kathryn? The shop looks open as usual as I approach. I can't see inside though, because of all the rain and condensation on the shop windows. I swerve into the parking space and hop out, leaving the key in the ignition. I should've sent her a message, warning her.

'Hello,' she says, as I open the door.

'Oh,' I say. 'Hello.'

'Are you all right? You look like you're in a panic.'

'Yes, thank you. I'm fine.'

'I had a strange visit before.'

'Ryan?' I hazard.

'Yes. His brother drove him here. He was in a very sorry state.'

'He left work in a bad way yesterday.'

'Well, that's what he came to see me about, kind of.'

'Really?' I held my breath.

'He asked if I had any work for him.'

I laugh. 'How can he think *you'd* give him work? Given the way he talks to you?'

'Well, that's what I thought. But then I thought: maybe that's just how he is. Maybe he just talks to everybody like that.'

'Well, that *is* how he is,' I say. 'That *is* how he talks to everybody. That's precisely the problem. He's a violent misogynist. So – what did you say?'

'I said no. I can't afford staff. And if I could – I wouldn't hire him, because he always has his hands down his pants.'

'Oh, right, yes,' I say. 'Of course. Can't have that when you're working with food.'

'Yes. But having said that, you work with food too.'

'I suppose we do,' I say.

'The usual?' she asks.

'Yes, please,' I say.

'How are you feeling about your mum?'

'Not very good. I keep crying.'

'I just think it's rough that the Bean won't give you any time off.'

'Yeah, I know,' I say. But actually I don't think I've asked for any time off. I try to remember. I can't remember.

'You're frowning,' she says.

'I'm just tired,' I say. 'Tired and confused.'

I REMAIN VIGILANT AS I move into the valleys. If Ryan's brother is driving him around, then he could be anywhere. I'm reassured that he's seen Kathryn and not hurt her, but then, if he's going to be angry with anybody, it's me.

I've got some milk to drop off at the Strands, and park up in the pub car park, as usual. And as usual, the smells of the microbrewery and the woodsmoke and the trees conspire to create a sense of well-being, a sense of belonging. I stand here in the rain for a moment breathing it all in. From inside the pub there's the sound of quiet talking, the clinking of cutlery and occasional laughter. I close my eyes, and then, after some time has passed, I quickly open them again in case Ryan is around.

I go through the back door into the kitchen and nod to the chef. She nods back, slightly dislodging her hat, and waves her meat cleaver at me.

'Hello,' I say. I put the milk down and open the fridge.

'Hey,' she says. 'Your friend was here earlier.'

'Ryan?' I ask.

'Dunno. Big guy, works with you.'

'Yeah, that's Ryan.'

'Looks a mess. He okay?'

'I'm not sure. What was he doing?'

'Asking for work. I told him, come back in the spring. Come back for the silly season. But even then, I don't think we'd have him.'

I nod. I put the milk in the fridge. 'Anything else you want?' I ask. 'Haven't had a full order from you today.'

'Quiet now. We'll get a big order in for Christmas.'

IT'S THE SAME AT the Wasdale Head, the Woolpack, the King George and the Bower House. Ryan has been round them all. He's even asked at the campsites. But it's the wrong time of year, and besides, he has a reputation. To be honest, I hadn't expected him to act on my suggestion.

BACK AT THE DEPOT I go inside the house and check the answerphone for new orders. Sure enough, there is one. Higgins. Whole milk, white bread and a catering pack of bacon. To go with all the eggs, maybe. I put it together and set back out again.

I pull into the Higgins yard and see him standing in his doorway, talking to a visitor. Then I realise the visitor is Ryan. Ryan turns and sees the van. They both watch me get out.

'Hello, Ryan,' I say. 'This is a coincidence, isn't it? I get an order from Mr Higgins, bring it straight here, and here you are.'

'I'm going to every bloody farmer on the round,' Ryan says. 'It's hardly a coincidence. Thought I'd've bumped into you a bit earlier, to be honest.'

'And besides,' Mr Higgins says, 'I rang the order in three hours ago. Where's the bloody Bean at these days? I never see her.'

'She's had to get out in the van today,' I say. 'Look, Ryan. I'm sorry about yesterday. I'm really sorry. I didn't want to hurt you. I never want to hurt anybody. Sometimes I can't control it.'

'I'm not coming back,' he says. 'You'll just have to do it all on your own.'

'Well,' I say. 'It might mean I don't get home until nearly four o'clock, but I think it's for the best.'

'And there's no work here, chump,' Mr Higgins says. 'Farm's on its arse. They all are. This bloody weather. I've got half a farmhand and I can't even afford that. Farmer Douglas has the other half and he's the same.'

'Aye, right,' Ryan says. 'What about those Poles?'

'Poles?'

'You had a load of Poles in a caravan.'

'That was Douglas, who hired the Polish. And they're long gone. Some fucker set fire to the caravan and they all went home.'

'Oh, right.'

Nobody says anything for a little while and then Ryan trudges across the yard to his brother's car. His brother gives me the middle finger and they drive off.

'Here you go,' I say to Mr Higgins, handing the box over.

'Thanks, lad,' he says.

The Undertaker

THE FOLLOWING DAY, I go to see the undertaker – Robinson, on Corney Fell – on my way to Bootle. Before setting off this morning I caught the Bean and asked her if I could do these rounds and make this stop, and she agreed once I told her what had happened to my mother.

'You want some time off?' she asked.

'Maybe,' I said. 'I don't know. I don't know what to do.'

'Work can help take your mind off it,' she said. 'You'll be on your own. Better than being on your own at home, because you'll be getting paid for it.'

'Okay,' I said.

She did the north way instead.

I pull over and hop out of the van and go straight to the outhouse where Robinson keeps the bodies, which is the same outhouse he likes us to drop the orders in. The door opens from his yard, but then the actual floor of the building is a few steps down. That's why he has to move the bodies when the river gets high. Once my eyes adjust to the gloom, I can see a few coffins laid out on old sandstone slabs. And my mother is in the one at the end. I walk up to her. He's done a good job of cleaning all the mud off.

'All right, lad,' he says, from behind me. I turn and see him standing in the doorway, at the top of the steps. A silhouette against the grey sky. He wears thick glasses and I can see their lenses catching the light. He holds a rag in his hands for some reason; he looks as if he's just been working on a car.

'What do I need to do?' I ask him.

'Nothing,' he says. 'All taken care of.'

'Oh,' I say. 'Okay then. But wait a minute. Do you know what she wanted?'

'No,' he says. 'Do you?'

'No,' I say.

'Well then.'

I look down at her dead body. 'Well then,' I say. 'I suppose.' I can't help but feel that something is dreadfully wrong. 'So what's going to happen to her?'

'She'll be getting picked up soon,' he says. He looks at his watch. 'Any minute now, in fact.'

I frown. 'The service is *today*? I didn't even know it had been arranged.'

'Service?' He seems as confused as I do. Beyond the doorway, the sound of a van pulling up. 'They're here now,' he says. 'Good timing on your part!' He turns and ascends out into the light.

I run up the steps. A Fallen Stock wagon has reversed into Robinson's yard. I realise that things are still not okay. I'm still living in a world that is a grotesque. I watch as the driver-side door opens and one of their drivers descends. How many of these drivers are there?

'Hello, there,' Ryan says, grinning, as he walks towards me. 'I found another job, as you suggested. Thanks for the push, old chap.'

'You're even dressed like one of them,' I say.

He gives us a twirl. He's wearing the obligatory wellingtons and plus-fours, with a white shirt, smart black braces and a tweed jacket. He wears a tweed cap and chews a long, golden piece of straw. 'Good, isn't it?' he says.

I LOOK BACK AND I see a past in which things made sense. Things were not always good – in fact, they were rarely *good* – but they made sense, and I could see a way to navigate through life, and help others navigate through life, and I could determine which things were connected and which things were not, and which things were important and which were not, and I could depend upon chains of cause and effect as tools for both making sense of the world and for exerting influence on the world. But at some point that changed. *There's nobody driving the bus.* Maybe there never was. I think about Kathryn. *The truth, and the revelation.* Either way, now I can't distinguish the sensible from the absurd, the insignificant from the important, or the mundane from the horrific. I watch as they bring my mother up out of the outhouse. I try to remember her being happy. The truth is, I don't think my mother has been happy since I killed her baby, and I don't have any memories from before that.

RYAN AND ROBINSON EACH have an end of the coffin. They put her down on the cobbles of the yard. I look at her lying there.

She has her glasses on, which I'm glad about. She wears a slightly bobbly fleece, and baggy trousers with a geometric turquoise design on them. Her white hair looks nicotine-stained in the daylight. Her arms are folded on her chest. I notice she still has some mud under her fingernails, but I decide against saying anything.

'Any last words?' Robinson asks.

I look at him. 'That's not what last words are,' I say.

'All right, then,' he says. 'Whatever. I don't care. Anything you want to say?'

'Didn't my uncle get in touch about the funeral? I gave him your details.'

'He did,' Robinson says. 'There'll be a coffin to bury in the churchyard. Don't worry about it.'

'It's not that I'm *worried*,' I say. 'It just feels wrong. Is the coffin what matters?'

'As long as nobody sees inside it,' Robinson says, 'I'd say so, yeah.'

I picture a politician presenting statistics. A climate change conference. A dick pic from a colleague using an anonymous phone number. A driverless bus, heading towards a cliff edge. I mean, maybe he's right. Who am I to know?

I kneel down and stroke her hair. 'I'm sorry about Robert, Mum,' I say. 'I'm so sorry. I just wanted you to get some sleep. I wanted you and Dad to stop fighting. I didn't mean for that to happen. I didn't mean it. I wanted you to get a break. Some peace. Five minutes' peace! Like the book.' I wipe my eyes. 'I thought I was helping. I was *five*. I was only five.' I break into sobs. 'Oh, God. I'm so sorry, Mum.' I lie down over her. My chest hurts. I try to speak but can't get the words out. I imagine a broken radio – its batteries gone, or something – and radio waves emanating through the air all around, there but not being picked up. Being transmitted but not received. It doesn't help.

After I don't know how long, I feel gentle hands underneath my armpits. 'Come on, old boy,' Ryan says, lifting me up. He's strong, like a bodybuilder. 'It's time.'

'Oh,' I say. 'Okay then.'

'Now, if I recall correctly,' he says, 'you've been wanting to see inside one of these vans for a while.'

'I have,' I say. 'It's true.'

'Well, given the circumstances, I think we can allow it this once.'

'I'd be curious too,' says Robinson.

'Not you!' Ryan snaps. 'You go and wait on the road.'

He waits until Robinson is standing out on the road, and then reaches up to operate the mechanism that opens the door. 'Are you ready?' he asks.

'I think so,' I say.

He opens the door.

I don't know what I was expecting. But what I see is just an assortment of bodies, jumbled up in a heap. 'Oh,' I say. 'Wait,' I say. 'Those are animals.'

'Are they? Look again. You have drunk of the blood now. You can see things differently.'

'Oh,' I say. I tilt my head. 'I'm not sure.'

'We all go to the same place,' Ryan says. He gets closer, so that I can feel his breath on my face. 'I'll tell you something. The bodies matter. The meat matters. But as much as the meat, it's the fear. That's what we're conjuring up with all of these apparitions, visitations and

277

manifestations, and that's what we're collecting. That's what we need. That's what we're drawing out. Your dear old mother gave us her flesh in death too, in the end, but it was the fear coming off her in life that was truly remarkable. It's as important as the flesh. Whenever you think of her in future, remember, please, how sad and scared she was.'

'And what for? What do you want either for?'

'To make the giant strong again.'

'It's real?'

'You know it's real. And soon it will be free, walking the world, and we will be walking with it.'

'People would have something to say about that, I'm sure.'

'It's real, but it's not . . . *physical*. Ordinary people won't even know about it. They'll *feel* different – a little bit meaner, a little bit crueller – and they'll see the world change – get *redder* and nastier and more difficult – and they'll see chaos and bloodshed, but they won't know why. They won't see the giant, and they won't see us, and they won't know that we're free again.'

He gives me a bit of a hug. I don't resist. He whispers into my ear. 'You will, though. You'll see it all.' He steps back and smiles. 'You really hurt me, Daniel,' he says, 'and I haven't forgotten that.'

The Wires, and
the Thing Waiting

'Hi,' I SAY.

'Hello,' Kathryn replies.

'I think we have to stop doing what we're doing.'

'Which bit?'

'All of it.' I look out at the mountains, misty and purple. 'They'll kill you if we don't stop.'

'What about your ghost?'

'I don't know. I'll learn to live with it.' I think for a moment. 'Or I'll address the cause. I know what that is now. I know where it came from.'

'Really? Where? Will knowing help all of the others?'

'Mine came from—' My throat seizes up and chokes the words off. 'It—'

'Are you okay?'

'I can't talk about it.' My voice is a croak. 'I want to tell you, but I can't.' She would hate me. She could report me. I don't know if the police are resourced well enough to get into a decades-old fratricide, but people would know. I don't want anybody to know. I especially don't want her to know. 'I'm sorry. But what I can tell you is, it's something from my past that the Fallen Stock men are using against me, to make me scared. They're doing this to the farmers too – summoning ghosts or memories or traumas – and then they're either harvesting the fear, or using it to blackmail people into providing them with meat. And the fear and the flesh feed something else. That's what they told me. And if the ghost or memory or trauma is somehow laid to rest, then . . .'

'Something else? Like what?'

'It's a giant,' I say. 'I've seen it.'

'What?' She sounds incredulous, but she's not laughing. 'What do you mean? When?'

'It was years ago. It was the day I left Ellie and Marianne. I – something changed. I had an episode.' The silence stretches out. 'That day, something tore, and I saw through the tear.' I'm lying again. Or rather, I'm not telling the whole truth. I suddenly know that there's another factor – a prerequisite that I satisfy. I have killed. 'Listen,' I say. 'They'll kill you. That's the important bit. Stop making the bottles. Stop all of it.'

'Let them carry on?'

'Yes. And we have to stop seeing each other.'

'Daniel,' she says, 'have you ever seen anybody? Do you think you need to see somebody?'

'I think it's a good idea,' I say, after a moment. 'But not because of the giant.'

'No. Not because of that. But maybe because of the episode that precipitated that.'

'It is real, though.'

'I'm not disputing it. But please. You need help with your relationships.'

'Yes,' I say. 'I can see that.'

'I think you're right about us breaking up,' she says, 'but if you ever want to talk, you know where to find me.' Then, 'I'm sorry about your mum, Daniel. Did you see Robinson today? Did you ask about the funeral?'

'Yeah,' I say, after a moment. I give her the date.

'I'll be there,' she says. 'Goodnight.' But she moves the phone away from her face before she finishes saying the word, and there's a catch in her voice, and she hangs up.

'Goodnight,' I say, after a moment.

That night I sit in the chair thinking about the wires trailing from the Iraqi man's arms and how they might drag along the grass outside my house as the entity stumbles towards the door. Or how I found him sobbing, sat in this very chair, wires lying on the floor. I jump up. I can't sit in this chair any more. I open the doors to the Juliet balcony. I pick up the chair and throw it outside. It crashes on to the paving below, beneath which the witch bottle is buried. The night is clear. A thin plume of smoke rises from the pub down by the river. I can smell it. A faint breeze rustles the trees, and an owl hoots quietly in response. The mountains are shapes cut out of the sky, revealing the blackness behind it. And there he is, coming out of the purpling night: the man with the hood and the cloak, slowly approaching across the grass.

By the time he is below the balcony I can see that he moves spasmodically, that every limb trembles. Somebody hurt. He trails the wires behind him. I go downstairs and find that he's entered the house, despite the door being closed. He stands before me, shaking and moaning.

Whichever room I walk into now, he is already there. When I'm in the kitchen, he stands nearby and watches as I chop and cook. When I sit at the dining table to try and write, he sits opposite me. I put my fingers on the keyboard, but never type a word. One night with a start I realise that I never really have; I've written, deleted and rewritten the first page again and again, and my current word count is zero. I stare at the screen and then snap the laptop shut. The ghost sits, shivering.

If there is a bed in the room then he is lying in it. He lies, trailing his wires, and I remember Ellie lying in theatre, the wires coming out of her arms, shaking as she shook, running out of her and off the bed and on to the floor and around my feet, in my memories now tangled around the legs of the surgeon, tangled around the nurse's arms, getting in the way like a thick black spider's web, and I remember her screams, during and afterwards, and the man with the hood screams too, and every night I listen to him and I think of Ellie, and Marianne, and Robert, and my mother, and I listen to the sound of something breathing, something outside of me and outside of the ghost, something far larger, the sound of something far greater inhaling and exhaling in the night, waiting.

The Email

I SIT DOWN ON THE floor, but I'm not resting. I'm just waiting, and I don't know what for. I drink whisky while I wait.

It's true that I can't much bear the attentions or even the presence of other people. It's one reason I live here. It's one reason that I work this job. One reason – of many, to be fair – that I didn't want Ryan in the van with me. It's why I was scared of acting on my attraction to Kathryn. I've long had this deep, subconscious fear that I'll hurt people around me, but until that memory – Robert – resurfaced, I didn't understand where the fear came from.

The dark evening becomes night. It's a cold night, but I feel hot. I showered after I got in but my skin is coated with a fresh sheen of sweat. My heart rate slowly increases as time passes, despite me not moving from the floor.

Eventually my phone vibrates. It's an email. My heart stops when I see who it's from. It's from Ellie.

Daniel,

I understand why you left, and I believe it was the right thing to do. I also believe that I have been justified in ensuring a distance between us. However, every day I imagine how I'd feel if Marianne was with you and I didn't know where you were. I should have kept in touch after we'd left the flat, and I apologise for not doing so. It was never my intention for us to vanish from your life. But every time I thought about sending you an email or a message, or ringing you up, I recoiled. The thought of it filled me with horror, and I couldn't do it. I could never even open the emails and messages you've sent me. Everything in my body told me not to. I don't know what to compare it to. Opening a door, maybe, when you know there's a monster on the other side and it's waiting to eat you. Not that I ever thought you were a monster. But our time together was a monster, somehow, and I didn't want to feed it, let it back in, or wake it back up . . . I'm getting my metaphors mixed up, but you know what I mean.

And so the guilt built up, and the monster grew larger, and getting in touch seemed scarier and scarier. Marianne kept growing too, and she's kept me busy. Parenthood is difficult. Of course, you remember the first few years. I don't know how to tell you everything about her. I can't. Obviously you will have to see her, and see her soon. It's the only way. She understands that you're out there somewhere, and that you love her, and miss her. She knows that her friends have fathers, so she knows what you are.

I am emailing now, after everything, because two things have happened that – when I put them together – compel me to write.

To begin with, I have to explain something. For a period of time that started before we broke up, I wanted to die. Our daughter is the only reason I'm still alive. Though there were times that I thought it would be better for her to die too. Looking back, I know that it was wrong to feel that way, but when I was in that place, it all made sense to me. It started with Marianne being born. I felt like the world had changed, or the relationship between me and the world had changed. Everything seemed darker and less forgiving. The world was closing in on me.

There were days after we separated when I'd get paralysed in the supermarket, knowing I had no time, knowing I had no money, stuck between this brand of nappy and that brand, knowing that if I chose the wrong one I'd be stuck with the choice, and Marianne would be stuck with the choice, and if she got nappy rash it would be my fault, and then she wouldn't eat or sleep, and then she'd be unhappy the next day, and I'd feel even worse, and the other things I had to do would feel even harder. I felt like this about every decision by the end. At the start it was just the big decisions – where to live, when to go back to work – but by the end it was all of them. What to wear, which room to try and feed her in, which direction to go for a walk. I'd freeze and cry. Every choice I made felt like the wrong one. Every time I made a choice all I felt was loss: loss of the options not taken. Every step I took resulted in my mind screaming about all the steps I could have taken instead. The future was collapsing in on me. Every day I felt this enormous pressure – not just the pressure to get everything right, though there was that – but an actual physical pressure. As if the air had turned to glass and was pressing against my skin, compressing me. Doing ordinary, everyday things like shopping – even online – felt like torture. I started to feel like all of those misogynistic clichés about female biology were true: I was a vessel that had fulfilled its purpose. I was an empty bottle. I started to think, if this is life then I don't want it. And I don't want it for Marianne. Because I love her. That was a constant. Love for her. But the love wasn't a warmth. It was just sadness. I just felt sad for her. My love for her met the world and immediately resulted in overwhelming, unbearable despair. The thought of her, so beautiful and delicate and wise, having to endure the darkness and pressure and loss that came with every day of life – life as a girl, then woman – was unbearable. I didn't want to endure it, and I was a horrible failure of a human who deserved it; she was innocent and perfect, and didn't deserve it at all. So maybe it would be kinder for me to kill us both. That was how I felt. And there were moments I came close. But revulsion at the act itself always stopped me. Fear stopped me.

And over time, something changed. My body healed. You will remember how badly the delivery tore me up and hurt my spine. I think I became so used to the pain that I forgot about it. In retrospect I could see that the constant pain was probably a factor in my mental state. Of course it sounds obvious now. But most of it has faded away. It has taken until now. I still get the occasional twinge, but it's nothing like it was. And Marianne grew a little bit older and started to walk and talk, and bit by bit things got a little bit easier. I'd have these infrequent moments – sometimes minutes long, sometimes hours, eventually days – of calmness, of not-panic, and they increased in frequency. And I'm glad now that we're both still here. Still alive.

Starting to feel better – that was the first thing. It was a prerequisite for getting in touch. When I felt bad, I hated you. I blamed you. So I would never have got in touch if I hadn't started to feel better.

The second thing – the thing that prompted me to actually get on and write to you – was a horrible dream. I can't tell if I've had the same dream for a few nights in a row, or if I dream different parts on different nights, or what – it's all a jumble in my head, but I know that it's connected. It's very unpleasant but I feel compelled to describe it in detail.

So it starts with you – as in you, my husband – being naked, lying on this lovely soft moss beneath a tree, and it's sunny and you're happy, and then all of a sudden you pull a face and you slap at yourself and you've been bitten or scratched or stung by some kind of insect. I don't know, the insect's not in the dream. But then the next thing is, you're full of its eggs. Your skin is coming up in all of these pustules, and you know that there's some kind of grub inside each one. Your arms and back are covered in them and every spot is black, with an angry red ring around it. And then the next scene is one of these things erupting, except it's not really coming out of your skin any more; it's the skin of the earth? If that makes sense. It kind of heaves itself up out of this chamber of blood, pus and black fluid, climbing up through layers of mud, until it gets to the surface. And the creature that crawls out is an ugly, saggy-skinned human, but its face is all mouth. No eyes. And these things are hatching all over the world. And now they're not larvae or anything like that – now the story is that these are ancient monsters that have been awakened by some great disaster. The news is reporting mass hysteria and everybody's scared and horrified. And then it changes again; suddenly, nobody's horrified. Everybody is completely fine with these things. They even have cults of followers who feed them, and they – the monsters – get bigger and bigger. They don't stop growing. They end up like giants. They live in big caves that they've dug out of the sides of the mountains. They can tunnel underground and walk along the bottom of the sea. And at the end of the dream, one of them rose up out of the soil of your mother's garden, opened its giant mouth and swallowed her whole. Like something out of a fairy tale.

Pretty horrible, right? But as I say, it prompted me to get in touch. It left me feeling disgusted, and scared for you.

I want your daughter to see you again. I want to enable healing, where healing can happen. And although the dream didn't necessarily mean anything, it made me think about wounds not yet healed, in you and between us. Please reply to this email and tell me how you are, and whether or not you think you can see us, and, if so, how and when.

Thinking of you,
XXX

The Dream Window

I THINK ABOUT THE EMAIL as I lie in bed, and I don't so much fall asleep as perceive a dream expanding outwards, superseding awareness of the dark room, superimposing itself across reality. It's a portal manifesting, similar to the portal that manifested when I opened the Travelodge room door and first saw the giant.

I walk along the side of the A595. Cars go past, each one stinking. I turn right on to a long gravelly lane, much like the one to the Bean's depot. This one ends in a gate – the only feature to break a high grey wall. The wall is like the one that demarks the Bean's yard from the one next door.

The gate is as tall as the wall and looks like galvanised sheet metal. Ugly and hard. I press a buzzer at the side of it, and after a moment the gate clicks and seems to physically relax. When I push, it swings open easily.

I don't want to step through but I step through.

The gravel lane continues and widens out into a yard. At the back of it is a squat, badly rendered farmhouse much like the Bean's.

Its walls are grey and stained with dark streaks where rainwater runs down it. Elsewhere are small sandstone outhouses. Where the ground is not gravel it is thin grass. The place is wholly depressing. I can hear machinery whirring away, but can't tell where the sound is coming from.

I'm inside the farmhouse, but it doesn't smell like a normal farmhouse. It smells of dust and warm plastic, and there's a sweet rotten element buried in here too. The walls are dark grey and they're scuffed and spattered with brown spots where people have splashed their teas and coffees. The carpet is old and worn and stained. There's no sense of it being a home; my first impression is that every room in the building has been converted into an oddly shaped office. I feel as if I've been teleported into low-rent office space on a twentieth-century industrial estate.

I'm in a room with a desk. The desk is covered in stacks of paper. Behind the desk, working at a laptop, is a spindly middle-aged man wearing a dark suit. His face is long and narrow, and his dark hair is neatly combed across the top of it. He is perfectly clean-shaven, with a pointed chin, and wears glasses with very thin wire frames. Dusty, buckled blinds are drawn across the window behind him.

'What is it I can do for you?' he asks. His voice is nasal and he has a slow, aristocratic drawl.

I'm not aware of saying anything.

'Quite,' he replies. The man behind the desk clasps his hands together and he looks over the tops of his glasses at me, wiggling his long fingers. Then something happens. For a split second, he changes. For a split second, he is a piggish creature and his fingers are longer, pointed and deep pink. The arms and torso are soft and bloated, unclothed and white, with cracks in the skin of its shoulders oozing something yellow. The face is long and raw and pink and snouted, with sharp yellow teeth bared by ragged, chewed-away lips.

Then he looks like a man again. He suddenly stands up, unfolding himself from behind the desk like something mechanical. 'Let's have a look.'

I'm standing with him – it – in another room. A machine noise is getting louder. There's another desk in here with another man sitting behind it. This man wears a white butcher's coat and hat, is very smooth-faced and has big blue eyes. His chin is cleft and he smiles a little smile as he transcribes notes from a jotter to a big ledger. He nods at the thin man. Now the machine sound is very loud; it comes from beyond a heavy plastic curtain that fills the next doorway and billows faintly. I watch the curtain move in and out. I feel as if it's moving with my breath. Or something's breath.

The thin man pushes the curtain aside and strides through. Then I'm on the other side of the curtain with him.

First is the sound. Grinding, whirring, sawing, as loud as insects stuck inside your ears. Then the heat. Like opening an oven. Then the dark, dank smells of blood and excrement and decay. Then the colours: black, grey, brown, red, pink and white.

I stare. I stare at the machines screaming all around. I stare past the thin man into a kind of basin. A conveyor belt protrudes from the walls at either side and prone, distended corpses slowly move along it. A man in a spattered butcher's coat stands over the belt. As I watch, he hits a big red button and the belt stops. He takes a great big knife and starts to skin the body in front of him. He slides his big hands beneath the hide, twisting and turning the body, peeling away the coat.

The basin itself is overflowing with skinless forms. Everything glistening, everything raw. There are small movements that after a moment I discern as rats and maybe worms of some description. The pile slowly pulsates, as if breathing. Maggots wriggle by our feet, just at the edge of the basin. Suddenly the grinding sound intensifies and the bodies in the basin judder, rise – as if pushed up from beneath – and then sink. They were being drawn down and out, from underneath.

The man at the conveyor belt throws the skin he's just removed over his shoulder. It lands on top of a heap of other skins. The heap reminds me of the pile of coats you get somewhere near the door at a winter house party. I stare at the heap. I can see a flash of turquoise in there. Scattered around it I can see either shoes, or hooves. I'm not sure.

The man inserts his big, pink, sausage-fingered hand up inside the body he's handling. It looks as if he's about to perform a puppet show. Then he takes the body's torso in his other hand. He roots about inside, and then yanks out a whole knot of internals. He places that on to another conveyor belt that runs along parallel to the wall. Then he presses the big red button again, and the conveyor belts restart, and the freshly skinned corpse slowly moves along its belt until it reaches the end and then falls. There are windows at the far end of the room, and through the windows I can see black towers and a dark orange sky.

The thin man stalks off to our right, and through another door that leads out on to a metal gantry. I follow numbly. The gantry overlooks another floor, another network of conveyor belts and machines. I watch as the slop of dead bodies flows through channels from one grimy assembly to the next. Everything seems to funnel together into one long, filthy trough, a deep and wide river of meat, of pure energy, all flowing slowly down towards yet another aperture in this lower floor, but this aperture is different, somehow fleshy, a big sloppy orifice in the ground itself, exposed by a hole in the concrete. It purses its puckered rim and then yawns to reveal slimy, white-strung pink walls, from which yellow nubs protrude like big blunt irregular teeth. The falling meat either splatters across it or slops directly down into the hole. The concrete around it is stained red.

The thin man turns and smiles.

More staircases and corridors.

The thin man stands by a door. The door is painted grey. The wall is painted grey too, and it's uneven, like the wall of an old farmhouse, but we must be underground now. The wall looks like unworked stone, done up in the same grim industrial-estate aesthetic as the rest of the nightmare. I can hear something moving on the other side of the door, but only faintly. I've got that white noise rising in my ears once again, drowning everything else out. A painful coldness grips my body.

'Do you want to see inside?' the thin man asks.

I don't respond. But I know what's inside; I've seen it before. And I see it again – whether I'm dreaming it, or dreaming the memory of it, I'm not sure, but I see it again. The giant, slouching at the table and demanding food, demanding feeding, screaming and crying like a monstrous baby.

'Quite right,' says the thin man. 'Everybody sees inside eventually.'

Back outside and the sky is now orange and red. Towers rise all around – lightless and monolithic, two-dimensional blacknesses standing sharply against the roiling fire of the space beyond. I watch as the three Fallen Stock vans trundle into the yard. The drivers reverse-park against one of the outbuildings and slither out of their cabs, looking human at first but then flickering into naked, oozing, pig-rat abominations, much as the thin man had. They bark and grunt at each other, open up their vans and then unload the cargo of dead bodies into a row of great, stained hoppers that feed the conveyor belts down below, which in turn feed the basin, which in turn feeds the giant.

The Expansion

'WELL,' THE BEAN SAYS, after I tell her I'd bumped into Ryan, 'those lot'll give him a glowing reference for his custody case.'

'Will they?' I ask. 'You know them, then?'

'Sure I do. They're the ones over the wall.'

'What?'

'Aye. The other half of the depot, there. The boss is very good with words. And it's one of those businesses that isn't going anywhere.'

'Well,' I say. 'I suppose.'

I'm sat in the Bean's kitchen, feeling a little bit shell-shocked. She's made me one of her bad cups of tea.

'I'm sorry,' I say. 'I think I need a few days off. I don't know if I'm getting enough sleep.'

'I understand, lad.' She sips from her mug. 'Do you want a cheese sandwich?'

'No, thanks.'

'Let's get outside. Some fresh air.'

'I'm just going to sit here,' I say.

'Come on, then,' she says, as if I've acquiesced to her. She takes the cup of tea from my hands. 'You haven't drunk this,' she says, and tosses it down the sink. Then she shoos me out of the front door.

BEFORE CROSSING THE YARD and walking the lane to the road, I stop. 'Wait,' I say. I walk along the side of the house towards the covered area where we load the vans and store the broken-down cardboard boxes ready for tip runs. Behind the trolleys full of cardboard is the wall that keeps us from the Fallen Stock drivers. I push the trolleys aside and put my hands on the wall. I place my head against the wall, side-on, so that I can look down the length of it behind the trolleys. There are no doors being built, no hidden holes, no ways through. I look the other way. I walk away from the wall, into the concrete area from which the fridges can be accessed, and go into the fruit and veg fridge. The back wall of this fridge is a continuation of the wall I just checked outside. I lean across the sacks of potatoes, place my palms on the cold stone and feel my way along it, checking its solidity. It *is* solid, but there's a vibration in it. The machinery beyond. I'm careful not to scrape my head against the rough corners of cheap wooden produce crates from the continent, overhanging precariously from a shelf just at eye level. Aubergines, courgettes, red peppers, yellow peppers, green.

Out in the yard I walk the length of the wall from the other side of the covered area all the way to the edge of the property, which is where the wall turns a right-angled corner and continues parallel to the A595 – though separated by some scrubland. From the corner

I look out across the uneven muddy field adjacent with its tussocks of yellowing grass. I can't see a way though the wall, but I'm not reassured. After a moment I turn and walk between the dormant vans and across the breezy yard towards the Bean, who stands waiting like a piece of rusty metal driven into the winter ground.

We walk down the lonning to the road without speaking. A steady stream of traffic drones past along the A595. The sky is scudding grey clouds, scattered with the black and white of crows and seagulls. The lonning feels very long. We turn right on to the road. Here the verge widens out beneath a chestnut tree, beneath which is an old wooden bench. In the autumn the grass is always thick with conkers. When I was a kid my dad would take me to that verge to collect them. There was never really any traffic round here back then. We'd fill carrier bags and then go back and tip them out on to the kitchen table and crack open the soft-spiked green cases. He'd get a little corkscrew and use that to make the holes in them and then thread them with shoelaces. I'd want them all done but he could never do them all. Too many. We'd put some in the airing cupboard to dry them out and toughen them up. But vinegar was cheating. One year I had a killer. It was a warm day for autumn back then, but probably about average temperature by today's standards, and I was at school. Playtime. We were playing conkers down by the hedgerow that divided the school field from the grounds of the old people's home. We were unbeatable, my conker and me. And the stakes were getting pretty high. Jonathon Cooper had bet me a pound he'd win. A small crowd of other schoolkids were clustered around watching, all of us in bright red jumpers. We were maybe ten years old. Neither his conker nor mine was showing any signs of damage, until it was my turn and I landed it squarely, and his conker disintegrated completely. He was pissed off but he gave me his pound. Next up was Lewis Beatty. He was one of those kids who was good at everything. His was the schoolwork that would make me ashamed of mine. The way he could draw trees made me feel so inadequate and sad that I used to cry in class. His cursive was perfect. He could do long division. I fucking hated Lewis Beatty, though I didn't quite realise it at the time. He lived on my street and I was always playing with him, so I thought he was my friend. He too bet me a pound that he'd win. He went first and didn't make a dent. My first turn I split his conker in half. I was so happy. I was so excited to tell my dad about this conker. This kind of thing didn't really happen to me. I think Lewis Beatty was embarrassed. He didn't give me his pound. He snatched my conker out of my hand and thrust it into his pocket. Then he shoved his hand into *my* pocket and found the pound that I'd won from Jonathon Cooper. He took that too. Then he pushed me into the hedge. The school tried to keep on top of the nettles but nobody can really keep on top of the nettles. I landed in a patch that was growing back, each stalk young and tough and sharp, and got stung all over. I couldn't tell my dad about it any more; now the story was humiliating.

We sit on the bench.

'Thinking about your mam, eh?'

'Yes,' I say. 'A bit.'

'Just a bit?'

'I'm thinking about being a kid. I just wish I'd helped her more. Made her happier or something. Been a better . . . just a better person. I don't know. And I don't just mean for my mother. For everybody.'

'Other people's happiness isn't your job.'

'I don't know,' I say. 'Sometimes that's true. But sometimes you can make other people *un*happy. Maybe I wish that I hadn't made her unhappy.'

'If a person makes a body unhappy, that body has to deal with it. Cut the person loose.'

'That's more difficult with family though.'

'Where are they?' she asks. 'Your family?'

'Ellie and Marianne? They live down south. I had a breakdown some time after Marianne was born. And then I left. I ran away.'

'Jesus. I'm sorry, lad.'

'Well, be sorry for her. I wasn't a good husband. It was my fault.'

'You can't say that.'

'It wasn't *just* me. We both needed help, and there wasn't any. Like Ryan. Ryan needs help, and there isn't any. You can feel it: people just silently, mentally, screaming for help, all around. That's why Kathryn – her from the La'al Tattie Shop – is in business. But that aside, there's no doubt that I was not good for her. For Ellie.'

After a long silence, the Bean sighs. 'I'm worried about Graham. Damned fool though he is.'

'Why?'

'Without the Craggesund contract that he stole from us, I thought we were going under. Would've lost the depot, including the building next door. Those Fallen Stock lads rent it from me. So I gave them the heads-up, start looking for someplace else, like. Anyway. The very next day, doesn't that Dawson's van turn up. And Graham hasn't been seen since. Didn't make the connection between me telling the boys about Craggesund and Graham disappearing – why would I? Seems a bit far-fetched. But to tell the truth, I don't like the fellas.

Make me uneasy. And like I say, it's not as if Graham's turned up yet. So it makes me think, maybe he's dead. That's what folks are saying. And it's not such a jump from there to . . . y'know. Maybe it's murder. And then it's just a tiny hop to – *maybe it was them.*' She pushes around an empy conker shell with the steel-capped toe of her boot. 'Especially considering their line of work.'

'Well then, we should go to the police.'

'I don't know. It still seems a bit outlandish. I'll go and see them, just ask if they've heard anything while they're out and about.'

'No,' I say. 'If they can kill him, why wouldn't they kill you?'

'I suppose I'm looking for a sense that I'm wrong. Like, if you've got a bottle of milk and you think *maybe* it's turned, like maybe you're ten per cent suspicious it's turned . . . you wouldn't just throw it away. You'd open it and have a sniff, right? Now say you're not ten per cent sure, but one per cent sure.'

'And it hasn't just turned, but it's murdered somebody.'

She laughs drily. 'The higher the stakes, the more reason to be cautious.'

'Exactly!'

'We're at different ends on this, I think. Listen. I can't just call the police. They've been good tenants and I want their money. I've got no real good reason to throw them under the bus. Besides, the police aren't up to much these days. I'm going to nip and see them now, lad, okay?'

'Please don't,' I say.

She claps me on the back and gets up. 'You go home,' she says. 'I'm thinking you do need a rest. I'm thinking I probably do too. We're both going mad.'

'I want to go and see my wife,' I say.

'You should,' she says. 'That's exactly what you should do.'

She walks off. She doesn't go back to the depot, but follows the road around the curve and out of sight. I can't move. I sit frozen to the spot and imagine going to see Ellie and Marianne.

I imagine the man with the hood and cloak standing next to me while the mechanic from the garage that services the Bean's vans fixes up my car. I pay her with the last of my cash-in-hand pay packets. The man with the hood and cloak stands behind me while I cut off my beard with scissors. I can see him subtly shake in the mirror as I shave. My skin feels soft and tender beneath the razor.

I imagine cleaning up the broken glass of the witch bottle and leaving my keys under the mat for my uncle. I throw my suitcase into the boot. What's left in the house was never mine anyway. Waves of cool fresh rain come down from the mountains. The man with the hood and cloak is sitting in the passenger seat when I get in the car. The grass and the hedgerows are vibrantly green, and the wet glass of the car windows refracts the colour into an enveloping emerald blur.

Before turning the engine on I take in the view for a little while and enjoy the sound of the falling rain. But then it's time to leave. The car coughs into life and I drive it down the driveway and on to the road. The ghost sits beside me. As I navigate towards the town in which I'm meeting Ellie and Marianne, the ghost starts to fade away. The town is just this side of the motorway. By the time I've reached it, the ghost is barely there, and as I drive slowly down the main street looking for somewhere to park, he disappears completely.

After I have imagined the man with the hood and cloak disappearing, I get up and follow the Bean.

Walking to the Fallen Stock depot is, as I expected, exactly as it had been in my dream, except the gate is not locked. I walk across the yard, noting that there are four vans. I can hear shouting coming from inside and break into a jog, and then a sprint, as I hear the Bean's voice rise from a yell into a wail.

I burst through the front door, expecting the layout from my dream, but it's not quite the same. The walls are that same head-ache-grey colour, spattered with specks of dried coffee or blood, but there are not as many rooms. There is a desk that looks as if it's been hurriedly abandoned, and the sounds of a struggle coming from the next room. I rush in to see the Bean fighting against five men – the blond one, the Londoner, the chinless one with the small red mouth, Ryan and the tall skinny one with glasses from my dream. She is stronger than all of them, except maybe Ryan. She has him on the grey concrete floor, hands around his throat, and she's forcing him downwards into some kind of meaty, lipped orifice that pulses and sucks. His head and shoulders are being enveloped by the folds of flesh. He's screaming. The other men are trying to pull her off him.

The Dead

As a teenager i liked to go out on my bike in the summers, on my own, and ride around the labyrinthine web of interconnected lanes that spanned the farmland between the local villages. I'd cycle completely aimlessly and almost completely thoughtlessly. Sometimes the lanes were edged by ancient hedgerows, sometimes they'd be worn-in tracks through fields. Grass head-height on either side, the insect buzz heavy in a way it just isn't any more. Bike tyres bouncing over mud that had been squashed into ruts and ridges and then dried solid and pale by the hot sun. The pollen was always up and my hay fever was worse then than it is now. I'd invariably end up with my eyes itchy, red and streaming, and my throat and nose would feel as if they were swarming with ants. There was something masochistic in me spending so long in the fields. I felt as if I was working something out. I'd go fast, as fast as I could. I'd enter the maze from the outskirts of town, where our house was, and from there could make my way almost ten miles without using the roads again. Occasionally I'd find that what I thought was a path wasn't a path at all, and the green would be too thick for the bike, and I'd have to turn back, or throw the bike over a fence or a hedge in order to progress. Sometimes I'd feel lost, but if I kept going I'd eventually hit some lane end or footpath or landscape that I recognised. Once I ended up sweating and breathless at the coastal line railway tracks, somewhere between Drigg and Seascale. I slowed to a stop as a fighter jet roared through the sky on exercises, and watched it disappear. Quiet, straight lengths of steel narrowed into the heat haze in both directions. After a few moments of silence, birds recovered from the sound of the plane and started up again. On the ground next to the track was a large swan, bright white and dead, its neck twisted almost to severance. Apart from the neck wound, the thing looked perfect; unharmed. Its wings were closed, its feathers clean. I stepped over my bike and let it fall, the clatter loud. I crouched down by the swan and put my hand on it.

Notes from the Rounds

A S SOON AS IT becomes apparent that the peristaltic motion of the orifice has Ryan well and truly in its grasp, the Fallen Stock men stop trying to pull the Bean off him and instead start trying to push her down into the suck as well. I find a knife on the floor nearby – streaked with wet blood, though I don't know whose – and I start to use it. I remember four wild kittens licking a dirty filleting knife in a margarine tub behind a pub kitchen. First I get the blond one with the wet lips and rumpled clothes. I remember ten to twenty wild cats roaming a pub car park looking for scraps. He changes into something else as the knife goes in, and then reverts back to human form as it comes back out again. The sound he makes puts me in mind of a rat. Once on the rounds I saw two fat grey cats under a bush where I put the milk, except it wasn't two cats, it was one cat and a huge dead rat. The rat remained there for days. Somebody is grabbing my arms and pulling me down and I don't know who. The very ground is slippery and soft. I can hear the Bean's voice, but not what she's saying. I hear her voice in my memory. Her loading something into the van last-minute in the morning and telling me just to get started. 'The door'll jink itself shut.' Or throwing some spare bread into the passenger seat and asking me to 'take it for a ride', or saying, 'There's somebody for you to talk to.' I feel like I myself am being vacuum-packed along with a load of other bacon. I stab the blond one again, and again he becomes a hairless pig-rat thing. It sinks long yellow teeth into me. I see a Prince Harry mask stuck to the inside of a second-storey window. A pale face in the pre-dawn dark that would make me jump every morning, and I laugh a little bit, in spite of the pain shooting through my body. I think I've just about killed the thing now. I can still hear the Bean, though her voice is weak. A child-sized doll in a conservatory, posed so that it has its head in its hands, like it's crying. Notes left out for me that have been nibbled by something overnight. Slipping a *Radio Times* through a letterbox and hearing excited grunting and slapping from the other side of the door. I start to stab indiscriminately around me, conscious that my legs have now been swallowed by the portal and I can't move them. I can't hear the Bean any more. At one house I delivered to there was a notice hanging on a front door, saying 'An Old Rooster and a Young Chick Live Here'. It used to make me feel ill every time I saw it. I grab a motionless pig-rat man and force it downwards. I twist the knife around inside an eyesocket and think about the sound of trays of eggs smashing across the back of the van due to a sudden brake. I realise that really nothing is moving now. A front porch so full of cacti that they had broken the wooden frame and cracked the glass. Waders hanging in a side passage like dead bodies. The spiderweb strands that are everywhere at 5 a.m. A house near the shore of Wastwater that looked and felt deserted, but we delivered milk to it and sometimes a small row of pound coins would appear on the windowsill. Garden wind chimes that sound utterly beautiful, truly magical, heard at the precise moment the sunrise begins. The names of houses – Sleathwaite, Wha House, Ravensview, Slapestones. Other names and other memories, held safe and tight at my core – Ellie, Marianne.

The Depot

I FOUND HIS BIKE AT the depot. I poked around a bit, but there was nobody there, and I didn't want to go into the house. I followed the sound of machinery around until I came to another yard that had the Fallen Stock vans in it. Found out later that the Bean had rented that half out to them. Thanks to Ryan's mum, it came out that they were paying her well over market rates so that she could cover the costs of her daughter's care at a home down in Cheshire. Another kind of blackmail. And the books weren't balancing, so it wouldn't have been easy for her to give them the push. Not that she knew what they were doing. I don't think anybody can have known what they were doing.

The story that eventually broke was a missing persons story: Daniel, Ryan, Graham and the Bean, all missing. That was why Ryan's mum ended up in the press. Nobody ever reported any of the other Fallen Stock men as missing, as far as I know.

I found a bloody knife on the floor in the Fallen Stock depot building, blood still wet, next to what I can only describe as the most compelling evidence of actual magic that I've ever encountered. A great orifice, through which I believe our missing persons went. A portal to another place. As I watched, it closed, grew still and then kind of solidified, in the end looking just like an uneven patch of concrete.

I looked again at the knife and the blood was dry.

There were trails of dried blood on the floor. Given what Daniel told me, I think the orifice must have opened when smeared with wet blood, or dead bodies, or something. I don't know. But I'm pretty sure it was through that orifice that the Fallen Stock men – though I doubt they were really Fallen Stock men, or men at all – fed the giant.

I miss Daniel a lot. Sometimes I think about getting in touch with Ellie, but I haven't yet. I don't know what I'd tell her. I don't know how things were left between the two of them. I hope he got in touch with her. I'd tell her that he saved us, I think, if I spoke to her; I really think he did, whether he meant to or not.

Though sometimes I have dreams about other giants. And sometimes I dream about a little girl – Marianne, I think, though I don't know what she looks like – and she's getting into a little boat and setting out across a stormy sea, and the sky's full of black clouds, and the sea is the future, and it's not good, and I think, *oh my God, oh my God*, and I wake up so scared I can't move or speak. And then I lie there and listen, and feel like I can hear something huge outside the bedroom window, inhaling and exhaling, slowly.

Acknowledgments

Thanks to Beth, first and foremost, for the support and the company and for keeping things moving in the right direction, always. I love you. Thanks and love to Jake and Arlo – somehow kind, funny, and wise every single day. Euan Thorneycroft at AM Heath and Jo Fletcher (at JFB, of course) for encouraging me to write this in the first place, being incredibly patient and supportive as I made a real meal out of it, and providing rock-solid editorial advice, as ever. Thanks to Milly Reid and Molly Powell for all of the help (also at JFB, now and before, respectively). The works of Naomi Klein, Haruki Murakami, Stephen King, James Tiptree, Jr, and Magnus Mills. Nicholas Royle for getting me started, still – forever grateful. Huge thanks to Redbane, the Squirrel's Feet, and the Emirates of Cronus. And thanks also to Pippin.

GLEAM

TOM FLETCHER

The Factory Trilogy Book 1

In this Gormenghastian world the Factory is the law – but Wild Alan is about to discover that law does not mean justice.

The gargantuan Factory of Gleam is an ancient, hulking edifice of stone, metal and glass ruled over by chaste alchemists and astronomer priests.

As millennia have passed, the population has decreased, and now only the central district is fully inhabited and operational; the outskirts have been left for the wilderness to reclaim. This decaying, lawless zone is the Discard, and Wild Alan's home.

Clever, arrogant and perpetually angry, Wild Alan is both loved and loathed by the Discard's misfits. He's convinced that the Gleam authorities were behind the disaster that killed his parents and his ambition is to prove it. But he's about to uncover more than he bargained for.

'Anyone looking for a science fiction tale of grim darkness should definitely pick this one up'
Starburst

Jo Fletcher
BOOKS